No Face

BRANDON KROGEL

iUniverse, Inc.
New York   Bloomington

No Face

iUniverse books may be ordered through booksellers or by contacting:

iUniverse
1663 Liberty Drive
Bloomington, IN 47403
www.iuniverse.com
1-800-Authors (1-800-288-4677)

ISBN: 978-1-4502-5184-6 (pbk)
ISBN: 978-1-4502-5185-3 (ebk)

Printed in the United States of America

iUniverse rev. date: 8/25/10

Contents

Prelude ix

1.) Drugs 1

2.) Cold hands 6

3.) New House Same Home 15

4.) The Lonely Mountain 21

5.) 4:30 AM 26

6.) The Despairing Mountain 41

7.) From Best Friends to Brothers From Brothers to
     Worst Enemies 55

8.) Reunion 73

9.) When the Dust Settles All I See is Grey 86

10.) Collecting Myself 103

11.) A New Era 132

12.) "The Times" 178

13.) Disbanded 203

14.) Crossroads 213

To the kids and teachers I grew up with at Heritage Christian School. You're not my friends, you're my family.

To 1814. We will find our way back home some day.

Prelude

They say that in life, what doesn't kill you will make you stronger. I was never sure what to make of that statement. It seemed too cliché to really be some sort of comforting or empowering advice. After witnessing the harsh reality of this world first hand, I contemplated whether it was all worth it. All the experience, knowledge, and wisdom I gained by somehow pulling through the traumatic crises I was forced to be a part of. Was it worth everything I had to sacrifice to achieve it? All the pain and suffering—not just mine, but that of others close to me. . . If I could build a time machine and go back and prevent the death, pain, agony, and poverty, would I? I decided I would not, even if I could.

Part of me feels crazy saying that, but the truth is I would not be the person that I am today if it hadn't been for every single thing that happened in my life, regardless of how big or small that thing was or whether it was good or bad. And the same goes for you.

We are all the product of our circumstances and our environment and often enough, our environment and circumstances are a product of us. I would be a different person than I am today if my life had played out differently. Although I wish I could have prevented all the pain and suffering that I have witnessed, without it, I would not be the same and therefore might not have that experience, knowledge, and wisdom that hardships have given me. I'm grateful for everything that happened. Hardships in life have molded me into a strong person. I know people who would not be able to handle some of the hardships I've seen and come out stronger. Some people would've come out a mess and some people might have not made it through at all.

It's easy to say "what doesn't kill you will make your stronger" but, if you lost everything would you still say that with such confidence?

I always thought that maybe it was somewhat conceited to write a book about your life unless you've done something heroic. That is, until I was browsing my local bookstore and saw that Paris Hilton had written an autobiography. At that moment, I felt justified, came home, and began writing. Everyone has a story to tell and this is mine.

Before I begin, let me tell you a little bit about myself. My name is Brandon Krogel and I'm 21 years old. I live with two friends and work full-time at a liquor store on the other side of town.

Right now I'm in a bit of a deadlock in my life. My little brother (who I guess is not so little anymore) just left for University this past September and my younger sister is preoccupied with everything that comes with being in the tenth grade. Watching my brother head off to University was kind of like a bucket of cold water to the face. I was confronted with a question: What was I doing with my life? I wasn't sure. I'm "surviving," working full time, making just above minimum wage. My bills mostly get paid every month. I go out for a beer with my friends a couple times a week. My life right now is alright. Maybe that's the problem though; it's just "alright."

I desire more in my life and one day I know I will reach my goals. For the time being though, I enjoy my mediocre, average, basic, almost-satisfactory life because for the past five years, my life was anything but satisfactory. In fact, it was a plain out nightmare which I thought was never going to end. So this life I'm living right now is a big step up from where things were before.

Perhaps one of the strangest things that have ever happened to me brought me here and now that I think about it, it's why I'm writing this book. About a year and a half ago, I woke up one morning and I was fine. Just fine. That was a big deal. I was lying in my bed, wondering what exactly I was feeling. "I feel. . . fine", I said to myself as though I had never understood what fine was.

You see if you haven't felt fine at all for five years, when you finally do, it's a big deal. My only concern, although I was grateful to be feeling fine, was why? Why was I feeling fine today and not yesterday? Where did all my "not fine" feelings go? Did they simply disappear? Did I move on from them overnight? Am I dead? All these questions filled my head and to be honest, I had no idea what happened. I'm hoping that by writing this book and revisiting my past I can find the answer to those questions. Why did things suddenly just get better for me? It doesn't make any sense. I didn't go through years of agony for life to just shrug it off as though it never happened. I need an answer. I need resolve.

A friend told me not to open up old boxes that you tapped up and locked away in your basement: They're tapped up and locked away because you've left whatever is inside of them behind you. I agree with him in some ways but in this instance, I didn't pack up those boxes, someone else did it for me.

I believe if I'm really ever going to put something behind me, I can't stuff it in a box and forget about it. Reason being is that box is still in my basement. One day I might go down there, trip over it, therefore opening it up, causing all the old stuff I had put "behind me" to come tumbling down all over the place. Then I'd be reacquainted with whatever problems I thought I had left behind. I believe in order to put something behind me, I've got to go through that box, organize it, keep what I want and throw away the rest. That way, if I ever stumble across it again I don't need to worry about it because I already know what's inside, and that is simply the resolve I made when I organized it.

This book is my organization and my goal is that when it's finished, I will have my resolve. My goal for you is that this book will be an inspiration to you and that you might help inspire others. If you are going through a difficult time then I hope this book will help you overcome whatever darkness you are facing. My mother always told me "It's always the darkest before the dawn." In your darkest hour, a light will emerge. I'm sure of it. All that you have to do is hold on until morning.

Chapter One

Drugs

It was Christmas of 1999 and I was 11 years old. I loved Christmas because it was the time of the year when my dad would come out and we'd spend the holidays together as a family. Whenever that happened it didn't matter that my parents weren't together because at that time, I felt like I was part of a normal family.

I remember hardly sleeping Christmas Eve in anticipation of Christmas morning, as I'm sure most kids do. When the morning finally did come around, my brother, sister, and I, would be screaming with excitement, it was 7:30 in the morning, and it was not too early to open presents.

Once again my father spoiled us with the latest toys, gadgets, and video games. As the morning continued and the afternoon approached, I wandered the house from room to room, trying out all my new stuff. As I came upstairs to try out a new video game I got, I noticed that my dad had been in the washroom for over 20 minutes. I shrugged it off as nothing but something didn't feel right. Just then, with my eyes already fixed on the direction of the bathroom, the door opened and out stumbled my dad, white powder on his nose, his speech distorted and his expression confused. My mom took one look at him and knew what had happened.

My father was stumbling through the house, shaking violently. He was completely incoherent, continuously muttering and stuttering about how the coffee was getting cold. I've never seen a man transformed into a child like that. My mother held him and guided him downstairs, all the while soothingly talking him through what I'd later discover was a cocaine overdose. She shouted at me in urgency to go next door to our neighbors and tell them to call an ambulance. At that moment my adrenaline kicked in and I ran next door faster than I'd ever run before.

Bolting down the stairs in my socks I threw the front door open and ran through the snow covered yard to our neighbors. In a frenzy I slammed my fists on their door, afraid that every second I wasted could cost me my father. Our neighbors opened the door to see me standing there out of breath, in my snow covered socks, in a panic. The expression on their face made me wonder what mine looked like. I yelled to call an ambulance because something was happening to my dad and before they had a chance to ask anything, I had turned around and began running back to the house.

Once inside I tried to calm myself. My brother and sister were standing on the top of the stairs, innocently listening to my father ramble. I told my siblings to go play in their room and that I would be up momentarily to join them. Once they turned and headed for their rooms, I quietly snuck down the stairs to the basement, getting close enough to the door to hear my parents speak.

A siren in the distance became louder with each passing second; the ambulance was near by. My father, learning that an ambulance was on route, sobered up slightly. Rambling incoherently changed to shouting profanities. "You called the fucking ambulance! I don't want to deal with the fucking paramedics, I'm fine! Now the fucking cops are going to show up and now I'm going to have to deal with their fucking bullshit!"

I didn't know the word "fuck" could be used so many times in a sentence as my father continued to exercise the term to its fullest ability. Behind me the door burst open and in rushed several paramedics and a couple of firefighters. Taking one glance at me and realizing I was not the one in need of immediate assistance, they rushed past me and followed the sound of screaming coming from the basement.

I remained close by the front door and did my best to listen to what was happening without getting in the way. I peered out the front door to see an ambulance, a fire truck, and two police cruisers parked outside our house. It was weird seeing all these emergency vehicles positioned around our driveway. "I wonder if the whole neighborhood knows what's going on here," I thought. I wondered what I would say to my friends if they asked what happened. My thoughts were interrupted as the paramedics calmly made their way up from the basement and out the door while two police officers made their way from the front yard to the basement.

I didn't catch the conversation the cops had with my dad but I'm sure my father didn't enjoy it. After all the emergency personal had left, my father grabbed his duffle bag and walked up stairs to the front door. For a brief moment he paused and caught my gaze, then turned his head and left the house, slamming the door behind him. I watched from the living room window as he drove away, his truck getting smaller in the distance. Refusing to cry, I stared out the window confused, upset, and afraid, while the sounds of my mother crying echoed from the basement. I looked to my right to see my little brother and sister standing next to each other in the kitchen perhaps even more confused than I was.

After that, I didn't like Christmas morning anymore.

I can't recall how long it was exactly before I saw my father again after that one Christmas morning but I know it must have been close to a year. Maybe he was embarrassed. Maybe he was mad. Maybe my mom told him not to come around for a while. I don't know what the reason was. My mom was pretty shaken up about the whole affair. Least to say, I think everybody was.

We all knew dad used drugs. We'd pray for him at every meal. I remember one time when my father was visiting and we were all at the dinner table. My mom, as usual, had asked one of us to say grace. My little sister who was only six at the time prayed that my dad would stop doing drugs. I couldn't help but open an eye to see his reaction. He didn't say anything but the look in his eyes told me that little prayer, coming from his six year old daughter, who had absolutely no idea what drugs were, hit him hard.

My father had a good heart and when he was around he was a good father; the best he could be considering he never had a father himself. My dad was not abusive. He wasn't a raging alcoholic (although I do remember him enjoying his booze from time to time). When my father came to visit, our family felt normal and I'd take that opportunity to tell all my friends at school that my dad was in town and how utterly cool he was.

The next time I remember seeing my dad after that one morning, was sometime in the fall of 2000. I had just joined a football team and told my father all about it. When he came to visit, he brought me a brand new football and showed me how to throw the ball properly and effectively. I remember passing the football back and forth in the front yard. The same yard that nearly a year before, I had run through in the snow to call an ambulance.

To be honest, I never really thought about what happened that one morning for a long time. Just to be spending time with my dad was all that mattered to me back then. I didn't care what his past was or what crimes he had committed. To me, he was my father and right now he was showing me how to throw a football.

After we had finished throwing the ball around we all decided to go check out this new bowling alley that had opened up in town. It was the first time our family had gotten together since that Christmas morning so everyone was excited for the trip.

When we got there, I was wowed by how big the place was. Prior to this bowling alley opening up, there were only two other ones in town; they were older than my dad. Having this new bowling alley around was quite the improvement.

We were there for a couple hours and I loved every minute of it. My dad was pretty good at bowling. I know he played a lot when he was younger so every time he'd get a gutter ball or not get a spare or a strike, you could see his lips move in frustration to form some profane word or another. At times I found it amusing. I never thought anyone could get so mad at a bowling ball. Then again, I never thought I'd get that mad at video games either. So I suppose if you love something challenging, you're bound to get upset here and there.

After the bowling alley we went back home and spent the rest of the evening just hanging around. I would just bask in the family atmosphere when everyone was in a good mood. I could hear my parents in the kitchen cooking supper. The sound of Lego pieces snapping together was coming from my brother's room, his mechanical and inventive mind always at work. It makes sense now why he chose mechanical engineering for his university studies. My sister talking to herself (or Barbie), I was never really sure which one. But as all the different sounds echoed from each room, they connected and formed this beautiful melody and all it sang was family.

That last autumn get together, that night, was the last time I ever saw my father. On December 6th of 2000 his way of life had finally caught up to him and he died from a cocaine and heroine overdose and thus, the first domino had fallen to begin the chain of events that would follow. This is where my story really begins, with the ending of my father's.

Chapter Two

Cold hands

My room downstairs was particularly cold that night, even for December. Mom always had the heat up in the winter so we were never too chilly. It wasn't even the temperature really. Something else gave me chills.

I was listening to music in my bedroom and playing some Tetris on this old computer we had when I heard a slight knock on the door. Before I could respond my mom slowly opened the door and quietly stepped in. When I saw her face and heard the tone in her voice when she called my name, I knew something was wrong. At first I thought I was in trouble for something and I sat there with my mind racing to remember what it was I did. Before I could find something to feel guilty about, my mom brought me over to my bed and told me to sit. Then she looked me in the eye with a look I had never seen on anyone's face before and spoke quietly. She said hesitantly "Brandon . . .your father passed away tonight."

When I heard the words, I could not speak. My mouth was open and I stuttered for something, anything to come out. For a good five seconds I was frozen silent and then when the words had finally registered in my brain and I understood what was happening in this moment, I began to weep.

For what seemed like an eternity my mother held me as we mourned the death of her husband and my father. I had never cried that much in my life and by the end, I felt sick with the bitter taste of tears that had reached my dry mouth, and sore from the movements the body makes when it mourns.

Thinking back now I'm actually surprised at how much I cried. I don't think I ever realized how much I truly loved my father. Despite the fact that we only saw him a few times a year, he meant so much to me. Regardless of his mistakes, regardless of anything, I loved him intensely. It was a realization that didn't truly surface until that moment.

When my mom and I had regained our composure enough to speak we decided it would be best to tell my younger brother and sister what happened tonight so that we could mourn as a family. We woke my siblings up and brought them into the living room. My mom broke the news to them and as she did her best to explain, I began to feel another wave of tears approach. My brother Eric sat there perplexed, unsure of what to do. His face smeared with agony and confusion. He was only nine years old and his relationship with our dad was not as developed as my relationship with him. I could see his pain even though he didn't shed a tear.

My sister did not cry although she understood what had happened.

In talking with my brother Eric in recent years he told me that on that day he wanted to cry. But for some reason he could not. The fact that he could not frustrated him. Angry with himself and unable to release his grief through tears, planted a seed inside my brother that day. To this day, I don't know what that seed has grown in him but I do know that I have virtually never seen my brother show genuine sadness or happiness since then. I know he continues to feel these feelings like every other human being, but to him, emotions are irrelevant and only get in the way. So he tries to suppress them. He's actually become quite good at it.

Our family changed a lot after that. My mom was ridden with grief. Although she did her best not to show it to us, I could hear her crying late at night. She tried to continue to function as a single mom and now, a widow, raising her kids as best as she could. To this day, I never stop hearing compliments from other people about what an outstanding job she did raising us and I agree. Considering our circumstances, she was a super mom and we all turned out half decent despite what the future had in store for us. It was a miraculous effort on her end to remain the glue that held our family together amidst the chaos when she was the one who was suffering the most.

After my father passed, I missed school for a good week or so and took that time to come to terms with what had happened. In the days and weeks that followed I would randomly burst in tears when a memory of my father would stir my head. A smell, a sound, a song, a place where we used to be together, all of these things would trigger memories of my father. When they came, all I could do was cry them away.

My mother was a devout Christian. She loved God and claimed that He was the provider for our family. Every good thing that happened to us was, according to my mom, from Him. Although I was raised Christian, my own understanding of God was virtually non existent. I knew the Bible stories and the concept of what it meant to be a Christian but to really understand Christianity and more importantly God, took me years to comprehend.

As a kid I prayed to God with as much faith as a kid can have and with the simplicity of a child's mind. Although He never really ever spoke back to me, it didn't matter because something in my heart just told me that I wasn't just speaking out into the nothingness, despite how much my heart and logic conflicted.

Probably one of the strangest and most comforting things that had happened to me back then was two dreams I had shortly after my fathers passing.

In the first dream I recall running in a panic to a destination I was unaware of. I knew the direction I needed to travel and I knew time was of the essence but other than that, I wasn't sure what I was doing. After running for a while, out of breath and confused, I had arrived at my destination which turned out to be a train station. When I saw that the train was boarding off in the distance, I spotted a familiar figure. My father was standing next to the train with a suitcase, calmly and casually waiting to board the train.

When I saw him my heart skipped a beat and I ran as fast as I could to where he was standing, overcome with fear that he would board the train and I wouldn't get a chance to say goodbye. Like I should've expected, he saw me running towards him and waited patiently for me to arrive.

I finally got to where he was standing and wanted northing more than to run into his arms but for some reason I couldn't; an invisible barrier was separating us. He looked me in the eye, his gaze was calm. He seemed at peace but saddened that he was leaving. He said to me "Brandon, one day I will see you again," and before I had a chance to interject, he turned and calmly boarded the train.

Our gazes met as he looked at me through the window of the train and I could do nothing as I watched him go off into the distance, off into wherever he was going. Although I was devastated to see him go, I somehow felt at peace and grateful for one last chance to see my father again. I had had a chance to bid my father goodbye. It was something I did not get the chance to do in real life but in this dream, it was a comforting and peaceful goodbye. I felt a burden lifted because I had a chance to say farewell. After that, it didn't feel like my father was stolen from me.

As the days and nights continued to pass, I had a second dream about my father. This time I felt as though I was watching everything play out from a third person's view. I had no say in anything. It's almost as if I wasn't even there but rather watching my dad like someone would watch a movie.

I looked around and the environment was a countryside setting. Endless fields of tall grass blowing in the wind and several hills off into the distance made me feel at ease. Various wild flowers each with different colors, stood tall in the grass making colorful patches everywhere you looked.

My father was running through the fields with the biggest smile I had ever seen on his face. He looked young, younger than I remembered him. It seemed as if he was playing with someone, but I couldn't see anyone else there. He ran through the fields and came to a hillside where he rolled on to the grass and with his arms resting comfortably behind his head, he looked up at the clear blue sky, a smile on his face and a piece of wheat hanging from the side of his mouth.

He wasn't aware that I was there. As I watched him run through the fields and rest so peacefully on the ground, I knew he was in Heaven.

I believe that dream was given to me to show me that my father was alright. That he was not suffering. The drug addiction that controlled his life no longer had a hold on him. All his earthly failings and faults as a father no longer mattered. All his regrets and mistakes were erased. The man I saw lying in those fields was my father in his perfect state. I still can see clearly the expression on his face in that dream and that's all I needed to know that he was okay.   At the train station I got a chance to say goodbye. In the fields I was reassured that he had reached his destination. Wherever the train took him, it took him to a good place.

Now this can be shrugged off as just a dream that was the result of his recent death. My mind was already filled with thoughts of him, it makes sense that I would dream about him right? Yet there was something about those two dreams that separated them from every dream I ever had before. Someone gave me those dreams; it was more than my own mind. It was one of my first experiences of truly understanding God.

Although I didn't make them myself, I'm sure funeral preparations are one of the hardest things anyone has to do. It was very tough for my mother. We were trying to find pictures of my father to create a slideshow that would be displayed at the funeral. Every picture my mom glanced at would set off another wave of tears.

My mom, along with my dad's sisters and mother, had all decided to have a viewing, something I had never heard of before. My father had requested my mother to have him cremated when he passed, as was the tradition in his family for generations. My mother wanted to see his wish completed so after this viewing, the cremation would begin.

While my mom and the rest of the family hovered around my father's body in this church-like auditorium, I stayed in the lobby, afraid to see the lifeless body of my father. Yet when everyone had finished their time with him, I decided to go and see the body, but I wanted to go alone. I walked into the room where my father's body lay and closed the door behind me. It took me a few moments before I began to walk down the aisle. I needed to muster the courage to take my first step. Like someone walking slowly, getting closer to inspect something, not sure of what they are going to find, I cautiously made my way to where his body lay.

When I got there all I could do was stare. The man in front of me resembled my father but this empty, lifeless body did not feel like him. I began to cry. In between sobs I managed to speak to him. Asked him why he had to go, told him that I missed him terribly. He never said anything back. I wanted to hold him and reached out to take his hand. I jumped back, startled, when I did. His hands were cold as ice. I didn't understand. Then I realized it didn't matter. It was still his hand. I took my father's hand in mine and stood there in silence, holding onto that moment. I knew it would be the last time I would hold my father's hand.

When the moment had ended, I felt it was time to finally say goodbye. I gently placed my dad's hand back by his side and whispered "I love you," as I turned my back and began the walk back into the lobby. Upon entering the lobby, my mother was waiting with arms open. I gave her a hug. No words were exchanged. Then I walked out to the parking lot and waited by the car, ready to leave this "viewing."

Later on that night, on the drive home I asked my mom why his hands were so cold. She told me they stored the bodies that were going to be viewed in a fridge to help preserve them. I didn't say anything after that. I just sat there in the back seat thinking about it. Thinking about this whole night and how messed up it was.

I contemplated what life would be like after this for all of us. How drastically would things change? Little did I know that the death of my father had just been the spark in what would ultimately be a raging fire that would destroy more than I could've imagined.

After a little bit of time went by, life began to carry on as it always had. Even though it seemed as though time had stopped for me, the world continued to turn. I eventually went back to school and was met with endless sympathies from students and teachers. I didn't know what to think of it all. Was I a charity case now? Did I like the attention? Or was I miserable?

Things at home started to become tense. Stress, pain, emotion—all these things built up as the weeks and months progressed after my father's death. My brother and I started to fight constantly. The more we fought, the more the fights would escalate. At first it was simply name calling but that changed quickly into screaming matches using only the worst profanity our minds could conjure. How my brother and I even knew such words is beyond me. The screaming escalated into violence. Throwing knives and scissors at each others heads was more common than not. At dinner time our choice of weapons were plates and chairs. My mom would always step in to break it up. Often times she would get more hurt than the two of us, being caught in the crossfire. She'd hold the two of us back as we used all of our strength to break free from her hold so we could tear out the other's throat. My sister would be crying in the background, afraid of the screaming and violence. Her ears forced to listen to the filth that we would sputter.

It pains me to recall this. All the damage our fighting did. My mother would break down in tears after each battle. I always felt terrible afterwards. I didn't understand why my brother and I were always fighting. I didn't understand why he drove me into such a rage. I've tried to understand my whole life and I still have yet to figure it out. In talking with my brother in recent years he once told me why he pushed me to such a rage. He said it was because he hated himself.

See my little brother at the time would contradict or argue everything I had to say. I'd point out the window and say the leaves on this tree are green and he'd say: no, they're purple. I'd say this pencil is a pencil, he'd say it's a pen. He always argued just because, to the point where my frustration would take over and another fight would begin. I didn't get it. I didn't like it. I didn't want it but it happened again and again.

I can remember a specific instance where he and I were playing a game of chess. I was about to win and in frustration my brother flipped over the chess board sending the board, the chess pieces and my win, all over the floor. In an instant rage I started punching him as hard as I could but for some reason he wasn't fighting back. All he did was lay there on the bed screaming for me to punch him more, to beat him harder. I stopped instantly, confused at why he would shout out something like that. Why would he want me to hit him? I realized something was wrong after that. I never enjoyed fighting with my brother but this made me hate our fights even worse. Why did my little brother want me to punch him?

Thinking back to this is devastating. I love my brother and couldn't imagine life without him. Remembering the details of our fights is something I avoided ever reflecting on until now. The memories stir something in me. Like a piece of glass buried beneath the skin, the pain isn't constant but when you do feel it, it's sharp and sudden.

My younger brother had always been a complex individual. I've tried to understand the way his mind works for years but I haven't even begun to crack the surface. All of our fights, our arguments and differences—they never really seemed to develop until after my father passed. His complex mind combined with the death of my father at such a young age—I would imagine it imposed a great many things in his development, as well as mine and my sisters. Anger, hurt, sadness—I feel as though all these things grew in my brother and his outlet was fighting with me. There were so many confusing emotions for him. When he screamed at me to beat him harder, was it because he felt like he needed to be punished? If so, for what? For being unable to cry upon hearing the news of our father's death? For being the middle child? For not feeling love and affection from his family? Did he not like himself? Did he hate me? I strain my mind to find the answer.

To make my brother sound like he was the one struggling the most is not my intention. As time carried on and my brother and I continued to fight, my mother felt that I was having anger problems and looked into what options were available for her. I ended up having to go to this group involving several kids my own age who had all been through one traumatic crisis or another and we apparently all had one thing in common. We were all very angry.

Therapy groups and counselors had never really been something I was interested in and after experiencing my first one, I concluded that I never wanted to be a part of either. For some reason, they seemed like they were made for stupid people. Not insulting the other kids in my group but the way the counselors would talk just drove me nuts. Something about the way they talked to you like you were simple minded, like you were an individual who had lost the ability to comprehend anything on your own. I felt like I already knew everything they were telling me. It was common sense why I was angry. I didn't need someone to explain it to me. The therapy group was short lived as I begged my mom not to send me back. I promised I wouldn't fight with my brother anymore and really meant that promise in my heart. Unfortunately the fighting wasn't done yet and wouldn't be for quite some time. Unfortunately as well, this was only the beginning and events had been set in motion that could not be stopped. My unsuspecting child's mind would have been overwhelmed if I knew what the future held. And if only I had known, I would've done so many things differently.

Chapter Three

New House Same Home

I can't recall how many times our family moved growing up but it was a frequent endeavor. It became even more frequent after my father passed. Money was tight, it always had been but after my fathers death it seemed like for the most part, we didn't have any money at all. Although my mother always did her best to make it seem like our needs were met, every day was a struggle for her both financially and mentally.

Just short of a year after my fathers passing, we moved again into a house in the upper part of town. Our previous house was in a small community on the outskirts of the city so there were more mountains and fields than houses and buildings. It was a good place to grow up for a while as a kid but now being almost 14, this house in the city provided me easier access to hang out with my friends and explore the neighborhood.

When we moved into our new house one of the things I had always wanted finally happened. We got a dog. She was a purebred black lab that we named Skyla and she instantly became one of the family. Having a dog was something that we had talked about for years but even though it seemed like a simple process to me, my mother knew better. Feeding, walking, and housebreaking the dog were things that I never thought about. I learned quickly that having a dog was more responsibility than I had previously imagined. Regardless though, we loved Skyla and it seemed like she had brought a small comfort to the empty space that my father had left behind.

I also made a new best friend. Prior to this, my best friend, whom I had grown up with since the second grade, had moved to Spain with his family for outreach work to help people with addictions and homelessness. After he left, I thought I was doomed to trek it through junior high without a best friend until I met Brian.

Brian was one of the few new people who entered my class in the seventh grade and since our school was so small, having new people join our class was always a big deal. For some reason Brian and I seemed to have a lot in common and we developed a solid friendship in no time.

Halfway through the eighth grade however, I found out that Brian's family was moving out of town, and I began to think about school without a best friend once again. I concluded that attending school without a best friend was pointless so shortly after Brian left, I asked my mom if I could home school.

Home schooling wasn't bad. My social life became almost non-existent, but I took satisfaction in passing the time with an extremely old (and very slow), computer that had somehow come into our possession. The fighting between my brother Eric and I was lessening. A computer program we had gotten from a friend occupied our time, and, in many ways, united us. Perhaps that's one of the reasons why I enjoyed it so much.

This program allowed you to create your own video games similar to those released on the Super Nintendo back in the day. For my brother and I, who were both big gamers, it was a good to let the creativity flow and spend more time on the computer and less time beating each other up.

My creativity also began to flow from me in other aspects of my life. Music was something I had always loved and just prior to my dad's passing, I had joined a band playing drums. Playing the drums was something I had loved since as long as I can remember. Although I was really never that good, joining that band allowed for me to develop my skills and gain a huge improvement. The band had disbanded just prior to me beginning home schooling so I had ended up not being as active musically as I would've wanted.

Several of my friends played the guitar and I decided this was something that I also wanted to learn. It took some time but I was finally able to save up enough money to get my first guitar. It was a piece of junk that I got from a pawn shop but at the time, it was the most beautiful guitar I had ever seen. Since I couldn't let loose on the drums anymore, playing guitar had become my replacement for the time being.

Writing was another thing I had become passionate about and I decided to combine my guitar playing with my writing in an attempt to make something similar to "music." Although most of it sucked, the experience was good and as time went on, I improved at both writing and playing.

I never knew what it took be a good singer. My mom was an incredible piano player and vocalist although she couldn't read a note of music. Of course she always told me I had a good voice but she was my mom, so that didn't count. A good friend's dad happened to be a widely known musician in the church and music community in general, and he encouraged me to continue to sing. I just sang for fun, not knowing or caring if I sounded good. But that day, when my friend told me his dad thought I had a good voice and that I should continue to develop it as I got older - this encouragement reaffirmed my desire to sing and so as time went on, that's what I did. Writing, playing, and singing music became a frequent pastime and I knew it was something I wanted to do for the rest of my life.

Among other creative things that were flowing through me, I began to develop strong ideals and values. I had never really been a bad kid in the sense that I didn't steal, I didn't get in fights in school, and I wasn't rude. My mom had raised me to be polite and taught me how to be a gentleman. I began to develop a strong sense of justice and what I believed was right or wrong. Girls became the most respectable creatures on the planet to me and although I had yet to develop any ability whatsoever to actually stand next to one and have a conversation, I knew that

17

a day would come for that and I would get a chance to display my gentlemanly gentleness.

Then one cloudy afternoon as I was sitting silently in my room, attempting to find a word that rhymed with love (all I could think of was dove, glove, and of), a familiar face came bursting through my bedroom door. I looked up from the love song I was writing (although I had yet to fall in love), to see my best friend Brian standing in the door way. His family hadn't found what they were looking for in the next town so they had decided to come back. I was stoked to be reunited with my old friend, even though it had been less than four or five months since he had left. Although I didn't go back to school right away like he did, our hangouts were just as, if not more, frequent than before. I was glad to have my best friend back to say the least and although it required time away from my newly discovered creative calling, the social aspect of hanging out with someone was definitely something I needed.

Brian's father was a cool guy. In many ways he was similar to my dad, the outback-hunting-fishing-camping kind of guy. As my friendship with Brian continued to grow, so did my friendship with his father. For some reason he was always quite involved in our hangouts. I felt like he genuinely cared about us. As time went on, Brian's dad Mark started to feel like the closest thing I had to father since I had lost mine and I began to enjoy the time I spent with him as much as the time I spent with Brian.

As Brian continued to bring out whatever small aspect of social abilities I had in me, I began to find it easier to meet new people and continue to hang out with the friends I already had. For some reason I had always enjoyed solitude over social interaction but since Brian came back, spending time with friends was becoming more common.

Brian and I, although we were best friends, were actually quite different from each other. Of course we had our many things in common, which really was the reason why we were friends in the first place, but there were several major differences in our personalities that separated the two of us in big way.

First of all Brian was an obvious extrovert, taking every chance he had to be involved in social encounters. All the girls thought he was one of the best looking guys around. He wasn't too fat or too skinny. He had a good build and naturally tanned skin. He was also quite the charmer; able to entice any girl he wanted with virtually no effort. He was liked by almost everyone and was generally the center of attention.

Now for myself, I was a devout introvert who was never the center of attention. I took every chance I had to avoid social interaction. All the girls thought I was nice, but that's about it. I had a similar build to Brian but my pale white skin was no match for his natural tan. If I had any charm in me, it didn't really come out that much. Getting a chance to sit and have an in-depth conversation with a girl was more my idea of charming. Getting to know her, what her hopes and dreams were, showing her that I actually cared to hear what she had to say. I was an old-school romanticist and this new age "charm" was something that took a lot to compete with. I was cute at best, but never hot. That description was reserved for Brian.

Despite these differences between us however, Brian and I remained the best of friends. In many ways Brian brought out whatever small extrovert was in me. He was always dragging me away from my computer and my comfortable solitude and making me hang out with friends instead. Most of the time I didn't mind the social aspect of it all when I got out there, it was just the getting out there that was difficult.

In the same sense I always felt like I brought a deeper part of Brian out in the open. When we hung out he talked differently around me than most other people. We would always divulge in the meatier issues of life and our conversations often went below the surface. In the end though, I concluded that there was definitely not a whole lot of introvert in Brian.

As a result of Brian's never ending social super powers he was always meeting new people and making new friends. One friend in particular that he had been recently hanging out with was a kid one year older than us named Jake.

Since Brian was hanging out with him all the time and I was hanging out with Brian, our duo quickly transformed into a trio. Jake was a cool guy and I bonded with him right away. I felt he was the balance between Brian and I. He was somewhere in between an introvert and an extrovert and therefore could relate to Brian and me on a different level than Brian and me could with each other.

Just as our trio started to strengthen and hang out sessions became more frequent, our family had to move once again. I wondered where we were going and if all this social development was for nothing. Living in the city had really helped me with the social aspects of life. Moving to the middle of nowhere would be last on the list of things that would continue to develop the extrovert in me. Sure enough, the middle of nowhere was exactly where we were headed.

Chapter Four

The Lonely Mountain

Our move from the city out to the middle of nowhere went smoothly for the most part. Brian and Jake both helped. Upon discovering where exactly it was that I would now be living, Brian and Jake couldn't help but relentlessly bombard me with jokes.

"So Brandon, I'm sure you and the Grinch will become swell pals while you're up here eh?" Brian would toy. "Let me know when you're going to be ruining Christmas, I'll come and join you," Jake laughed.

Although hardly amusing the truth was that we went from the middle of the city to the middle of nowhere. It was a small community about a twenty minute drive up a mountain from the airport. The airport was already a good ten to fifteen minutes out of town as it was. I knew this could be problematic to my social status. Although scenic and adventurous, I was just beginning to enjoy hanging out with friends more often than not. Now I was stuck on top of a mountain with no way down.

It was interesting. We went from renting a house in the city to living in a mobile trailer home in the middle of the woods. Although it wasn't exactly my dream home and location, it grew on me quickly.   Being so far out of town and having no means to enter the city pretty much turned me right back into my introverted self. Hangouts with Brian and Jake, although still occurring, were less frequent.

I spent most of my time in my room listening to music or writing. My siblings and I were all being home schooled by this point. A bigger Christian school in town that somewhat rivaled the one I had previous attended offered a program for home schooled students. Every Tuesday home schooled students would come to the school campus and spend a day exploring various studies with several teachers in a classroom environment. Basically, you went to "school" one day out of the week. My mom thought the program would be good for us, so every Tuesday that's where we went.

Having been in real "school" for most of my life made this concept simple but for most of the other kids, it was something new.

Home schooled kids are an interesting bunch. Some are a little strange. Some are reserved. Some are smart. Others are idiots. Most of them weren't very outgoing. When I realized that last part, I took that as an opportunity to step up to the plate and show off all my social interactive abilities that I had recently acquired (which really wasn't all that much). Since I was pretty much the only one who talked at first, I somehow became the outgoing adventurous kid right away. As time went on though, my class became more and more comfortable with each other and before long it felt like for one day out of every week, I was back in school; only this time I was the life of the party.

So life for me at this point in time pretty much consisted of listening to music, doing my school at home for most of the week, attending a real classroom every Tuesday, and spending my remaining time either on the computer or exploring the wilderness that was my back yard. The environment was spectacular. Before my father passed, we lived in a similar setting. Although the community was much larger and it only took about seven minutes to get into town instead of half an hour, being surrounded by mountains and fields a second time, allowed for the adventurous child in me to be released once again. I spent a good portion of my childhood hiking through fields and forests, searching for new unexplored territory (or at least something that hadn't been turned into a golf course yet). Having a similar environment where I was living now re-awakened that thirst for adventure.

In many ways living way out of town wasn't bad. It gave us a break from the hustle of city life. There were no weirdos traveling through our backyard in the middle of the night and the constant noise of sirens piercing the air day and night was less common. One thing I enjoyed especially was the amount of time our family spent together. Since there was no one else to hang out with, we'd spend time with each other. Soccer games in the backyard (which was also a forest) were common. Eric and I stopped fighting as much. Instead we traveled the wilderness together in search of anything worth searching for.

Being out in the middle of nowhere served me. I had developed a disastrous case of acne that didn't look like it was going away anytime soon. Combine that with my extremely pale face and my already somewhat social awkwardness and you have a recipe for social insecurity. I avoided hang outs as much as possible because I hated the way I looked. So instead my guitar, computer, notebook, and three oranges I used for practicing juggling (which I had to replace regularly), had become my sole companions.

Not having to attend the classroom every single day gave me leverage in my free time. Turns out Brian's dad Mark needed some help with his job. He had his own business installing exteriors on houses. He asked me if I was interested in helping out. I had worked for Mark before with Brian doing clean ups of the work site and other random jobs a year or so ago. Working just him and I sounded a little more profitable and since money was something I had none of, I jumped at the opportunity.

Working with Mark was rewarding in more ways than one. Not only was I making money but I got a chance to spend some good quality time with him. We'd talk about life and politics, science, and religion. There was nothing I didn't enjoy about Mark. He was interested in me. He was genuine and sincere, and I accepted him as a father figure. I knew I could count on him if I ever needed anything.

While living at this house in the woods, my mom started seeing someone, a guy named Darren. I was fifteen now. It had been about two years since my father's death and it was weird when I discovered that my mom was interested in this guy. But I wanted to see my mom happy and when Darren was around, she seemed to be. I didn't hate him, he seemed like an alright guy. He wasn't bad looking either, which was important to me because my mom was always great looking. No matter how much older she got, it always seemed like she was always getting younger. Whenever we'd go out and about, whether to a gas station or the grocery store, at least one guy would try to get her number. She would always laugh it off, nice but never really interested. For some reason Darren was different.

Darren was an architect, who would take my mom out to dinner regularly and take her shopping. Sometimes he would come over after my younger brother and sister went to bed. Usually the lights in the living room would turn off at that time and that's when I decided I should just stay in my room, not wanting to interrupt anything.

He was divorced, and after awhile my mom started to hear things about him from other people that weren't very pleasant. Even his ex-wife warned her about some of the things that had broken up their marriage. My mom, always putting her family before her personal feelings was in an awkward position. Here comes a guy, the first real thing that's happened since my father's death but on the other hand this same guy also has some problems and this was not something our family needed more of.

My mom talked with some of her friends about it and concluded that she needed to make a choice. Either things were going to progress with Darren or she was going to have to call the relationship off. I imagine that this was a difficult decision for her and my imagination was right because after she called it off, I hadn't seen her that sad since the death of her husband.

After that, things became really strange. Something in the atmosphere had changed. I could feel it. Something was lurking, hiding in the shadows. I didn't know what it was, but I tried to keep my senses sharp. I knew it was something below the surface, something I would never know just by looking at it.

Before I could dwell too much on my suspicions I was faced with another change. We were moving again, this time back into the city. Little did I know that for the time being, I would become oblivious to my initial suspicions and instead become preoccupied with my own life. If only I had known that this was the most crucial time to be suspicious . . . I wouldn't have let my guard down.

Chapter Five

4:30 AM

Moving back into the city was refreshing. Although I had enjoyed the serenity of the mountains, I felt at home amongst the traffic and the buildings. I never knew why we moved from our little mobile home in the woods back into the city, or why we even moved up there in the first place. I suppose I never really thought about it. My mom would just say "we have to start looking for another place to live," and for some reason that was normal to me. I didn't really ask any questions, I'd just start packing my stuff.

We had moved into quite a large house, which sat right next to a go cart racetrack. It was one of the few attractions our city had. The owner of the go cart track was also our land lord and my mom had worked out a deal with him to get the house. We'd do some renovations in exchange for a cheaper rental rate. He agreed and the house was ours.

It was nice having a house again, and a big one at that. The small trailer home in the mountains was starting to get a little stuffy. Being back in the city gave me the ability to spend more with Brian and Jake and although it still took the both of them coming over at noon to drag me out of bed. When we finally did go out, it was always a good time.

We had moved just before the summer and I was still stuck in the isolated mindset that living up in the mountains had given me. I got a job working at the go cart track next door and so I spent the summer working there and continuing to nerd it up on the computer and with video games in my free time. Whenever

Brian and Jake would come over and yank me out of bed, I'd reluctantly go hang out with them. Sleeping in until 3:00pm was not uncommon.

I felt as though a year and a half of home schooling was more than enough and now that I was back in the city, returning to my old school seemed like the right move. Apparently my brother and sister felt the same way and returned to regular school as well.

The summer drifted on with Brian, Jake, and I sitting in the car that Brian had recently got, fantasizing about taking a road trip down to California. We were young and even though the car was in no condition to be driven at all let alone across the country, we fantasized anyways.

Things continued pretty much the same for the rest of the summer. Jake and I really got closer during that time. I hadn't realized how much we had in common until then.

We were both in love with our celebrity crush. His was Beyonce from Destiny's Child and mine was Hilary Duff from the show Lizzie Mcguire. We started a collection of teeny bop magazines and smothered our bedroom walls with the posters that came in them. Thinking back, it was a little corky and when friends came over our rooms probably looked like they belonged to twelve year old girls, but we had fun so it didn't matter.

Jake and I both had a passion for the arts. Drama, film, television, and of course music. We always talked about how one day we'd be famous, chilling with all these super stars. How we'd make our music and it would be at the top of the charts. Brian wasn't very musical although he did try to sing (even though everyone told him not to), so this was one of the things that gave Jake and me our own friendship aside from the trio.

The summer began to fade and school was just around the corner. Going back to regular classes after a year and a half of home schooling made me a little nervous but it was mostly overwhelmed with the anticipation of seeing all my old friends.

When I entered grade ten I left a good part of my introverted self behind. For some reason I actually really wanted to be more social this time around. So that's exactly what I did. I ran for class representative and won making me the ambassador of the grade ten class to student council. It was a lot of fun.

After reuniting with some old friends, a few of us decided to start a band. Surprisingly enough, all that time alone in my room playing guitar and writing had paid off and I was now somewhat decent at playing the electric guitar. Also surprisingly enough the band didn't sound half bad considering our drummer was still in grade nine and our bassist, who was my long time friend Ryan, learned how to play the bass just for this band. It became known as "pulling a Ryan" whenever anyone would spontaneously learn something new.

Along with Ryan and our younger drummer Adam, our friend Aaron had joined in, providing an extra electric guitar. We all got along well which, believe it or not, is not always the case for bands. As well as that, everyone was dedicated to the project so as time progressed, our music tightened up and we even started to collect a few fans (although most of them went to our school).

In our school, grades seven to twelve would go to a camp retreat on the outskirts of the other side of town to create unity in the school and to give new kids a chance to get to know other students. Since I was in the seventh grade, this camp had been one of the biggest highlights of my school year. Since I missed the last one, I was definitely excited to make up for lost time. Traditionally the middle schoolers would only get to stay the day while the grade ten to twelve's would get to spend the night. This year however, all the grades got to spend the night.

About a week or two into the school year, the time to head out to the camp had arrived. I was stoked for two days of missing school to go have fun.

We arrived at the camp and everyone was assigned a cabin. This was generally chaos as everyone scrambled to call first dibs on their bed of choice. Since I generally didn't rush around as much as everyone else, I usually got stuck with one of the "less pleasant" beds. It didn't matter though. I was happy just to be up here hanging out with friends.

It had been a couple of hours since we got off the bus and the dinner bell was going to ring soon. Everyone had free time until then so my friends and I just hung around talking about this and that when a group of girls caught my attention. Not far from where we were standing was another group composed mostly of girls. While some of the guys in our group did not have this problem, I still found it somewhat difficult to communicate with the opposite sex. Conversation usually started with pathetic attempts at forming words to create a sentence that would generally come out as an assortment of intangible sounds. They usually ended that way as well. For some reason though, in this moment I knew I was going to have to work on that.

What had caught my attention so suddenly was what I believed to be the most beautiful girl in the universe standing not far from me. When I turned my head to change my view from the corner of my eye to full vision, time stopped. I'm not sure how long it stopped, probably enough for my brain to process what I was looking at. When time resumed, it had decided to move in slow motion. I watched with my mouth wide open as she threw back her hair and the most beautiful smile I had ever seen elegantly spread across her face. I was speechless. I couldn't move. I could feel something like drool trying to escape from my mouth and luckily before it did escape, Ryan punched me in the shoulder and brought me back to reality. "You're spacing out again dude," he joked. "Who is that!?" I half screamed half whispered. Ryan looked at me confused "Who's who?" I pointed in the direction of the group of girls in front of us. "That girl, the one with the dirty blonde hair, the angelic smile . . .she's a goddess." Ryan burst out laughing. "Well stop staring so obviously or you're going to creep her out. Her names Amy, she's in the eighth grade. I guess you wouldn't have seen her since you weren't here last year. "Grade eight," I thought to myself. "That's kind of young."

I contemplated these newly discovered facts as I made a pathetic attempt to hide my relentless staring. I concluded that since I was in grade ten, we were both somewhat young. I figured two years wasn't enough of a difference that it would be weird for me to like her. I tried to focus my mind on hanging out with my friends and enjoying the rest of the time at this camp, but the only thing I could think of was Amy and how time stopped when I looked at her. I had never felt this way before and the mystery of it all contributed to what I was convinced, was love. I found out later on in life that this feeling was called infatuation. Like many times before, little did I know. Little did I know that this feeling would get me into quite a bit of trouble in the not so distant future.

We came back from camp and school continued just like I knew it would. I never forgot the feeling I got when I saw Amy for the first time, but I focused my attention on my friends and on the band. Although I tried to distract myself from thoughts of Amy, she was always somewhere in the back of my mind. Her and that magnificent smile.

My life was seemingly becoming better than it ever had before, I had good friends, a band, decent grades, popularity in school and now a love interest, yet still, there was something stirring in my heart. I didn't know it at the time, but it was.

We had what somewhat resembled a small suite in the basement of our house. Since finances were tight, my mom decided to put an ad out to rent the suite. She needed the cash and when some guy came to look at the suite with first months rent in hand, my mom gave him the place.

Usually my mom was always an excellent judge of character. Since she let this guy move in with virtually no hesitation, I assumed he was a good guy. Turns out I was very wrong. He was an active coke head among other things. Screaming, banging, and swearing started to become a regular tune that was sung from his part of the basement.

One time, Ryan and Aaron had come over after school to work on a class project our group was assigned. On our way into my room, which was also in the basement, the guy living downstairs opened the door connecting the basement to his suite and gave me a good long stare. Ryan and Aaron stopped behind me as we all watched this guy stare at me with his mouth hanging open. His eyes were wide kind of like he just witnessed the apocalypse or something. He was sweating and although he wasn't moving around frantically, he definitely seemed in a panic. "Where's your mom?" he asked in urgency. "I need to talk to her." He looked messed up in some way and before he could have another chance to freak out me and my friends, I told him she wasn't home. Upon saying that he closed the door mumbling to himself and withdrew back into his part of the basement.

When I thought about it, it was weird. Then it occurred to me that my mom had been out quite a bit lately, at least more than usual. I hadn't really thought of it until just then. I shrugged it off as my friends and I continued onward towards my room. Yet over the next few weeks, I started to feel a churning, sick-like feeling in my stomach as if I was missing something very important, something that was right in front of me.

It was Friday and Jake and I had made plans to watch a bunch of scary movies at my place until the early hours of the morning. My mom said she was going out for a couple of hours to meet with some Christian friends. I didn't think much about it and said we were just going to be watching movies in the basement. She left and Jake and I began our movie watching marathon.

Some time went by; when we looked at the clock it was three in the morning and my mom still hadn't returned yet. That was strange. I couldn't recall the last time my mom had stayed out that late. In fact, I couldn't recall a time she ever stayed out that late.

When she finally did arrive back home, which was just before 4:00am, I plagued her with a mountain of questions. She replied simply by saying she was spending time with Christian friends and getting prayer. I thought it was weird for people of any religion to be gathering so late in the night. I had never heard of anyone my mom's age, let alone Christians my mom's age hanging out into the early hours of the morning. I shrugged it off because I believed what she said, as bizarre as it sounded, went downstairs and Jake and I crashed halfway through Urban Legends 2.

The next night my mom said she was going out again. She had already tucked my brother and sister into bed before she left. I asked where she was going and she gave the same response as before. She was going to hang out with her "Christian" friends again. "Don't you think it's a little late to go out?" I asked gently. She replied saying she was only going to be gone a short while and would be back before midnight. After she left I noticed there were still some movies left over from our movie marathon from the previous night. I decided to watch the rest of the films we didn't get to the night before. Midnight rolled around as I waited in anticipation for my mom to get back. I had to work at 6:00am the next morning at the go cart track but I didn't want to go to sleep until she got home. I popped in another movie while I waited.

One o'clock came around and she still hadn't showed. She hadn't left a number and didn't have a cell phone so I had no way to get in touch with her. Waiting was the only thing I could do. Two o'clock rolled around and still no sign of her. I started to worry. Maybe a car crash. No, it couldn't be that. Maybe it was just a really long prayer session. I decided it was weird enough that Christians were gathering this late anyways that it would be unlikely they were having a prayer that lasted until two in the morning.

It wasn't until 5:00am, me half asleep on the basement couch with the TV on that I finally heard her walk through the door. The sun had already gone down and risen before I had gone to bed. I was about to run upstairs to the front door when she walked down to see me on the couch. "What are you still doing up!?" she asked worried. "What were you doing out until 5:00am!?"

I asked in the same tone. She gave me the same response as before but this time, it didn't sit right with me. I expressed my worry and slight anger as she brought me into my bedroom.

"I have to work in an hour," I mumbled already half asleep. She said she would call my boss and let him know that she was out late and I waited up for her so I could get the day off from work. I remember being grateful for not having to work and instead catching up on some much needed sleep but something was bugging me. Something wasn't right. I couldn't shake this weird feeling inside me but before I could think anymore, sleep took over and I was off somewhere else. Somewhere where this feeling couldn't find me. Although I escaped it that night, I would have never expected it to catch up with me in the coming weeks and it would come back with a vengeance.

A couple weeks had passed since that night my mom stayed out until five in the morning. Although I managed to continue on with my day to day activities, that weird feeling stayed with me.

I had walked home from school and when I arrived the house was the same as it usually was. Mom was in the kitchen preparing dinner. My brother was in his room trying to figure out some new crazy invention and my sister was enjoying a movie in the living room. Everything seemed fine so why did I still have this feeling? I shrugged it off and went downstairs to unwind the day with a solid guitar jam out.

The night carried on as most weekday evenings did. My younger siblings went to bed at their usual time and I spent the last hour before bed doing some work on the computer.

It was after eleven and I figured heading to bed would be the wisest course of action since I did have school in the morning, despite my desire to continue being nerdy. I turned off the computer, said goodnight to my mom and headed downstairs. The crazy guy in the basement suite didn't seem to be screaming so I figured he was asleep or out somewhere. Knowing that always made sleeping downstairs that much more comfortable. I set my alarm for 7:15am, the time I usually woke up in the morning, and did a quick scan of my room. Everything seemed to be in place. The closet looked fine, although it was missing the door. The light in the hall outside my bedroom door shined in just enough to gently illuminate the room. I never liked sleeping in the light but complete darkness was never any better. I compensated by having the bedroom door open just a crack. It was enough to make out objects in the room but still dark enough that the light wouldn't interfere with my sleep. After one last check of my alarm clock and one more glance around the room, I concluded everything was in order, and rolled over to go to sleep.

When I awoke some hours later, I didn't quite feel as well rested as I should have. Glancing over to the clock provided me with the reason for that. It was 4:30am. I rolled over on my side back into a comfortable position, demanding that my body return to sleep. It was while rolling over that I noticed something out of place in my room. I sat up to take a better look.

My desk, which sat directly across from my bed, was for some reason replaced with a door. Rubbing my eyes to make sure I was actually awake, proved that my desk had indeed been removed and a door had been installed in its place. "What on earth?" I said to myself, trying to figure out what was going on.

A combination of curiosity and a slight build up of anger for someone installing a door in my room while I was sleeping, compelled me to, without question, open the door and see what the deal was.

Slowly but steadily getting out of bed, I walked towards the door. For some reason my room seemed bigger. I reminded myself that I was still half asleep and didn't think much of it. Upon approaching the door I noticed something peculiar. The door was just slightly hovering above the floor giving anyone the ability to tell if the light was on or off in the next room. Glancing at the foot of the door, a light was definitely on. Looking closer however, I realized that it wasn't a light at all but actually what appeared to be a line of fire underneath the door. Concerned that there was a fire in the next room, I opened the door quickly. Upon doing so, I wished I hadn't.

There before me was an infinite blackness and amongst the dark was an endless fire that was burning everything and nothing. A stone path from the door into the infinite blackness stretched on as far as the eye could see. Walls of fire danced menacingly on all sides. The heat of the flame guided the sweat down my face and the endless blackness put horror in my eyes.

Before I could grasp what I was looking at, a small spec appeared off in the distance. It traveled down the path at a rapid speed. I knew it was heading in my direction. As it got closer the spec became clearer. It was a face. No . . .it was a skull and it was seconds away from me. Its mouth was opening and closing, not like it was saying something but more like the movements of a machine, just opening and closing. Nothing I could do would stop this thing and so I did the only thing I could. I screamed in utter fear and terror as the skull opened its jaw and devoured me.

I sat up in my bed like a dead man coming back to life, out of breath and in shock. "A dream . . ." I gasped as I tried desperately to collect myself. "No not a dream, a nightmare." With my head in my hand, I spent a couple of minutes trying to forget about the horror I just went though. "That was one of the worst nightmares I've ever had," I thought. "At least I'm awake now."

After calming myself down I felt like I could finally go back to sleep. I checked the alarm clock. My eyes widened. It was 4:30am. Convinced that I was now truly awake, I slowly turned my head towards my desk knowing, without a doubt that it would be there.

I couldn't breath. There again, instead of my desk was the same door with the same fire lit beneath it. I continued to remind myself that I was awake and there was nothing behind this door. I did that about a hundred times before I mustered up the courage to approach it once again.

This time, I didn't rush in. Instead, I opened the door slowly; afraid of what lurked on the other side. I continually reminded myself that it was impossible for there to be anything on the other side of the door. In the end though that didn't even matter because upon opening the door, there before me was the same infinite blackness and walls of fire that I was convinced I just woke up from.

I stared at the vision of darkness I had just tried to forget in utter shock and terror. I didn't understand how this could be happening. The same stone path, the walls of fire, the endless darkness—it was all there. It was all the same as before. Not one detail had been changed.

Before I had a chance to register what was happening again I saw a spec off in the distance, this time traveling towards me much faster than before. I knew what it was and I knew that it was coming for me but again all I could do was scream as the skull opened its jaw and devoured me.

For the second time I sat up in my bed with more intensity than the first. Panting and sweating I frantically searched the room for signs of normality, for something that would prove that I was awake.

I glanced over at the clock. Once again it read 4:30am.

I started to panic, questioning my sanity. For the first time in my life I couldn't tell if I was awake or dreaming. I had woken up twice already, or at least thought I did. Was I awake now? I could only hope to escape this madness. My eyes scanned the room a second time and upon seeing the door and not my desk, I was almost in tears.

I jumped out of bed full of panic and fear. I needed to get out of my room, I needed to get upstairs. The moment I was on my feet something bizarre happened. Standing in the center of my room, I noticed that two flames about the size of a small coin had appeared on either side of me. One was directly to my left on the wall, the other on the right. Both were perfectly parallel to each other and to me.

I took a step forward and the flames followed me, creating a thin yet frightening line in the direction that I was going. I took a step back and they returned to their original spot. Nothing had been burned and there were no marks on the wall.

I tried to asses what was happening despite the fear gripping my throat. The flames had appeared the moment my feet had touched the ground and they seemed to be following me in whatever direction I took, creating a thin line of fire on either side of the wall. Since there was always a wall on either side of me in the house, there would always be a flame on either side of me.

Feeling anxious and tired of trying to make sense of everything, I bolted out of my room and ran like a mad man up the stairs to the kitchen. The thin line of fire on the walls had followed me out of my room, all throughout the basement and even up the stairs but when I got to the top, the flame disappeared.

I ran into the kitchen to find my mom just standing there, staring into the living room. I bolted in front of her and grabbed her shoulders yelling that there was a fire and we needed to wake up Eric and my sister Lisa and get out of the house. She didn't respond to my urgency so I started to shake her shoulders. When that still did nothing I realized something.

The expression on her face—she didn't have one. I looked at her and she looked empty. She stood there with the eyes of a zombie, hollow and unaware. Her body did not move. Her feet seemed rooted into the ground. She never looked at me once the whole time I was yelling. Her gaze seemed fixed on something past me.

Still holding her shoulders I turned around to follow her gaze. When I understood what she was looking at, I couldn't move. There in front of me was the living room, engulfed in the fire and darkness that I had so vividly seen behind the door in my room. I watched in horror as once again a spec appeared off in the distance of the living room, somewhere in the fire and the dark.

"No . . . ". "This can't be happening." I took one last glance at my mom and her expressionless face then returned my eyes to the living room. I was just in time to scream a bone chilling scream, as the skull devoured the two of us.

For the third time I sat up in my bed once again out of breath, utterly afraid and on the verge of insanity. I wasted no time and looked frantically for the door. To my relief, it wasn't there and in its place was my desk sitting quietly and calmly just like it always had. I was finally awake and rejoiced in my consciousness.

Relieved to finally be out of what seemed like a never ending nightmare, I quieted my mind and relaxed myself. I waited for a moment for the tiredness to kick back in and it did rather quickly. I got back under my blankets and turned on my side to check my alarm clock one last time.

When I saw the digital numbers display the time they did, I felt sick. There on the screen it clearly stated that the time was 4:30am.

I couldn't believe this. "The door was gone!" I fearfully whispered to myself. "I'm not dreaming anymore." It seemed as though sanity had left me alone to die a crazy and very afraid fifteen year old. It was in this moment of question that I stopped asking questions. For in this moment I realized that I was not alone in my room.

Out of nowhere I couldn't breathe. I couldn't move and I couldn't talk. I lay stiff as a board on my back, paralyzed from whatever intensity was gripping my very being.

My eyes made their way to the closet in my room. I knew this feeling was coming from there. An evil presence leaked sourly out from that closet into my soul. I tried to see the appearance of whatever was standing before me but the crack of light that leaked into my room made it difficult to see the dark. After a moment I realized I didn't need to see it to make out its shape, the overwhelming fear gave it an outline and it was massive.

This thing couldn't even fit in my closet. It was bursting at the seams, feeding off my fear. It continued to grow and so did my terror. I had never felt like this before. I had never been paralyzed with fear. I could not move my body. I couldn't speak. I couldn't do anything.

I tried desperately to call for help but nothing came out. I tried to call out the name of Jesus but His name never escaped my mouth. "Death," I thought. "This is death and it has come to take my life." Suddenly, for just a split second, I felt like I could move and without wasting any time, I burst out of bed running for my life up the stairs and into the living room.

It was true. I was awake but this was no better than my nightmare. I sat on the couch against the wall in the living room. This allowed for me to see anyone or anything entering into the living room. If I was going to die, at least it wouldn't be by surprise.

As I stood there shivering in fear I tried to make sense of what had happened. A terrible nightmare in my mind and then an immense evil in my room—just what was going on around here? I had never dealt with anything like this before.

When I was finally convinced that everything had passed, I concluded that sleep wasn't possible. I was too awake and there was no way I was going back into my room. So I turned on the computer and played some games until the time came to get ready for school.

I told my mom about the dream when she woke up but her response wasn't very satisfying. She said it was just a bad dream and everything was fine now but I knew in my heart that this wasn't the case.

Experiencing that whole thing reminded me that despite what people might think, there is a darkness in this world that cannot be explained or denied.

Some people believe that what you could call "evil entities" is just superstition and no such things exist yet all throughout history there is reference to evil, super natural beings in our world like demons, the devil, ghosts etc. that desire to scare or harm us. Even all these paranormal TV shows that were seeing prove that enough people believe there are evil forces beyond our understanding at work in this world. I try to talk to some people about angels and demons and they just laugh. I tell them about my nightmare and they get a frightened look in their eyes.

That night, I was reminded just how real evil is, in whatever form it might be. To this day it is the most terrifying experience of my life. No film or image could compare to the fear and terror that night brought me.

At first I shrugged it off as just a nightmare, but what I would learn in the not too distant future is that it was more than that. It was an explanation of things that were right in front of me, but I did not see, and it was a forecast of things to come.

Chapter Six

The Despairing Mountain

Shortly after the winter had come and gone it came time for us to move yet again. We were several months behind on our rent in the house by the go cart track and our landlord was not pleased. Once again I began the process I knew all too well: packing and moving.

Our destination this time was another mountain paradise that was just a little farther out of town than the previous one. Before we were living on the west outskirts of the city, this time we'd be living on the east.

I was sixteen and thoroughly enjoying myself in school. I had plenty of friends, the band was making progress, and I was liked. I thought this was awesome and worried that moving away from the city again might put me back in hermit mode. Not having a choice or say in the matter, I did my best to be grateful for a place to live and tried to make the best out of the situation.

We were once again in the forest. It was somewhat enchanting you could say. There definitely weren't very many houses around and the ones that were up here were scattered all over the place. So basically this part of town had yet to discover the concept of a neighborhood. We did have something close though. Our house was actually a four-plex composed of yes, you got it, four housing units. Definitely not the newest accommodation to have come out in recent years but the old brown barnyard color gave it a "cozy" feeling I suppose.

The move in was a huge pain. Every time we moved it seemed as though we had more and more stuff. My mom was a bit of a pack rat, collecting virtually anything that seemed valuable in the moment. She had endless boxes of keep sakes that my siblings and I had made over the years. I didn't have a problem with that but all the random junk and toys and just nothing stuff was certainly piling up.

Luckily for my brother and I, one of the families in the four-plex had two sons. One whom just so happened to be my brother's age and the other who was just a couple years younger than I. Since there was virtually no one else to hang out with out there, we became good friends quickly.

Regular adventures included hiking, building tree forts, shooting pellet guns, and arguing. It was great. In many ways it reminded me of my activities as a kid just a few short years before my father passed and our recent adventures living out by the Grinch. It was actually quite nostalgic . . . again. Having fun and building tree forts was great but for some reason my desire to relive childish moments left as quickly as it came. I was sixteen after all and there were other things on my mind.

I had stopped working at the go cart track a month or two before we moved and instead got a job working at a gas station which, oddly enough, wasn't that far from our house (only a good 20 minute bike ride if you took the short cuts).

Along with the job something else had progressed in my life. The girl I had seen at the beginning of the school year was actually talking to me. It was a miracle for me. I had never been interested in someone and in return have someone show interest in me. Of course it took a little bit of undercover work before I made my first move.

Posing as a "Chad Matthews" on an instant messaging program on the computer, I claimed to be a friend of myself. As carefully as possible I asked her what she thought of my good friend Brandon Krogel. Surprising enough at the time she didn't think of me as the loser I thought of myself as most of the time.

Despite the fact that I had good friends, a cool band, and while people in general enjoyed my company, my self-confidence level was about a zero. Acne had taken over my face. My pale skin was whiter than ever. When I'd take off my shirt my friends would joke that the second coming of Christ was underway. I could already grow a beard if I wanted and when I looked in the mirror, I just didn't like what I saw.

That's why I felt like I needed to pose as Chad. I didn't have the confidence to approach Amy myself until I knew for sure that if I did approach her, she wouldn't shut me down before I could speak a word. After hearing what Amy told Chad, I definitely felt more confident than before and luckily for me, that confidence would last a lifetime because I never felt the need to pose as anyone again.

It would be premature to say that Amy and I were a thing but we were definitely getting to know each other. I'd approach her at school and say hi. Then she'd say hi back. Then I'd let out a nervous chuckle. Then she'd giggle and then our conversation ended. Yup, we were definitely exploring the depths of each other's lives. In the coming weeks we'd even sometimes make it as far as "So how's it going?"

Although our relationship was nothing yet, I was really feeling something for Amy. She inspired confidence in me and every time I was standing next to her, butterflies would swarm my stomach. Throughout my life and especially after my dad passed away, I had always felt more mature than most of the people my age. In fact that was one of the biggest things Brian and I had in common. While everyone around us was acting like undisciplined adolescents, we were exploring life from the mature perspective of a man. Roar!

Of course there were times when we were both dumb and immature but for the most part, we were ahead of the game. How we handled conversations, encounters, responsibility, and commitment—these things made others our age seem unworthy of our attention. I mean don't get me wrong, I had many friends who I didn't feel were on the same level as me maturity wise but I loved them all the same. It was just that when I tried to discuss deeper things with my friends, all they wanted to do was go to the mall. Brian on the other hand generally got what I was saying.

When you grow up in a single parent home, you perceive the world differently than if you had both parents. When a youth experiences the death of a parent this can also impact that individual's perspective on things. Some people say maturity comes with age. I'd say maturity comes with experience and since I had lost my father before most of my classmates had lost their grandmother, I saw the world differently than they did.

As a result my perspective on relationships was different from most of the people I knew. I always wanted something real and genuine, not a week long fling. I wanted something passionate and overwhelming, not a relationship out of boredom or necessity. So while all my friends were taking turns dating everyone all throughout middle school, I did not. I didn't see the point in these meaningless flings. I wanted something real and I was willing to wait.

Of course waiting didn't really give me much experience so when I finally found someone I liked, found something that could be real, I wasn't really sure what to do. All I knew was that I needed to hold onto it.

As time went on I started to think Amy was the girl I was waiting for all these years. This in turn led to perhaps an unhealthy outlook on our developing relationship. I never considered that this ideal that I had would possibly lead to over attachment and I didn't think about the consequences of that if things went sour.

Time in our little four-plex on the mountain carried on. At school I enjoyed my time with friends and especially every chance I got to see Amy. The band was making progress, sounding pretty good. My brother enjoyed his time with our neighbors and my sister had made a friend or two as well.

On the surface, things seemed fine and I hadn't had that weird feeling for a little while now. Despite that, I couldn't help but notice that things were getting a little more messed up around the house than usual.

For one, the house was always a mess. Not that it was generally ever clean but it had never been this bad. There was stuff everywhere. The dirty dishes were piled high in the tiny kitchen and a mix of clean and dirty laundry littered the floor and couches. I tried to tidy up as best as I could to help my mom out but after noticing that she was making virtually no effort to clean, it got harder.

Things were starting to get strange. I'd wake up in the middle of the night and my mom wasn't home. She didn't even tell us she was leaving. Some times I'd get a ride home from school and find her passed out on the couch in the middle of the day. Then I realized that she had been sleeping a lot lately. In fact, for a good part of every day she was sleeping on the couch.

Time went on and her late night encounters seemed more frequent than ever before. One night I asked her where she was going all the time. Her reasons were always vague and sometimes they didn't even make sense. From what I gathered, she was meeting with people. Well at least I knew she wasn't out in the woods hunting wild animals or turning into a werewolf but her explanations brought me no comfort.

I started to feel uptight as the days went by. My mom was always sleeping. The house was always a mess. She was always gone in the middle of the night. Now there wasn't even food in the fridge half the time.

One morning I awoke to get ready for school and went downstairs to find my mom asleep on the couch. It took several minutes but I finally woke her up. "Mom Eric, Lisa, and I need to be at school in half an hour and there's nothing to eat for breakfast."

She looked up at me half asleep with one eye closed and one hardly open. Her response was a barely audible mumble that I couldn't understand. I repeated myself and she dragged herself off the couch into the disastrous kitchen to conjure up something for breakfast.

As we headed out the door, I was the one directing everything. Checking to make sure my siblings had everything and telling everyone to hurry or we were going to be late.

Upon reaching the car my mom spoke to me in a barely audible mumble. "Brandon I can't drive right now." I looked at her a little confused. "Why not?" With her eyes barely open she tried to give me a response but with no avail. Since I had just recently got my learners drivers license, I could technically drive as long as she was in the car.

She got into the passenger seat with as much grace as an octopus getting in a limousine. Her eyes were closed looking pretty much asleep. I wondered why she was so tired. Did she just go to bed? Why was this whole situation completely messed up?

I drove my brother and sister to their school, which was directly across the street from the gas station where I worked, and, after wishing them a good day, I drove myself to my school with my mom asleep in the passenger seat.

I couldn't stop thinking about that whole experience for the rest of the day and when I got home there was another surprise waiting for me.

After arriving home from school I unwound with some video games. The fridge was empty, so there was nothing to eat, and even if there was, there were no dishes to eat off of.

My mom was in the shower, she seemed a little more normal when we got home that day. I thought maybe it was just an off day for her and everything's fine. Turns out what I thought was about to get smacked in the face by reality.

While my mom was in the shower I was sitting in the living room doing some homework on the computer when suddenly out of nowhere our front door burst open and in walked an extremely haggard looking lady and a skinny guy with a leather vest.

The woman was short with messy blonde hair that looked like it hadn't been kept in at least a few months. She looked in her late forties but something told me she was younger than that. The guy she was with was tall and thin with a black leather vest. His black hair had some length but nothing over the top and I could see the light reflecting off his greasy hair.

The moment this crazy lady burst into the house she started screaming my mom's name demanding that she pay her the money she owed her. Her screaming caused the dog to start barking, which caused my sister to start crying, which caused me to run and get my baseball bat in case I needed to take out these people myself.

"Linda!" the crazy hag shouted. "Where the fuck is my money?" I stood up, wanting to say something but not knowing what to do. This whole situation was so unexpected, I never imagined what I'd do if someone just burst through my front door screaming before.

"Its okay, calm down," the slimy guy said soothingly to the lady as he tried to tame a clearly untamable rage. "I'm sure she's around here somewhere." The woman looked wild as she scoured the house for my mom. I knew she was whacked on something. "Linda I'm going to fucking kill you if you don't get down here right now!" she yelled up the stairs. This woman was relentless, her screaming echoing off the nearby mountains. The guy continued to try to calm her down and our dog at the same time with no success. After a few moments my mom came downstairs in a towel and when she realized who was here, her face became afraid and she started to tear up.

"Linda where's my fucking money?" the woman screamed. My mom was trying to calm her down. Looking over at her face, the fear in her eyes was apparent. "Please . . . my kids are here. Can we go outside?" my mom pleaded in between sobs. "I want my fucking money!" the woman shouted back.

I stood behind a wall with my baseball bat, waiting for these people to give me a reason to beat them senseless. I was afraid but my adrenaline provided me with more than enough confidence to face these lunatics if I needed to.

I saw my brother out of the corner of my eye hiding at the top of the stairs leading to the basement. His expression was more intense than mine. I knew if these guys touched mom that he would be on top of them before I even got there. I had never seen that look in his eyes before.

"I'll have your money soon, I promise!" my mom assured the lady with tears of fear dripping down her face. "You fucking better Linda. You won't want me to come back here." Seeing the situation for what it was, the man put his hand on the woman's shoulder. "I think she got the message, c'mon lets go."

They left the house, leaving the door wide open. My brother stood at the top of the basement stairs, gritting his teeth in anger and fear. My sister was crying in the living room. My hands were shaking as I continued to firmly grip the bat. And my mom was sitting there on her knees in nothing but a bath towel, weeping profusely.

I stood there not knowing what to do. I knew that this was what everything had been leading up to. The late nights, the extreme tiredness, the messy house, the empty fridge . . . it had all lead up to this and what exactly was this? I did not know.

The adrenaline still pumping through me, I picked up the phone and called Brian's dad Mark. He was the only person I could turn to. For my family's sake, I needed to find out what was going on.

Mark was calm as I tried to explain to him everything that had happened. He told me to lock the front door and not to let anyone in. He told me to pass the phone to my mom and to just sit tight as he was on his way over.

When he got there he checked in with me first asking if I was alright. I told him I, along with Eric and Lisa, were fine and that my mom seemed to be shaken up the most. My siblings and I all huddled together in the living room. I threw on a movie to help take our minds off things. We didn't say much although I knew everyone had a hundred things they wanted to blurt out. We just sat and watched the movie while Mark and my mom talked upstairs.

It was a while before they came back down again and I had no idea what their discussion had been about. Mark took me aside as he was leaving and told me to call him anytime if something like this were to happen again. I gave him my word and after a solid hug, he left the house and I somehow felt a little more at peace than before.

I can't remember how long it was exactly before the shit hit the fan but I know it wasn't long after the events of that day. What I can remember is the day when my life would change more drastically than I could imagine.

Sleepovers at Brian's were a common thing. Sometimes Jake would even spend the night as well. Since all three of us spent most of our time hanging out with each other anyways, it made sense and was convenient for frequent sleepover endeavors.

One day, no more than a couple weeks after that crazy lady burst into our house, Brian and I were hanging out at his place. It was early summer with only a couple weeks left to go until the end of the school year and we were both looking forward to an awesome summer vacation.

We had a pretty decent day. Got out of school at 3:00pm, played some basketball, met up with some friends and then stopped for some food before heading back to Brian's.

Seven o'clock had rolled around and nobody was doing much. My mom was going to be there any minute to pick me up so we decided to watch some TV until I had to leave. After forty five minutes had passed I started to wonder where the heck she was.

Eight rolled around, then nine with still no contact from her. "You'd think she'd at least call," I thought to myself. "She always makes me call when I go out".

By the time ten o'clock came around I was as equally frustrated as I was worried. It was in this moment when Mark came out of his room after having been on the phone for several minutes and asked to speak to me in private.

He took me outside in the backyard where no one was around. The night sky was starless and empty but the air was warm and soothing. I had a feeling what Mark was going to say wasn't particularly good news.

"Brandon, your mom is in the hospital" he said bleakly. "She had an overdose of anti-depressants and can't pick you up tonight so you're going to spend the night here". I thought about it for a moment. "Anti-depressants?" I replied confused. "I didn't even know she was on anything."

Mark tried to be reassuring for the rest of the conversation, which was basically him telling me that everything would be fine, yet I wasn't feeling very positive. I wondered if this was why she was so tired all the time, if this was why she stayed out so late.

I decided to go for a walk after Mark had finished talking to contemplate everything I had just heard. It made no sense but perfect sense. Although Mark said they would be, I didn't think things were going to be okay. Something in my gut told me otherwise. This weird feeling I had gotten all that time ago was now churning in my stomach more intensely than ever before.

The next day at school I was anything but myself. All I could think about was what was happening with my mom. I found out my brother and sister had spent the night with some friends of the family and I was able to chat with them on the phone when I got home from school.

Along with chatting with them I was also able to talk to Mr. Morris who along with his wife, was currently looking after my siblings. The Morris family had been friends of ours for quite awhile now and I knew that if Mr. Morris knew something about my mom, he was going to give it to me straight.

"So Brandon . . ." he said trying to decide exactly how he was going to word this. "We found out today that your mom was not on anti-depressants. She's been using cocaine".

The world stopped before me. I couldn't believe it. Never in my wildest dreams, in a million years did I think my mom would ever do drugs. It killed my father. My mom was relentless all throughout my life making sure that my siblings and I stayed as far away from drugs as possible. To hear this was devastating. Suddenly it all made imperfect sense.

Drugs would explain the late nights, the tiredness, the messy house, the empty fridge, the frequent moves and the fact that we were broke all the time. I wondered how she was able to pull this off without anyone knowing until now, especially me. Then I realized that all the symptoms had been in my face for the past eight months, but I had just been to naïve to see them.

Now that my mom's addiction had come out from the shadows, things were about to change. Social services became involved in the situation and my school was notified that I wouldn't be attending for a couple days. Out of nowhere my life went from semi-normal to being completely whacked.

Social services wasted no time in making arrangements for my siblings and I. The Morris family agreed to take my sister in for as long as necessary and Mark said that Eric and I could stay with him for however long we needed. I was grateful once again for having Mark in my life. Already he had done so much for me and my family. But it brought little relief from the situation at hand.

The following day we learned my mom had gotten an eviction notice because she hadn't paid rent once since we had moved into the place. Turns out today was the last day for us to get our stuff out. Mark, Eric, and I went up to what just a few days ago was my home, to get all of our stuff out before the landlord hired someone else to do it.

Junk. We had so much junk. Mark took one look throughout the house at everything that was lying around and then called me over. He told me to make a pile of stuff that we would keep: keepsakes, personal possessions, and other things of sentimental or significant dollar value. Everything else was to get thrown in the biggest moving truck we could rent, and be taken to the dump.

I knew we had a long day ahead of us so I wasted no time. Sorting through as much stuff as possible, separating the valuable from the junk. I could not believe how much crap we had. I knew stuff had been collecting over the years but when I saw this huge moving truck filled to the brim with junk, it was sobering. "Mom would kill me if she knew half the stuff we were throwing out," I thought.

After many hours, several breaks for food, a small fortune in dump and truck rental fees, we finished the job. It wouldn't have been possible without Mark. He paid for the whole thing. If he hadn't been there, we might have lost all of our family's possessions forever.

The end of that day was the hardest. We had to take Skyla to the animal shelter. Mark said this was our only option. I knew he couldn't keep the dog and my mom wasn't in a position to make arrangements, so I tried to accept what needed to be done.

The entire drive down to the animal shelter was spent in silence. It was just Mark and me in the truck. Eric and Brian were at the house. I sat there in the passenger seat with Skyla on my lap. I remembered when we first got her and how excited I was. I remembered for how long I wanted a dog growing up and now I had to give her to a shelter. I racked my brain trying to think of an alternative, but there was nothing I could do to keep Skyla. I had a taste of bitterness in my mouth. "This isn't my fault," I muttered to myself. "Why do I have to do this? Skyla nor I deserve to be in this position." I wrestled with these thoughts as we got closer and closer to the animal shelter. When we arrived at the parking lot, I sat in the seat, not wanting to move. For several minutes I sat there quietly, hoping that if I waited long enough, this situation would pass.

"Brandon . . . " I heard Mark call my name gently. "We have to do this." I looked up at him desperately, trying to say something to stall for time, to come up with an alternative that didn't involve letting my dog go. When nothing came out of my mouth, I hung my head in despair.

I let out a heavy sigh, grieved with what was happening as I opened the door. With Skyla's leash in my hand, I hesitantly led her to an unfamiliar place, a place where anything could happen to her. Would she be adopted? Would she be put down? I couldn't think about it.

We went into the shelter and one of the workers there came to greet us. Mark explained to her the situation and she nodded her head understandingly. She reached out her hand, motioning for me to give her the leash. I knew I had to but I couldn't let go.

Why was I forced to lose so many things so quickly? My family, my house, and now my dog that I loved? Skyla was a part of my family, a family that was falling apart. I didn't want to give her away to the uncertainty that awaited her and me. I stood there pushing out the world as I waged a war inside my head. The expression on Mark and the shelter workers face brought me back to the task at hand and I reluctantly handed her the leash with the bitterness of someone spitting on the ground and the sadness of someone condemning a friend to die.

I knew I had to get out of there as quickly as possible or I was going to break down. I could feel the tears swelling behind my eyes and I didn't want to make a scene.

As we walked back to the truck I looked behind me for one last glance at the dog I loved. She was crying and barking as it took two workers to restrain her from running after me. At that moment I felt the dam burst and as much as I tried, I couldn't resist the trickle of water that had begun to fall down my face. "I'm so sorry . . ." I whispered as I turned my back and got back into the truck.

Mark must have seen the look in my eyes as we left because when we got in the truck he put his hand on my shoulder and said "I know that was hard for you Brandon, and I'm sorry that's something you had to go through."

I appreciated his thoughtfulness but in that moment no words could ease my sadness. I could only return his words with an expression of anguish and so we sat in silence as we drove home.

After a few days I had somewhat come to terms with letting Skyla go. Mostly I just tried not to think about it. My siblings and I finally got a chance to talk to my mom on the phone. It was an emotional experience to say the least but by the end of it, things were looking somewhat up.

My mom had already made plans to go into treatment and would be beginning that as soon as she got out of the hospital. The program was three months long; she'd be done at the end of the summer.

I went back for the last two weeks of school and did my best to pretend like everything was normal. Living with Brian wasn't bad. I spent most of my time here anyways. I was glad to still be close to my brother and my sister was only an eight minute drive from Brian's house.

So as the summer began as did a new phase of life. Not just for me but for the rest of my family, Mr. Morrison and his family, and Mark and Brian. Since plans had been made, I did my best to remain positive and not to abandon my social life or my own goals. I figured I'd just wait until the fall, enjoy my time living with Brian, and then our family would get back together and everything would be just like it used to.

One thing I should have learned by this point in my life is that nothing is really ever that simple. And nothing goes according to plan.

Chapter Seven

From Best Friends to Brothers
From Brothers to Worst Enemies

Living with Brian was pretty good. We got along well and living there enabled me and Mark to spend some time together. He always had something to say; anything ranging from advice to his personal thoughts on the state of the world. Mark was an old-fashioned kind of guy. Computers were untrustworthy, if you wanted food, you go up in the mountains and shoot a moose, using bear fat as lip balm was the only way to relieve chapped lips, and many more ideas that I found quite interesting and, sometimes, utterly ridiculous. Regardless, Mark had a great heart and a true desire to help people in need. It showed in the way he tried to develop a solid relationship with Eric and me during the time we spent together.

That summer seemed longer than others. I continued to work at the gas station, which gave me some cash of my own. Amy and I got together to go for walks around the park or hang around the mall and just chat. I still thought about my mom frequently, but considering my circumstances, I didn't feel all that miserable. I did my best to remain optimistic but in the end, I may have been a little unrealistic.

In my mind, things seemed to have a predetermined way in which they were going to unfold. I was convinced that my mom was going to get better. I was convinced that Amy and I had something real going on. And I was convinced that Brian and I would always be best friends. So since I was so convinced about everything, my optimism and feelings for Amy continued to grow.

There's hardly a feeling that can compare with loving someone and being loved right back. As my relationship continued to develop with Amy, she made it clear that her feelings for me were as strong as mine were for her.

We'd write each other letters throughout the day at school, talking about anything and everything. At the end of the school day, we'd meet up, exchange letters, and go home giggling as we read paragraphs of flirtatious content.

Every day at school was a rush. Every chance I had to hang out with Amy would send butterflies through my stomach and beyond. At lunch or after school we'd just lounge around on the grass, accomplishing nothing but the silent communication of thoughts and feelings.

One night, we decided to go see a few local bands that were playing a show downtown. We called up all of our friends and ended up getting a decent mob together for the night's adventures. It was great hanging out with all our friends and sharing good music. But for me, sitting next to Amy was all I was soaking in. As I sat there enjoying the show, I couldn't help but think about how much I cared for this girl. I had told her on many occasions and she had always replied with a similar statement but I really wanted to show her. I wanted her to feel my love for her instead of just hearing it. I wanted her to feel safe when she was with me, confident and happy. I had never done anything like this before, but after fifteen minutes of sitting there, attempting to muster the courage to put my arm around her, I finally did and when I did, I breathed a sigh of relief as she rested her head gently on my chest. In that moment I knew she felt safe and in that moment I felt loved.

Mark and his family lived in a basement suite with two bedrooms, one bathroom and a tiny kitchen. Unfortunately the size of the suite didn't match the number of occupants that were living there. Mark and his daughter Jenny each had their own room while Brian, Eric, and I had designated spots in the living room. After a month of living in that tiny basement suite, it was starting to show that people definitely needed their own space.

Brian and I were beginning to disagree on almost everything. I felt he didn't understand me and he felt I didn't understand him. We both thought the other was an idiot and we no longer felt like hanging out.

Eric was my brother and I expected him to side with me in my arguments with Brian, but most of the time he did not. This frustrated me, always having to face the two of them. Our fights were never serious. Nothing ever escalated into physical violence. We'd just leave pissed as hell and then come back a few hours later calm enough to both watch TV in the living room at the same time. We needed more space in the house; I was not the only one to notice that. A few weeks later Mark had secured quite a large house not too far from where I had lived in the eighth grade. Everyone had their own room and the living room and kitchen had plenty of space to maneuver about. Upon getting the house we also all chipped in for a trampoline which became a regular means of letting off steam when things got heated. A couple front flips, a few ridiculously high jumps in the air and you didn't have the energy to be mad at anyone.

Despite the new house, Brian and I continued to argue and our friendship was weakening. We rarely hung out as we saw each other whether we wanted to or not every day. As our friendship began to wither, my friendship with Jake began to grow. I started to spend more time with him, which in itself created conflict. Brian also wanted to spend time with Jake. In the end it was always a race of who could get together with Jake first. It was silly.

Because Brian pissed me off most of the time and I didn't trust him with anything, I began to confide all of my secrets in Jake. I'd talk about my plans and goals and in turn he would confide in me. We were still convinced we were going to be famous celebrities in the now even nearer future. It began to seem like Jake and I were hanging out more often than Jake and Brian. At times though, we could put our differences aside and hang out as a group, and when we did, there was little or no conflict.

Time went on, summer passed, and once again it was time to go back to school. I was in grade eleven and was excited to be that much closer to graduating and to not having to spend the majority of my time with my head in a textbook.

The year started off good. We reacquainted with friends who we hadn't seen over the summer and made some new ones. We had a couple of new teachers, which was always a big deal in our tiny school and they seemed like solid, down to earth people. All in all, this year seemed like it was getting off to a good start.

Seeing Amy every day continued to be a daily highlight. I had fallen completely head over heals for this girl. We'd hang out at lunch; I'd buy her a coffee and bring it back to the school in between classes. We'd write each other notes and talk online when we got home from school. I was in love and didn't hide it.

Brian noticed that I had been acting different lately and had overheard me talking to Jake about Amy. On one of our good days at school he asked me to point her out. I was reluctant to comply at first. I had avoided telling Brian about her because I wanted him to stay the hell away from the two of us. I knew Brian was good with the ladies. He could get any girl he wanted and I was afraid that one day, that girl would be mine.

Not wanting to make our friendship any worse I reluctantly pointed her out of the crowd and he nodded in approval. "She's not bad," he said. "Not really the kind of girl I'd go for but good for you." Despite what he said I wasn't reassured and returned his comment with an uneasy half smile. He must've picked up on that because in that moment, something changed and I felt sick.

The school year carried on and for some reason Brian and I seemed to be getting along much better than before, though I knew he wasn't sincere. Although I wanted him to stay away, he had interrupted Amy and I hanging out with some friends one lunch hour, to come and introduce himself. Before anyone could say a word he had somehow taken over the conversation and instantly became the center of attention in our group.

When he wasn't around, I had confidence, I had thunder. The moment Brian stepped in, I became that quiet and socially awkward hermit. I had known that this day would come but it didn't stop my anger at Brian for barging in. Brian was now acquainted with the group I had joined to get away from him, and I was going to have to be cautious.

I wondered why he was doing this, why he was being so friendly and why he suddenly was interested in a group of people he never was before. I wondered but mostly I was afraid. I was afraid I was going to lose the girl I loved to Brian, a guy who would like her for two weeks and then leave her high and dry. I couldn't let this happen and I decided that I would do everything I could to counter Brian as best as I could.

One day Brian, Jake, and I were walking home after school when I got right to the point and asked Brian flat out: "Man, would you go for Amy?" He looked at me surprised and caught a little off guard but he quickly caught himself and his expression changed to one of fake shock. "Whaa? No way man. I'd never do that to you," he said trying to sound convincing. "Yeah dude, Brian wouldn't do that," Jake tried to reassure me. "Were all friends here."

I would've believed the both of them if it wasn't for the uneasy feeling that stirred inside me but for the time being, I tried to sound assured and replied "I know. I didn't think you would, Brian. I don't think either of us would throw away years of friendship over something like this."

Brian looked over at me, a nervous expression his face. "Of course not!" he exclaimed. "We're friends for life!"

We continued to walk home, now in awkward silence. Jake, seeing the moment for what it was chimed in to reset the mood. "So what are we doing tonight?" he asked trying to get the conversation flowing again. As Jake and Brian started talking about the plans for that night I couldn't help but think about what just happened.

"He said he would never do anything like that," I thought. "For the time though, I'll try to do something that friends do and trust him. I'd like to believe I can give him the benefit of the doubt."

Although I told myself I would, I didn't trust Brian at all and I knew that before the end, my trust in him would be put to the test and the result would be exactly as I predicted: that I couldn't trust Brian, and I had known it all along.

Jake and Amy had become good friends, which was fine by me and often times, just the three of us would spend hours hanging out together. After Brian had introduced himself that one day, our hangouts of three became hangouts of four. For some reason Brian always knew when and where we were getting together and he would always invite himself along, of course being the center of attention the whole time. It drove me nuts.

Our school was putting on a big fashion show and Amy happened to be one of the models in the show. After school one day we were all hanging out and helping get things in order for the upcoming show. It had gotten dark and was close to dinner time so we all decided to call it a day. Jake went home and Mark was coming to pick up Brian and me from the school. Brian, Amy, and I were all just hanging out, sitting on the grass by the parking lot when Mark arrived.

"Hey guys, you ready to go?" Mark asked as he drove up and rolled down the passenger side window. "Sure thing," I replied quickly, wanting to separate the three of us as soon as possible. "What are you doing now?" Brian asked Amy in an overly interested tone. "Oh I'm just waiting for my mom, but she said she probably won't be here for about an hour or so." Suddenly Mark, with his generous heart, blurted out a nice yet unfavorable idea.

"Well there's a burger place down the street. How about we all go down there for an hour? It would kill some time and I don't know about you guys but I could eat." I glanced over at Mark nervously. "C'mon," he said. "It'll be my treat."

Brian and Amy exchanged a look. "Alright, well that sounds like fun!" Amy said cheerfully as she climbed into the truck. "Let's do it!" Brian exclaimed, following behind Amy. "Hooray," I muttered to myself. "This should be interesting."

"Brandon, you coming?" Mark asked in my direction. I looked around to realize that I was just standing there while Mark, Brian, and Amy were sitting in the truck waiting for me. "Oh uh yeah!" I said trying to sound excited as I made my way towards the truck. I squeezed in next to Brian and closed the door as we drove off.

I couldn't help but feel a little uneasy as I recalled the smirk Brian sent my way when he got into the truck behind Amy. It was almost as if he was saying "So this is the girl you care about. Now watch."

I didn't like the fact that he was sitting next to Amy and I was sitting next to the door but judging from the grin on Brian's face, I'd say he already knew that. I tried to put on a smile as everyone talked about the upcoming fashion show. After a few minutes I realized fake smiles are difficult to hold.

We got to the burger joint, grabbed some food and after our meals were done, we just sat and talked. Mark had brought a deck of cards (which he always seemed to have with him), and was determined to teach Amy how to play Texas Hold 'Em Poker. I wanted to interject and teach Amy how to play, but Brian was one step ahead of me. He had already grabbed the cards and begun to work his legendary magical charm.

I went over to sit next to Mark, who was at a different booth inside the restaurant reading a newspaper. "Can you believe they're imposing another new tax?" Mark said half to me half to himself. "I tell yah if I was running this country things would be done a lot differently!" Mark continued to ramble about government and politics but all I could do was watch Amy laugh as Brian in that moment became the person I should've been. There he was, flirting with the girl I loved, and all I could do was watch in horror as she indulged him.

I thought maybe she didn't know what he's doing. Regardless, I knew that he knew what he was doing. At one point he looked up at me and I could tell he was pleased by the bitter expression on my face.

I confided my suspicions to a select few friends, Jake being my primary counsellor. My friend Bill, who was also friends with Brian, said he wanted to talk to me in private after I mentioned my suspicions to him at school one day. I followed him outside behind the school. After looking around to make sure no one was listening, he spoke. "Listen man. I don't want to get involved in this whole thing because it already sounds like a gong show but if you didn't know already, I feel like you should." I stared at Bill with an ill expression on my face, having a feeling that I was about to hear some unpleasant news. "Brian is going after Amy, a bunch of people know. He doesn't even like her; he's doing it just to spite you. He's trying to make you mad. I don't know what you did to him to piss him off but he does not like you right now."

For a moment I just stood there, soaking up what I already knew. Hearing it from Bill confirmed that I wasn't paranoid. After staring at the ground for a few moments I turned to face Bill. "Does Amy know?" Bill cleared this throat before he said "She doesn't have a clue."

After hearing that I knew I was going to come across as obsessive or something like it if I tried to warn Amy what Brian was doing. Guaranteed she would never believe me and guaranteed Brian wasn't going to confess. I thanked Bill for letting me know and headed back off to class.

I knew why he was doing this. He was jealous. Jealous that unlike to him, relationships were more than hobbies to me. I had been seeing Amy for several months now and the best he could do was hold down a relationship for three weeks. He was jealous that I had found something real. Since he hadn't, he decided to take what I loved so we'd both suffer. I knew this and it ate me up.

I was a mess. Always paranoid of what Brian was doing at every moment of every day. I knew it was only a matter of time before something would happen, before he would make a move. I watched every day as Brian would flirt and charm Amy and her friends. I couldn't even hang out with all of them at the same time because of the rage Brian would stir up inside of me. I made myself sick with worry.

The fashion show was approaching. I was hoping Brian wouldn't attend since this was never something he had ever been interested in. But of course because Amy was modeling, he had every intention of being there.

Back at the house, Brian and I rarely spoke to each other. I knew what he was doing and so did he. I tried to avoid him as much as possible throughout my daily routine. I wondered why Brian would do this. Did he hate me that much that he wanted to take away the only person I had ever loved in this way? Yes, we had been fighting and arguing in the previous months but I never thought it would lead to this. I always believed our friendship was thicker than that. I was wrong.

The big day of the fashion show arrived, and it was going to be held at a fancy hotel in town. I remember being in my room preparing to leave. I put on my best clothes and spent twenty minutes looking in the mirror to make sure that, aside from the brutal acne, my face looked as good as it could. Finally, content as I could get, I left the house to snag a ride with Jake down to the hotel.

Upon arriving at the hotel, Jake and I just walked aimlessly around, killing time before the show started. I saw Amy a few minutes before she was about to go on. She was already in one of the dresses she was modeling. She looked stunning and I had to tell her that. I wished her the best of luck and then made my way into the show room to find a seat.

"Is Brian here?" I asked Jake as we sat down. "I haven't seen him yet since I've been here." Jake looked at me and laughed. "Dude, he's been here all day helping set up!" Jake continued to laugh as he saw the expression on my face change dramatically. "He helped set up the stage and helped the models get ready. One model in particular."

Jake knew how I felt about Brian and sided with me most of the time when I talked about how much I despised the guy. He also knew all my suspicions about him. Yet for some reason he always found it funny when I didn't know something that directly affected my situation was going on. In this instance, the fact the Brian had been here all day with Amy. I sighed as I settled into my seat and began to contemplate everything that had happened recently.

Things had been really weird between Amy and I since Brian came around. I didn't like it. She wasn't talking to me about anything anymore. I'd ask her if there was something on her mind and she'd always reply with a smile, saying everything's fine. I knew that wasn't the case but I didn't want to pry. Still, I couldn't help but wonder what false information Brian had given Amy about me because I was sure he had.

I was interrupted from my thoughts as the show began. It was a fantastic performance. All these models, most of which were girls I went to school with, all looked so good up on this stage. It was really quite impressive. Of course my favorite was Amy. No matter what, she always looked better than all the other girls in my eyes.

I tried to make eye contact with her several times throughout the show but she never looked my way once. I told myself that she was just concentrating on the show, but I couldn't help once again thinking about how wrong everything was.

Amy had recently told me that she wanted us to not get physical because she just wanted to take things slow. I was fine with this. It kind of came out of nowhere but I was fine with anything. Amy's happiness and comfort was all that mattered to me. If she didn't want me to show my affection physically then that was fine. Just being close to her was good enough for me.

But still, things had been compromised ever since Brian infiltrated our group of friends and my relationship with Amy. I knew he was the cause of her uncertainty and I was afraid that Amy would fall for Brian. After all, I had never seen Brian not get a girl that he wanted.

I tried to suppress these thoughts and feelings as I diverted my attention back to the stage, where the show had ended and all the girls came out on stage to take a bow. The crowd loved it and everyone was cheering. I stood there, feeling the sting in my hands as they clapped together with a strange ferocity, all the while holding my happy smile which was becoming increasingly difficult. "Who am I kidding," I thought to myself. "I didn't enjoy the show. I was miserable the whole time."

With that thought I left my seat and headed into the lobby to wait for Amy. Jake looked at me confused, wondering why I was walking out of the room. "I'll meet you out there," I stated as I passed by him. All I could think about was all these questions in my head. "I need to talk to her. I need to say something, anything!"

Jake came and joined me out in the lobby shortly after I had left the show room. After a short wait there, Amy walked in with her friends, smiling and laughing. I couldn't help but let a smile sneak across my face as well seeing her in all her glory. That smile quickly turned upside down when I realized why the girls were laughing. Brian came into view. He had been waiting for Amy backstage and now walked into the room with her by his side, with a grin on his face that boasted Amy was his girl. I had never felt so furious and helpless at the same time.

When our groups met, I immediately complimented Amy on her excellent performance and expressed how I thoroughly enjoyed the show. She returned the compliment with a half smile and a simple "thanks."

Before I could come up with anything else to say, Brian took the floor. "So are we all still going to see the movie?" I looked at Jake and whispered "You guys are going to see a show?" He looked back at me confused. "Yeah, didn't you know?" I shook my head. "Well whatever, you're coming," He reassured me.

Just then Brian looked over at me and said loudly: "Hey Brandon, you can come to if you want." Everyone glanced in my direction. The awkwardness of the situation made it difficult to respond. "Uh yeah," I said. "I was already planning on it." I could hardly finish as Brian nearly cut me off and with more enthusiasm than necessary, he conducted the parade to the movie theatre, which just so happened to be down the street from the hotel.

In the back of the group I walked with my head hung low as I realized what was happening. Brian had completely taken over. He was in control now and all I could do was speculate whatever was going to happen next.

We got to the theatre and Brian and I both attempted to buy Amy's movie ticket. She insisted that she buy her own ticket after seeing the situation for what it was.

We found some seats and I sat next to Amy because as far as I knew we were still a couple and she and Brian were not. Sure enough, Brian had to sit next to her as well. So there we were watching *The Incredibles* on this huge screen in this theatre, expecting to be entertained. Or perhaps *The Incredibles* were watching our vicious love triangle through the screen as Amy sat with Brian on her left and me on her right, expecting to be entertained. Mr. Incredible probably also would've seen something else that was happening during the show. It was something I could not see but something I would discover soon enough.

If it hadn't been for Amy's request to refrain from physical affection, I would've considered this a perfect opportunity to hold her hand. Slightly disappointed but still content, I sat and tried to enjoy the film and the fact that the girl I loved was sitting right next to me.

When Brian and I got home that night tensions were high. Earlier that morning when I had gone to brush my teeth I had realized that my toothpaste was missing. I searched the whole house but had no success. There was no toothpaste in the house at all.

I suspected Brian. He was always taking, borrowing, or using my stuff and without fail every time I would never see what was borrowed or taken again and if I did, it was usually generally destroyed or in unusable condition.

When we got home, I asked him where the hell my toothpaste was. He said he put it back but clearly hadn't. Suddenly the toothpaste became the vessel for my frustration and fury.

All my emotions were released on Brian in that moment and we stood outside of the house yelling at each other for a solid fifteen minutes. When we finally ended our argument, I went inside and headed right for my room, pissed as hell. I hated Brian. I hated how he was ruining my life. I hated everything about him.

I went to bed but hardly slept. The next morning I woke up hoping that today would be the day when things started to look up.

Amy seemed different at school all day. We hardly spoke and when we did, it seemed like she had something else on her mind. I of course asked her if everything was okay and she of course gave her usual response, "I'm fine, thanks."

Arriving home after school that day brought an odd sense of relaxation I hadn't felt in awhile. I hadn't seen Brian all day and no one was home so I figured I'd just unwind with some food, a hot shower, and some video games. For the first time in what seemed like forever I let the stress of my relationship with Amy and Brian fade for a few hours and it was exactly what I needed. This moment of relaxation ended abruptly when I got a phone call from Amy.

I was excited that she was calling me but upon answering the phone the tone in her voice changed my excitement to dread. She was crying, attempting to piece together a sentence, which was not working out so well. I tried to calm her down and asked her what was wrong. When she finally was able to talk I understood what she was saying.

She claimed that the previous night during the movie Brian was holding her hand. She said it was eating her up all day and she needed to tell me. I asked her to explain how it's possible for holding hands to be done without any effort from the other person. She tried to explain that his hand was just on top of hers. She didn't move it because she was unsure of what to do at the time. She told me she was sorry and didn't intend for it to happen.

When I heard this my adrenaline began to pump though my veins. My rage began to swell up inside of me more intensely than ever before in my life. As calm as I possibly could I told her that everything was fine and not to worry. I said I was going to go talk to Brian and sort things out. After hanging up the phone I just stood there, chin raised in the air, fists clenched, and eyes closed. I was trying to calm myself down but I couldn't.

I marched downstairs into Brian's room. If he was there, I was going to lose it. Luckily for both of us he wasn't there. I paced around in the basement trying to think where he would be when I remembered that he was at the school tonight.

Every Thursday night for a few months in the fall, people would gather at the school to prepare food and bring it downtown to the homeless. Brian attended this group regularly, and as soon as I realized where he was I wasted no time and began the twenty-five minute walk from our house to the school. I had picked up a wooden club on the ground on my way to the school. I hid it in my jacket not sure if I was actually going to use it or not.

When I think back to this moment, how I was feeling and what my intentions were, I am very glad that I had that walk to think. Because if Brian had been in the house when I got that phone call from Amy, I believe I would've done something that I would've regretted later. In fact, I think if Brian had been in the house, I would've done something that might have compromised the rest of my life.

Holding hands may be the lowest on the scale of ways to cheat, but it was a big deal at the time. We were all attending a Christian school. Sex wasn't an option, not even for Brian. Making out was something I hadn't even done with Amy, and it was unlikely Brian would be able to pull that off. Holding hands was a big deal for a 16-year old love sick kid.

Never in my life had I been that enraged. When rage takes over like that it completely controls you and in that moment, I was not myself. I was a time bomb whose time had run up. All the tension, stress, and my suspicions that Brian was going for Amy had all come out. They had been building for so long and now this was the last straw. There was no more room inside of me to contain these feelings. When Amy confirmed what I had feared so long, that Brian was trying to take away from me the girl I loved, I lost it. I wanted to shout "I told you so!" at the world. I had known in my heart that this was coming. My friends all disagreed, saying, "Nah, there's no way Brian would do that." I knew better. I called it. I saw it coming.

The walk to the school seemed shorter than usual. I wasn't paying attention to my surroundings. All I was doing was walking at a steady pace with my head low staring at the ground, cursing under my breath thinking only of what I would do to Brian when I saw him.

A group of guys in their late teens huddled together on the sidewalk I was walking on. I saw them just up ahead. Two were on BMX bikes. One was smoking a cigarette and the other a joint. They looked intense and normally I would've ventured across the street to avoid them and any conflict that might begin but in that moment I was already so enraged, I didn't care and I wasn't moving.

I continued to walk in their direction. They were directly on the sidewalk, forcing anyone heading that way to go around them. I knew that one of us was going to have to move over. Normally I'd be the one to do that but not this time.

My head was still hung low but I knew they were watching me approach. There wasn't a drop of fear in me as I approached the group on the sidewalk and finally raised my head. Upon doing so I made eye contact with the huddle of wannabe gangsters and they, upon seeing the expression of anger and bitterness that covered my face, quickly got off the sidewalk to make room as I walked right through.

I must have looked somewhat frightening to have forced a group of punks that may have otherwise initiated conflict, to scatter in order to make room for my path, which went right through them. It felt pretty good to have pulled that off but my mind quickly returned to the situation at hand. I was not thinking clearly and so before I got to the school I stopped in at a burger joint to think; after a brief while, I had calmed down enough, left the restaurant and threw my wooden club into the bushes. I had decided that to fight Brian would only make things worse but at the same time I couldn't let this go. I concluded I would release my anger through words and that's what I did.

Upon arriving at the school, Brian was standing outside with a couple other people I recognized.

"Hey Brandon!" a girl I knew said cheerfully as I walked past her. I gave her a brief glance and watched her expression change dramatically once she saw mine. "Oh sorry, I thought you were someone else," she said apologizing. If it wasn't for the mood of the moment, I might have laughed. I must have looked down right pissed to have someone recognize me and then believe that they were mistaken upon seeing my face.

I didn't care who was watching though. This was between me and Brian and without wasting a moment, I marched up to him and told him that Amy had called me and that he had stabbed me in the back. For a good five minutes I used the most profane combination of words that I could think of, I told him that he was garbage and that I wanted nothing to do with him. I threatened to beat him if ever tried to pull a stunt like this again. I told him he was lucky that I wasn't beating his ass right now.

As I continued to scream at Brian, I felt as though I had left my body. I stood there watching myself just lose it on this kid who was once my best friend. I watched the expression on Brian's face as I continued to bombard him verbally. He looked terrified. It was an expression I had never seen on his face before. By the time I was finished unleashing my fury I paused only to soak in what I was seeing. Tears were swelling up in Brian's eyes and his voice was shaky as he kept repeating "I'm sorry, I'm sorry." My words had hit their target and this encounter was over.

Without saying anything or looking back, I walked away from the school as Brian sat down on the curb with his head in his hands. The nearby spectators came to console him wondering who or what had taken over Brandon's body.

As I continued to walk away, my anger changed to sadness, and, not knowing what else to do, I called Mark. He came over right away to pick me up, and when he asked me what was wrong, I blurted out everything. How I had suspected Brian would try to make a move on Amy for a while. How the tension had been building between us. How it finally happened and how I had just brought him to tears with my words.

Mark sat there for a moment in silence. He must've seen the pain in my eyes because as we drove home, he called Brian and demanded him to wait outside the school because he was picking him up right away.

Mark dropped me off and told me that he was going to deal with the situation. I went in the house and headed straight into my room. Ten minutes later Mark and Brian came through the front door. Mark seemed pissed as hell. He yelled for Brian to get into his room and wait for him there.

My room was quiet and I heard Mark come down the stairs. He was heading for Brian's room. When he got there, he walked in and slammed the door.

Their conversation was loud enough that I could hear it through the walls in my room.

"What the hell are you doing?" Mark asked Brian angrily. "Do you know what kind of scumbag move that was?" Brian didn't say anything. "I thought you two were supposed to be friends? At the very least you're living under the same roof so I would think that you would have some kind of respect for each other!"

Mark continued to lose it on Brian. In the midst of the yelling I could hear Brian apologizing in between sobs. Mark could be an intimidating guy at times. I certainly wouldn't want to be shouted at by him. And Mark had taken my side. Here he was screaming at his own son for my sake. It was at this moment that I knew Mark cared about me and it said a lot about his character. I respected him greatly already. This only added to that.

I suppose I felt some comfort in that fact that justice had been served, at least as good as it could be from Mark's end. I heard Mark walk out and slam Brian's door behind him. "You are not to leave this house! You're grounded for a week!"

I had never seen Mark get so angry before. I lay there thinking about everything that had happened that night. I wondered what kind of consequences awaited in the days that would follow. To me this was the climax of the series of events that had happened thus far.

I learned in English class that every story has several key components that make it a story. There's the introduction, then character development, then the rising action followed by conflict. Finally that conflict and rising action would lead to the climax of the story, and then finally the conclusion. If tonight had been the climax then I knew the conclusion would follow soon.

What would the conclusion be? I wasn't sure, but my biggest question was: Did this mean that the story was about to end? And if so, what story was going to end? The story of my life at Brian's? Or perhaps the story of the relationship between Amy and I? I wasn't sure but I knew that the events of that night played a big role in determining this story and what happens next.

Chapter Eight

Reunion

It was the end of October, almost six months since our family had split and my mom went off to rehab. While staying at Brian's I had gone to visit her several times over the summer. Eric and I would bike down to the recovery center and visit with her. It was always good to see her, a little strange in many ways but she kept our spirits high with all her upcoming plans. When she graduated from the rehabilitation program in September, she got her own place in town. It was quaint. I'd go over and visit her frequently to make sure she had some company.

After that whole thing exploded between Brian, Amy, and me, I was desperate to make new living arrangements. I told my mom that things were way too stressed at Mark's and I needed to get out. It might have been too soon and I may have put to much pressure or raised too much concern, but my mom got a place and regained custody over Lisa, Eric, and me. This was what I had been waiting for all summer long, the reunion of our family and a fresh beginning.

I took this opportunity to quit my job at the gas station as I wanted to devote all my time to enjoying life with my family and concentrating on my school work.

The house we got was a miracle in itself. It wasn't brand new or anything but it had a main floor and a basement along with more than enough bedrooms for our family. We had just moved in and already I was feeling better. Eric and I called the rooms in the basement while my mom and Lisa took the ones upstairs. That left one room unoccupied upstairs which we decided to turn into the computer room. I was pretty excited not only to be back together with my family again but now we had this great house where I could play my guitar as loud as I wanted and for the first time in a while I just felt free, at peace, and at home.

Things got even better when my mom showed up after going grocery shopping one night when, through the front door and into the living room, with her tongue hanging out of her mouth and the biggest grin on her face, came running my dog Skyla. I couldn't believe it. Warm relief washed over me and I kneeled down as she ran into my arms. "Yes . . .," I whispered, getting a little more emotional than I wanted anyone to see. "Everything is finally back to normal." It was nothing short of a miracle that all this had happened and I was so grateful. I sat there with Skyla in my arms as she slobbered all over my face. I was drenched in saliva, happy to have my dog back and by the looks of things, she was glad to be back home. It was evident that she had not forgotten about us.

The days went on and Christmas was approaching. Amy and I talked about what had happened and things seemed to be fine between us. I stayed as far away from Brian as possible for the time being. I figured he had interfered enough in my life. I was writing more music than I ever had before and it actually wasn't sounding half bad. Most of it was sappy romantic stuff but I didn't care. At that time of my life, that's what I was all about.

My relationship with Amy at this point had blossomed into something real. That incident with Brian had almost brought us closer it seemed. It's like we got a taste of what it was like to lose our love and as soon as the bitterness flavored the mouth, we held onto each other for dear life. In fact, we actually started pumping so much energy and emotion into our relationship after that, I wondered if I was simply going to explode from it all.

We started saying "I love you," which was a big deal. Amy was making it clear more than ever before how she felt for me and this in turn stroked my passion for her. Below is an e-mail that Amy had sent me at around this point in time.

BRANDON,

hey! :)..how are you?..I am tired. haha soo tired. where to start..
When I looked at my email messages and saw the one from you
i was like YESS SCORE..cuz i was really disappointed we didn't
get to talk today and i missed you lots too..so that email was
just what i needed :)..I am babysitting right now..unfortunately
my computer is still broken..urg it makes me soo mad..it sure
better be fixed by friday! or that'll just not be cool..

There's soo much i could tell you that happened like today
haha but now i just forgot everything..It would probly take
up like soo much space too haha.. Chapel today was soo
fun!.. great great.. you looked very fantastic today yourself
:)..which i would have told you if i had a chance to talk with
you..hee.. ahhh im soo tiredd im going to like collapse.. hey
i didnt get much sleep cuz i was thinking of you too..what a
coincidence..well i think you you like everynight so its not
really a coincidence..well maybe it is..i dunno haha..

I want to talk to you right now soo badly! i miss youu..urg im
mad i missed you on msn earlier..getting this email from you
though makes me happy :) ..today was such a crazy day..
haha pe and basketball..now babysitting..tires me out hha..
So how's the new house coming?..that's awesome that your
back with your mum..really good..and you're getting net on
friday?..that's awesome tooo :).. man i can't wait to go home
and go to bed..cuz then i get to wake up sooner..and go to
school..and see you :) woohoo.haha uhh yeah.. so we should
definitly have so catch up talking time tomorrow (woa catch
up talking time..long one..haha) i dont know if you'll get this
email before then..im guessing not but yeahh..

I shall see you tomorrow :) :)
I love you Brandon. LOTS.

Amy
P.S. you can for surely hold me. anytime. haha. alright,
goodnight! ;)

Everything seemed like it was going great. Our family was back together, we had Skyla back, things were going good with Amy, and I was more in love than ever before. Eric and I hardly argued and actually spent a decent amount of time hanging out. My music was flourishing and things at school were going well. Everything seemed perfect. It was this "seemingly perfectness" however, that made me a naïve fool.

I'm not sure if I was choosing not to look at or be conscious of the reality of things or if I was just that dumb where I didn't even realize what was really going on. Perhaps I was trying to be as optimistic as possible, doing everything in my power not to consider the chance that things might not stay this way or that things might not actually be better. Maybe I was in denial. Truth be told, my outlook on my life at that point in time was much different than how it really looked.

I had caught my mom using cocaine twice in the first three weeks that we got back together. Before we had moved in, she had confessed to using once when she had her own place for that short while. I told her that if we got back together again using was unacceptable and when I found out she had used twice now, I was in an awkward position.

I had already talked with her the first time I found out and thought that this would be our only conversation. Now that it had happened twice, I needed to let her know that I was serious about her not using. I told her that if it happened again I would call our family friends who were involved in the last segment of our lives and that she risks breaking up our family again. I told her that I couldn't live with the fear that her addiction would cause utter chaos on our family once again. She assured me that this would not be the case. Unfortunately, despite her reassurances, it was the case.

Christmas Eve rolled around and my mom had been out a lot in the past couple of weeks. Mark had stopped by to see how we were all doing and to hand out a couple Christmas gifts he had gotten for us. When he asked where my mom was I nervously told him that she was out and would be back soon. I could tell he knew something wasn't right. He looked around the house for any signs to support his theory but upon finding no immediate evidence he just turned to me with his gaze firm and said "You'd tell me if something was wrong, right Brandon?" I looked back at Mark and tried my best to keep a straight face. "Of course Mark. You know that." Not looking super convinced, we continued to chat for a minute or two before he took off.

I wanted to tell Mark that things were probably not as fine as they should be, but I was afraid that our family would split again and I couldn't let that happen. I told myself unless I knew for sure my mom had used a third time, I wouldn't bring this up. Turns out I'd have to bring it up sooner than I thought.

On Christmas Eve, the Christmas tree stood proud in our living room with an assortment of gifts underneath, which made this place seem like home. It was late, but my mom said she was going out to get some more gifts and wrapping paper. I glanced over at the clock, it was 10:00 p.m. and my sister was already in bed. It struck me as odd that she was going to get these things at this hour, but, wanting to give her the benefit of the doubt, I nodded in approval.

By the time midnight had rolled around I got off the computer and made my way into the living room. Mom still wasn't home. Generally I couldn't sleep on Christmas Eve out of pure excitement for the upcoming morning, but this time, I couldn't sleep because of the worry that my mom was somewhere out there doing cocaine or God knows what else.

Eric came up from his room and joined me in the living room. He sat down on the couch and we both just sat there quietly for a couple minutes. Finally Eric spoke.

"Mom's using drugs again isn't she?" he asked, already knowing the answer. I looked down at the ground trying to figure out how I was going to say this. "Eric, maybe we shouldn't get too comfortable living here." We were silent for a few moments, and then, to take our minds off the circumstances at hand, we spent the remainder of the night talking and joking around in the living room. It was good to just spend the night with Eric chatting about life and how crazy things had been. It felt like I really got to know my brother that night.

At 7:00 a.m. my mom finally showed up. Eric and I both knew what she had been doing but we refrained from saying anything as to hopefully not upset this already dysfunctional Christmas.

My mom woke up Lisa and to her, it seemed like a normal Christmas morning, although Eric and I knew better. We opened our gifts but to me it felt more like a funeral then Christmas morning. Every time I looked over at my mom, I was reminded by her eyes that here in this moment, during our Christmas morning, my mom was high as a kite.

Mom made breakfast while Eric, Lisa, and I all tried out the new stuff we had gotten. I wondered how on earth my mom was able to get enough cash to buy all this stuff. After breakfast she passed out on the couch for the rest of the day and got up some time in the early evening. I knew this wasn't just the third time she had used. Judging from her old patterns, I'd say she had been using every day.

I swore that I would not ruin our family by ratting out my mom until something substantial happened that left me no choice. I didn't want to be the one who always had to do this but if I didn't who would?

My mother stayed home that night and did some cleaning, so I was finally able to go to bed with peace. That peace however was short lived as I awoke in the morning to find that my mom was not home. I went out to the carport and my suspicions were confirmed. The car was gone and so was she. I knew she had gone on another all night binge.

This was it. This was the substantial event that was going to lead to our family breaking up again. I sat there on the couch trying to figure out what I was going to do. I decided we weren't going to school that day. When Eric and Lisa woke up I was going to have to sit down with them and let them know what was going on. Lisa was still only ten years old and Eric just thirteen. Trying to explain to Lisa what was going on was difficult. Eric already knew so he did his best to help me explain things.

We had breakfast and everyone just kind of did their own thing. I started to do some cleaning after noticing how disastrous the house really was. The kitchen was a mess with no clean dishes and hardly any food in the fridge. The living room was covered in random junk. I was amazed at how much stuff we had already collected since being together for just over a month and a half. I also realized how much the house looked like it did before our family split for the first time. I realized then how out of hand things had become once again.

Sometime in the afternoon my mom finally called. As soon as I picked up the phone I asked her where the hell she was. Her response was a series of excuses that made no sense whatsoever and all she kept saying was that she'd be home soon and she'd bring a pizza for dinner. I screamed into the phone that nobody gave a shit about pizza and that she needed to get back here right away. I thought, "My mom is out binging on cocaine and who knows what else, she left in the middle of the night without letting anyone know where she was and now she's talking about bringing home a pizza and that this is going to make everything okay? This is ridiculous!"

Eric wanted to talk to her, and also expressed his frustration and anger for what was happening. Lisa, with tears in her eyes, got a chance to throw her two cents in after Eric and begged my mom to come back home. After she passed the phone back to me I couldn't take any more of this insanity and told my mom to get home or I was calling Mark. As quickly as I had picked up the phone, I hung it up.

We waited for hours for her to come back with no avail. I knew Eric and Lisa would be getting hungry again so I decided it would be best if I figured out how to cook something. Rummaging through what was left in the cupboards I came across a box of macaroni and cheese and figured this would be as good as it would get.

After eating I spent some time in my room trying to figure out what I should do. I knew that I didn't have a choice and would have to let someone know what was happening. Reluctantly I went upstairs and called my mom's friend Jane who had been helping our family out here and there for quite some time now. I was going to call Mark but I figured he had done enough for us and I didn't want to burden him with our family's trouble any more than we already had.

When I called Jane and told her what was going on she was clearly choked that this was happening all over again. She said she'd get in touch with the right people and that she'd come by as soon as she could.

When she arrived I was relieved to have someone to talk to. "Hey Brandon," she said sympathetically. "Hey Jane, thanks for coming by." Jane put her hand on my shoulder comfortingly. "I'm so sorry that you have to go through this again. If you need anything at all please don't hesitate to call me." I just kind of looked around like I didn't know what was going on or like I was zoning out while I attempted to reply. "Yeah . . . thanks. I really appreciate it."

"Are you guys going to be alright here for a few hours?" Jane asked concerned. "I think we'll be alright for a little bit," I tried to reassure her, not really knowing if things would be okay or not. Jane looked down at her watch to see the time. "I've got to go pick my kids up from school. I already made some calls and arrangements are in the works. I'll stop by again later. Call if you need anything before then." I thanked Jane for stopping by and promised to give her a shout if we needed anything.

Hours passed. It was dinner time and it had been a good five hours since we last heard from my mom. I knew everybody was going to need to eat once again so I somehow figured out how to make some grilled cheese sandwiches and luckily that held us over for a while.

At around 9:00 p.m. my mom finally came home. She looked like hell. In fact I had never seen her look anything like this. Her finger nails were black and her body was twitching as she talked. Huge bags hung under her eyes and her face looked noticeably thinner. Her eyes were sad and exhausted. When she leaned in to give me a hug she smelled as though she hadn't showered for several days. What appeared to be a bruise around her eye made me panic that someone had hit her. When I asked her, she of course denied it, but I knew I couldn't believe anything she said.

I had already put Lisa to bed not knowing what else to do. She was of course still awake when my mother finally came home. She went into Lisa's room, but Lisa gave her the cold shoulder. My mom tried to hug her but Lisa wouldn't have it. Instead between tears she kept asking why she was out for so long. It was difficult to watch my little sister be so hurt. I was mad at my mom for putting Lisa through this, for putting all of us through this.

Some fresh air seemed like just the thing I needed so I walked out the front door and decided to go for just a brief walk, as it was completely freezing outside. Upon passing the carport I looked to discover that our car was not there. Upon questioning my mom when I got back inside, I had realized and concluded that the car was used to pay her drug debt, although she claimed to have given it someone who was in need.

Frustrated and upset I told her that I had informed Jane who had passed on the information to other friends of our family about our present circumstances. Once again our family would split and this time I had a feeling it was going to be longer than six months.

In order to kill a weed you must pull it out of the ground by its roots. If you don't pull out the roots, it will seem that the weed is gone but really it just needs a little bit of time and it will grow right back to its original size or even bigger.

When my mom went to rehab her weeds were trimmed down, it seemed like they were gone when truthfully, the roots remained. When our family reunited, everything seemed great at first but slowly the weeds of addiction began to grow back. The source of her addiction was not uprooted. As a result her rehabilitation was ineffective, which in turn made the reunion of our family short lived.

My mother didn't have an easy life. Growing up, her mother divorced and remarried several times, not always to the best of step-fathers. At sixteen my mom was sent to a private Christian school where things started to look up. She married my father after she graduated and loved him dearly but his addiction seemed to be more important than anything else. She separated from him for the sake of her kids.

The seeds that were planted in my mom throughout her life turned into a garden of thorns and weeds that left no room for good things to grow. Her mind became a tangled mesh of pain, sadness, and anger. Raising three kids as a single mom wasn't easy either, and the death of her husband, the one man she loved, added to the already enormous burden that she carried. Meeting Darren and getting a taste of what it means to be in love again and then having it stripped from her, was the last thing she could handle. All these things combined formed a monster that was taking over her life, and, during a weak moment, someone offered her cocaine with promises of relief and happiness. That snake full of lies poisoned her, took advantage of her weakness, and promised her freedom but really it was slavery. Some of my friends say that when they did cocaine, everything seemed fine. When you were high on coke you were always looking on the bright side of things to an unrealistic level. Everything was okay. Someone close to you could have just died and somehow cocaine would help you come to terms with that. Well, at least for a short time.

Perhaps it is that feeling that my mother fell victim to, that feeling that everything is "okay." My mother is a great woman with a great heart. She did the best she could with what she had and I admire her courage. Despite her mistakes, she always has been my hero.

Not too far before this point in time, when my mother's addiction was beginning to take control, I endured the worst nightmare of my life. I described it in the chapter "4:30 a.m." I've always believed that dreams can have meaning and I've spent quite a bit of time contemplating whether that nightmare had a deeper message behind it then I originally thought. As time went on I attempted to interpret the dream. Although I cannot say for sure that I am correct, it is the closest I have come to explaining that night.

I believe the recurring time in my dream, 4:30 a.m. was symbolic for the cycle of addiction that my mom could not break. The new door in my room that had replaced my desk symbolized a new door that had opened up in our home, and beyond it lay death and destruction. The skull that tried to devour me was the addiction itself. It had already consumed my mother. The stone path that stretched endlessly through the blackness and the flames was the path my mother was walking down, the path of despair. The fire beyond the door represented the destruction of everything we held dear. When I ran up into the kitchen and shook my mom, telling her that we needed to wake up Eric and Lisa and get out of the house because it was on fire, she did not respond but instead watched helplessly as the flames engulfed the house. That fire represented the fact that my mom could do nothing as her addiction took control over her life and she watched helplessly as her home and her family was burned to ash. Those flames, her addiction, consumed everything. She would loose it all. The zombie like state my mom was in represented the mental state she was in due to the drugs. The drugs had voided her mind and slowed her body, giving her that zombie like appearance.

That nightmare was more than a nightmare; it was an explanation for what was going on right in front of me. I just wish I could've interpreted it sooner and maybe prevented those flames from consuming everything.

As Social Services got involved with our family again, arrangements needed to be made for Eric, Lisa, and my living situation. The Scott family, old acquaintances, offered to take Eric and Lisa in. They lived a good half hour drive out of town in a huge log house that Mr. Scott had built himself. Their property was vast and the lifestyle there resembled that of a small farm. The Scotts already had six kids, two girls, and four boys. I wondered how adding Eric and Lisa into the mix would turn out.

As for me, I had talked to Jake who talked to his mom and it seemed I would be living with him. I anticipated living with Jake would be much different than living with Brian. We got along much better and rarely ever argued, let alone fought. Living at Jake's didn't seem half bad considering the circumstances.

I remember thinking how messed up it was for us all to be bidding each other farewell. It was like "Okay well bye Eric and Lisa. It was good growing up with you. I look back fondly on our childhood memories. Keep in touch!" Saying goodbye to my brother and sister was surreal and indescribably tough.

It would still be a couple weeks until my mom left for rehab and I told her that I would come visit her at the house everyday until then. After many hugs and kisses, I left to head to Jake's, all the while feeling completely messed up that just a few days ago we were all a family again and now suddenly, it was gone.

Upon arriving at Jake's place I learned that I would have the whole basement to myself, which I thought was pretty cool. I loved having my own space, a small comfort in those circumstances.

After settling in, which I somehow pulled off in that same day, I lay on my bed reflecting on everything that had happened. It was all so crazy.

I lay there and recalled a memory I hadn't thought of in quite some time. It was just after my father passed and around that time I would hike up the nearby hills and through the forest to clear my mind. I remember one time standing on the top of this hill that overlooked the city and wondered what I would do if something happened to my mom. I vowed I'd never go to foster care and that I wouldn't let Eric and Lisa go either. I imagined us all running away, moving from town to town trying to avoid Social Services as they tracked us down.

I thought about it. It seemed like an adventure, like something out of a movie. Here I was, in that situation I had thought about all those years ago. Something had happened to my mom and wasn't I supposed to take Eric and Lisa and run away? I felt like I failed to protect them, especially now that they were living out of town. Taking Eric and Lisa and running away seemed like ludicrous now and I was pretty sure they wouldn't even join me to begin with. All I could do was trust that they would be safe and well at the Scotts' and that I would be safe and well at Jake's.

Fortunately for my siblings, they were safe and well. Unfortunately for me, I would soon be not. A dark cloud was approaching in the skies of my heart and soon I would be plagued with something that I did not expect or know. Soon another domino would fall, forcing the rest into motion. What awaited me, I never could've anticipated. It is a part of my life which I would never want to endure again. It was getting dark . . . and I had nowhere to go.

Chapter Nine
When the Dust Settles All I See is Grey

It was crazy how fast I got settled in at Jake's. I had my whole room set up the day I moved in. When the social worker came to inspect the room that I would be living in, she was noticeably surprised to see how settled I was. I guess I was just used to moving all the time.

Jake and I shared the house with Jake's mom Rebecca (who refused to be called Mrs. Jennings) and his sister Amanda. Like my mom, Rebecca was a single mother as Jake and Amanda's father had left shortly after they were born. In many ways I felt it was the similarities between our two families that allowed for Jake and me to connect on a deeper level.

The first couple weeks at the Jennings were alright. I visited my mom almost every day back at the house and kept her informed of what was going on in my life. I visited her one last time the day before she left. I wished her all the best and told her I would be waiting for her when she returned. It was tough to say goodbye again but I tried to remind myself that I would see her soon.

As I started to get more and more accustomed to living with Jake and his family, I started to develop a good friendship with his sister Amanda. Although Jake told me to just ignore her, she was fun to hang around and she always had some sort of helpful advice to offer me when I needed it.

I spent four out of the seven days of the week at the only decently sized shopping mall our city had. Without fail, Jake and I were there at virtually the same time every day. Our activities included aimlessly walking around the mall and occasionally finding enough change scattered about (and the odd pop bottle that could be returned for a refund), until we had enough cash to split a side of fries from the food court.

We talked a lot about pretty much everything. Most of it though revolved around Amy. It seemed like in the past few weeks Amy had completely fallen off the face of the planet. She just stopped talking to me. She avoided me at school and every time we did chat, it was awkward. I had no idea what was going on and she wouldn't tell me. She was even spending time with other guys, mostly the drummer from our band: Adam.

Amy and I never really recovered from the whole incident with Brian. Things just weren't the same after that. The way she looked at me, the way she talked to me, nothing was the same. I was still head over heels for her, so blinded by the way I felt that I couldn't see that she was beginning to lose interest in me. In many ways, she already had.

I didn't know what changed but whatever it was, it changed so fast it left me more confused than I think I'd ever been. One day we were telling each other "I love you," and the next she just stops talking to me altogether. It didn't make any sense.

As time carried on so did I in misery, not knowing where I stood with Amy. If we weren't together anymore then I was hoping she'd just tell me instead of just pretending like I never existed. I needed a conclusion, I need resolve and until I got those things I couldn't be at peace.

It is nearly impossible for me to relate any other word that describes how I was feeling at this time other than misery. Because my feelings for Amy were so strong, when she rejected my feelings, all the insecurities and negative emotions that being with her had helped me overcome, came back tenfold. I was afraid again. I was insecure again. All I wanted was to stay at home in my room and never see anyone again. But I didn't really have a home; I had a room in my friend's home. And unfortunately things were getting a little messed up back there at the Jennings too.

After several weeks of living with Jake and his family I came to learn that Rebecca was utterly illogical and unreasonable. Things were all right at first, but after a while Rebecca imposed a rule that I wasn't allowed in the house until 4:30 p.m. and I had to be out by 8:30 a.m. every day. Apparently she needed her "own space" during those hours of the day. I tried arguing that rule was unreasonable but there was just no getting through to her. Since school got out at 3:00 p.m., I always had an hour and a half to kill before I could go home. During this time I'd usually skateboard to the mall which was a good twenty minute ride away or stay at the school and do homework.

One time I came home at 5:00 p.m. and Jake, Amanda, and Rebecca were already at the dinner table. When they let me in the door, Rebecca acted surprised and said "Oh Brandon I didn't know you were going to be here for dinner. I only made enough food for us." I thought, "Well of course I'm going to be here for dinner, what did you expect? It's not like I have money to go out and buy my own dinner." Pissed as hell I said nothing as I went down into my room to take my mind off the hunger in my stomach. After that little incident I always made a habit of asking when dinner would be ready each night. Rebecca would always say she didn't know. After a while I stopped asking because it really wasn't doing me any good.

At around this time I got a phone call from Jane with some bad news. My mom hadn't made it to the treatment center. She had gotten off the bus at some point and abandoned the plan for her recovery. She had most likely hit the streets in search of something to quench her addiction. This news devastated me and only added to the incredible misery I was already feeling. She was on the streets in a city that neither she nor I knew. Her whereabouts were unknown and thus some friends of the family had called the police and reported her as a missing person. For a very long time, my mother was missing and not a day went by when that didn't eat me up.

As I continued to be forced away from the house I was supposedly living in, my grades in school began to drop due to stress and no resources or a place to do my homework.

In another instance, it was the end of February and Amanda, Jake and I had gone to a friend's birthday. Amy was there with Adam so I was miserable as usual. Jake and Amanda were getting a ride home and they asked if I wanted to join them. I said I was going to stay for a little while longer and that I'd be back at the house soon. After some time went by I tried to snag a ride home with no success. Since I had brought my skateboard I figured this was going to be my only way to get home. So after leaving the party I embarked on the most insane skateboard journey I had ever made across town in the freezing cold wearing nothing but a hoodie.

I was still a little choked up as I had somehow lost my wallet earlier at the party when I had for some reason decided to jump into the ice cold lake to receive a point for our team for a scavenger hunt we were all doing. Somehow I lost my wallet in the transition of taking off my clothes and putting them back on. Was it worth the point? No.

So there I was skateboarding across town in the middle of winter. Luckily there was hardly any snow on the ground but that was little relief compared to the wind chill. About an hour and a half later, which was much longer than I was hoping it would take, I arrived back at the house. Upon approaching the front door I noticed all the lights were off.

"Don't tell me everyone's in bed this early," I said to myself. "It's only just after 11:00 p.m. Rebecca doesn't usually go to bed until midnight."

After knocking on the door and ringing the doorbell several times it was clear that Rebecca was not going to let me in and she had obviously told Jake and Amanda not to open the door either.

Pissed as hell (which was a feeling I was starting to get a lot those days), and freezing cold, I made the journey up town to a doughnut shop that was open all night. When I arrived I was grateful to finally be somewhere warm and I took a seat to rest my legs, which were extremely sore from the close to two-hour skateboard ride here. I was famished. I decided to purchase some food to fill my stomach and in hope that by doing so; the staff wouldn't kick me out of the shop. It was in that moment that I remembered I had lost my wallet earlier and my heart instantly filled with more dismay than before. So I sat in the most uncomfortable chair I had ever sat in as I watched, while starving, a display of freshly prepared food, rotate again and again in a glass casing about two feet away from me. It was torture.

For the entire night until 7:00 a.m. when the store started to get busy with the morning rush, I sat in that chair watching the rotating food and trying to fall asleep. I did not sleep at all but I had a good chat with a homeless guy who was also spending the night in another chair at the table across from mine.

At one point I thought that sleeping in a cardboard dumpster might be more comfortable than this chair, so I went out to the bin behind the doughnut shop. After crawling in and burying myself under the cardboard I was surprised at how warm it was. After lying there for about half an hour though I became nervous that a truck might come in the morning when I was still asleep, dump the cardboard and myself into the back of the truck where I would be compressed. Not wanting to take any chances at a flatter body, I went back in the doughnut shop to wait out the night.

When 7:00 a.m. finally rolled around, I made my way back down to the house. It was even colder than it had been just hours ago and all I wanted was to eat some toast and get some sleep.

I got to the house to discover that no one was up yet but being as tired, cold, and pissed off as I was I didn't care. Still though, not wanting to face any more wrath from Rebecca, I gathered some small pebbles from the ground and threw them one at a time at Jake's bedroom window in hopes that he'd wake up and let me in.

After a few tries he looked out his window and I motioned for him to let me in. When he came downstairs and did, I was overjoyed to finally be allowed entry into the residence where I was pretty sure I was living. Jake yawned as he mumbled "You woke up my mom as well with the rocks you threw at the window." I looked at him, the expression on my face probably more than enough to get the message across. "I don't give a shit," I said bitterly as I grabbed two pieces of bread, shoved them in my mouth and went downstairs to go to bed.

Luckily for me it was Saturday, which means I could probably pull off sleeping in until noon. Unfortunately that wouldn't happen either because at 10:00 a.m. Rebecca woke me up from the top of the basement stairs, mad at the amount of noise I had made with the rocks earlier that morning.

As time went on, my misery worsened. I suffered from insomnia and slept no more than two or three hours a night. I always had bags under my eyes and falling asleep in class was a common occurrence.

On top of that Jake was acting weird. He had always been a touchy feely kind of guy and Brian and I had always accepted it as just part of who he was. Lately though he had been a little over the top and it was making me uncomfortable.

I went to bed at around 9:00 p.m. every night but rarely fell asleep before four or five in the morning. After a while my insomnia started to really get to me. Messed up shit was happening in my head when I closed my eyes. My mind was overly active and it wouldn't shut up. If I lay in my bed for too long I'd start to get random itches all over my body that would pester me until I left my bed. At certain points I was starting to feel like I was on the verge of insanity, often times not knowing where I was or what was going on. The following is a journal like entry I typed on the computer one night during one of my worst nights of insomnia.

Sleeping Problems   *Brandon Krogel*
Written: Night of April 4, 2005

It is almost impossible to describe what I've been feeling these past nights. For a couple of weeks now I am finding my sleeps, or lack therefore of, to be more aggravating and frustrating than anything else. What I can only describe as a slow moving madness that makes me question my own sanity, I find that the strangeness of my mind seems to merge with me as I am still awake, which confuses reality from my dreams.

It starts like this. I get in my bed and spend a few minutes thinking about anything and everything until I get comfortable and that drowsy feeling starts to kick in. Then I close my eyes and rest on my most comfortable side, my left. This is crucial. I know that if I do not fall asleep before switching to lying on my right side more than once (once the left side becomes uncomfortable), I will not fall asleep for many hours to come, or even at all. If I haven't fallen asleep by this time I know that the rest of my night is going to be pretty much just plain horrible. It will start by me tossing and turning, I will be very tired and crave sleep, but my mind will be awake and active. Other messed up things happen as the night continues. I will be itchy all over my body until I finally fall asleep, if I do. So I am scratching away, and how can you fall asleep if you keep scratching yourself all night? My mind is running wild. Random words and thoughts are moving through my head very quickly. I have conversations with myself. I am not yet asleep.

If I do fall asleep I tend to dream huge, complex, and bizarre dreams that usually relate to my current life, and sometimes they forecast things to come.

This entry, although vague and poorly written, was my attempt at trying to communicate what it was that I was feeling these nights. To say that I was on the verge of insanity is almost an understatement. I tasted the life of a man who had lost his sanity. Luckily these sleepless nights would not last forever, but at the time, they were certainly taking a toll on me.

At this point in time, I began to loose all feelings and emotions except for sadness and anger. Other emotions had become unattainable. No matter what I did, this feeling remained. This feeling of "grey." When all the dust had settled from the chaotic events that had happened in this past short while, all I could see was grey. It was an endless road that stretched as far as they eye could see.

There was grey colorless grass on each side of the concrete road and the sky was neither black nor white. My life had become an emotionless abyss and I was starting to become unable to function in day to day activities. Most of my conversations took place in my head as I felt no one understood what I was feeling. Hell, I didn't even know how to explain how I was feeling. I was always tired but could never sleep. It took everything I had to just get up from my bed in the morning. I realized I was not well and went to the Ministry to request to see a counsellor. After a week or so I was able to meet with a counsellor by the name of Dave.

When I first met with Dave I was eager to tell him everything that I had been feeling in hopes that he'd know what was wrong with me. After hearing my story he asked me why I thought I was feeling emotionless and grey. I replied by saying I figured it was a self-defense mechanism that my body had initiated in order to protect my brain from insanity. He said it was an interesting way of putting it but I was pretty much right. He claimed I had extreme anxiety and stress from everything that happened thus far in my life and this in turn led to what he called depression.

I learned that depression introduces you to a world without color, emotion, and feeling. He said the best way to cure this is to find out what the roots of the depression are and to deal with those first. In time, when things have improved and loose ends have been tied, I would emerge from this depression and everything would eventually be alright.

At the end of our first encounter I felt good. I felt like I had taken my first step in getting out of this grey void that I had fallen into. As the weeks went on I continued to meet with Dave every Thursday and even though I'd be miserable going in to see him, I would come out optimistic and refreshed. Despite this though, that optimism only lasted a few hours before reality would grab me by the throat and pull me back into misery.

I knew that there was only going to be one way that I could make a drastic change to the way I felt. I needed to get out of the Jennings. So many of my problems were a direct result of living there. But where would I go? If I had another option aside from foster care, I would've taken It before moving into Jake's.

I spent a lot of time thinking about other options but nothing came to mind. I knew I needed to change my living arrangements or I was going to lose my mind. I felt as though pressure was building up in me and soon I would explode like a balloon filled with too much air. I needed to do something before that happened. Unfortunately though, life wasn't going to cut me a break just yet, but it would be just this thing that would give me enough momentum to enter into a new phase of life. I was about to experience the worst day of my life but it would be this day that would spark a new beginning, or something like it.

I had woken up that morning with no more than two hours of sleep. As usual I had to be out of the house by 8:30 a.m., but I left earlier as I loathed spending unnecessary time in this place that I hated to call home.

The counselling sessions had been good at first but I had reached a point where nothing was making me feeling any better. I was at the peak of my depression.

At school, Amy continued to avoid me and every time I saw her and Adam together, my misery worsened. More than ever I needed her to speak to me, to tell me something, anything. I needed resolve and I needed it soon or I was going to lose my mind.

My report card arrived that day, which didn't add any joy to my current state of affairs. I was nearly failing every class I had. I was concerned that I wouldn't pass grade 11 and would be forced to stay back a grade next year. I knew this was because I never had a place or a chance to do my homework.

After school I didn't even bother going home as I knew my efforts to get inside would be futile. Instead I went to the mall as usual and spent my time reading at one of the book stores there until I figured it would be alright to go home. I didn't bother to try and make it in time for dinner as I generally didn't get one.

I arrived home at around 5:30 p.m. and as expected, everyone had already eaten. After being let in the house, I made my way to my room, barely saying a word.

I was so tired. I needed sleep. I needed a new life. I lay on my bed wondering how I was ever going to get out of this mess. It seemed impossible. After a few minutes of lying there I heard the door to the basement open and suddenly the lights turned off.

"What the hell?" Just then I saw Jake making his way down the stairs. "I'm too tired to hang out man, I'm just going to go to sleep," I said as I rolled over to my side. Before I could see it coming Jake jumped onto my bed and pinned me down. "I'm not in the mood, man," I said a little agitated and annoyed. He said nothing as he continued to pin me down. "Piss off dude!" I yelled as I tried to push him off of me. He wouldn't budge. Jake was a bigger guy than I was and it generally took all my energy to overpower him. Then things got messy. While being pinned down Jake reached down and grabbed my dick, attempting to act innocently. When he did I knew that I wasn't just imagining things now and I was convinced Jake was coming on to me. Not needing any more stress or uncomfortable feelings, I went into a rage and threw him off my bed and stood up immediately. Although I knew in my heart, I didn't want to accuse him of coming on to me so I silently and quickly made my way up the stairs.

"Where you going?" Jake asked innocently. "Out," I snapped back as I put on my shoes and headed out the door.

I walked up to the school to clear my head. All I could think about was what just happened. Not only could I not come home half the time but now when I did I had to worry about Jake coming on to me. I felt like I was going to lose it.

"FUCK!" I screamed with enough ferocity to scare nearby pedestrians as I walked up the sidewalk. "I can't believe this shit," I continued to mutter to myself. "Why is this happening to me!?" the desperation in my voice made it seem like I was calling out to someone. Noticing a nearby patch of grass, I stopped and sat down to take a breather.

"Where the hell am I supposed to go? How can I function in this mess?" I looked around for some sign of an answer. There was nothing. "I'm alone," I whispered to myself. In that moment I seemed to have finally realized that fact. After a few moments I got up with my head hung dejectedly and continued my trek towards the school.

When I arrived I realized that it was youth night at the church next door to the school. I knew Amy would be there and since I figured this day couldn't get any worse I decided that tonight would be the night that I got an answer out of Amy no matter what. I needed her to give me an answer and I was going to lose my mind if I didn't get it that night.

I sat outside the church contemplating how shitty I had been feeling these past weeks. I tried to understand this "feeling of grey," this emotionless world that I now inhabited. I wondered what happened to my life, my joy, my happiness, and my optimism. It was clear I had become a much different person in these past weeks than I was before and I didn't like who I had turned out to be.

Suddenly an interesting concept appeared in my head as in that moment I remembered that, for the past two weeks I had been having an interesting recurring dream (when I was finally able to actually get to sleep).

In this recurring dream the concept was the same, although the situation or scenario was always a little different. I was stressed, sad, or angry and for some reason I would have a cigarette and feel better. Since I had never smoked before I had no idea why people smoked. I thought people just smoked for the hell of it. I didn't know there was more to it than that. Since in my dream smoking was providing me with some kind of relief or comfort, I wondered if this might be the case in real life. "Perhaps that's why people smoke," I thought.

Of course I couldn't take any facts from what smoking seemed like in my dream, considering I had never done it before. Yet still that curiosity that this dream had brought me was difficult to suppress. Now in what seemed like my darkest hour, these cigarettes were on my mind along with the idea that they could make me feel better.

I remember thinking how bizarre it was that I was having these thoughts. I had been against smoking my whole life. Telling smokers to not smoke was a sermon I preached at every opportunity I had. Some of my friends who were older had even started smoking and I came down on them hard with my conviction of how bad smoking was. I must have annoyed a lot of people thinking back on it.

The point is smoking was the farthest thing from my mind. It had never been appealing or cool to me. I had refused cigarettes countless times in social encounters with my peers with ease. Why now was I so intrigued with smoking?

This recurring dream was responsible. For two weeks, every night without fail, my dreams were filled with the idea that smoking cigarettes brought comfort and relief. I had never cared to understand why people smoke but these dreams made me ask that question. I wondered "Why would people put that garbage into their bodies unless it did something pleasant for them? Killing yourself probably doesn't feel very nice but I suppose if you could kill yourself over the course of thirty years or so and feel good the whole time, you might not actually care."

Before I could carry on with my thoughts, people started to leave the church. Youth was clearly done and I knew Amy would be one of those people coming out of the church doors. I waited patiently until I saw her lovely face in the crowd. Upon seeing her I approached and asked if I could talk to her alone for a minute. She agreed and we wandered a little ways from the crowd.

I took a deep breath before beginning. I was nervous, even though I knew what the outcome of this conversation was going to look like.

"Amy . . .I need you to talk to me. I know you've avoided this conversation for awhile in hopes that I'd get a hint and leave you alone and I got that hint, but I need to hear you say it. I need you to tell me that there is nothing between us and that you feel nothing for me."

Amy looked down, obviously not wanting to be in the position she was in but knowing that if she didn't deal with this now, it would continue to cause more problems. She let out a heavy sigh and met my gaze. Her eyes seemed sad but I knew they were that way for me and not her. "Brandon, there is nothing between us. I have no feelings for you. Its over."

I hung my head in silence for a moment. This was the answer I was expecting. This was the answer I knew she would give me. Yet it was still so hard to hear it. I did my best to keep my composure.

"Thank you for bringing closure to this," I said quietly as I glanced once more into the eyes of the girl I loved. Staring into her eyes brought me back to the moment when I had first seen her that day and time had stopped. It almost seemed as though time had stopped again as I watched everything from then until now flash before me. But we can't be frozen in time forever and so that moment continued and I turned around and took my first step away from Amy.

I knew she was watching me as I walked away and I turned around just in time to see her ride show up and her leave the parking lot. The church that was just a few moments ago filled with people had been closed and locked as everyone went home. Here I remained in an abandoned parking lot, looking up at the dark night sky which reminded me of the darkness that seemed to have overtaken my life. I felt a swelling of energy and frustration build up inside of me and before I could calm myself I screamed into the heavens, perhaps at God or perhaps to no one, yelling that tonight I would smoke a cigarette, that tonight I would stop giving a shit about anything. And that's exactly what I did.

As I left the parking lot and headed to the street, I searched the ground for cigarette butts. I knew this was dirty and gross but I didn't care. The same intensity of the dream I had been dreaming overwhelmed me and somehow I was convinced that a cigarette would bring relief to my suffering.

After several minutes I had found a butt with a decent amount of tobacco still left on the stick. Before I could pick it up, an older lady sitting at the bus stop a few feet away from me shouted in my direction.

"That's disgusting!" she blurted. I looked up at her wondering if she was talking to me and if so, why did she care? "Here . . ." she said as she beckoned me over. "Take these." I reached out my hand as she gave me two fresh cigarettes from her pack.

I looked down at my hand and the two cigarettes that lay there, then back up to the woman who given them to me. "Uh thank you," I said not sure what to say. "Don't worry about it," she replied. "Just don't pick up butts on the ground. You could get sick that way." I nodded at her and said thanks again as I made my way back to the school.

I figured since this was the place where so much shit had gone down, this would be the place where I would have my first cigarette.

Sitting down on a set of stairs, I took one of the cigarettes and brought it to my lips. Brian and I had the odd cigar from time to time back in the day, although we never inhaled, but actually breathing in tobacco smoke was a whole new idea. I understood the concept. You light the end and inhale the smoke. I had seen people smoke for the first time and they would burst into an insane coughing fit so I cautiously lit the smoke and inhaled lightly. I didn't cough. Feeling brave, I decided to take a decent inhale the second time around. Still, I didn't cough. "This is great," I thought. "I'm not even coughing."

I sat on the stairs and continued to puff. The taste wasn't that bad although it was safe to say that it certainly didn't taste good. I noticed I was feeling better somehow. I was more relaxed and calm than before. Although this feeling was not nearly as good as how I felt in my dream, I was grateful for any relief I could get my hands on.

"So this is why people smoke," I thought. "It calms you down. It relaxes you." I continued to ponder the concept of smoking until my cigarette had reached the filter. "I'm assuming you don't smoke this part," I concluded as I chucked the butt away.

After spending a few more minutes on the stairs I decided it was about time to head back to the Jennings. I didn't want to get locked out of the house again after all.

As I walked back to the house I thought about how bizarre this all was. Look at me, I was smoking cigarettes, something I had been against my whole life. Why was I doing this? Then I realized after going through as much shit as I had lately, it was no wonder. I no longer cared. Nothing mattered. I had lost everything. My family, my dog, my girlfriend, my sanity . . . when I really thought about it, I had lost my life. So since I didn't have one, I figured it didn't matter what I did.

Another week had gone by. I bummed cigarettes whenever I could. Since I was always at the mall, it made getting smokes easier. Also I found that they reduced my appetite which was terrific because I was never eating at the Jennings anyways (because I was kicked out of the house for most of the day), so this was a great alternative for my hunger. Still though, I knew that even with smoking, I needed to change my living situation.

It was while I was enjoying a smoke and a coffee outside the mall one afternoon, that an idea came to me. The Williams family had been friends of my family for years and had helped us out in difficult times. I wondered if maybe I could live there. The more I thought about it the more the thought became appealing. If this worked out, maybe it would be the thing that would save me from this hell that I was currently living in.

Without wasting any time I hit up the nearest pay phone and called the Williams. After speaking with Mrs. Williams and asking her what she thought about that idea, she invited me to come up to the house for dinner the following night and we'd talk about it then.

More excited than I had been since I could remember; I hopped on the next bus and headed home to await the next day when hopefully my life would change for the better.

Despite the fact that I had once again gotten no sleep the previous night, I woke up and jumped out of bed with more energy than I had had in a long time. I got dressed and headed to the school early like I usually did to take a shower (for some reason I was only allowed to shower at the Jennings once every three days), and prepare for my day.

When school got out I wasted no time and walked with anticipation up to the Williams house. About a half hour later I arrived and the moment I stepped though their front door, I felt a peace that I had forgotten existed in this world. After a wonderful dinner I explained to them my situation.

I told them how I wasn't allowed to come home for most of the day, how I was never eating anything. I explained how Jake came on to me and how I suspected he might be gay. When I had finally finished describing the horrors of my current living situation Mr. and Mrs. Williams sat silently thinking about everything I had just said. After a few moments they gave me a response and it was the most beautiful, amazing words I had ever heard. They said I could move in to the spare bedroom downstairs by the end of the week.

Finally. Finally I was getting out of this house. Getting out of this miserable, insane house that was such a factor in my miserable, insane life. This had to have been God Himself stepping in and saving me from certain doom.

The Williams said I could spend the night in the spare bedroom if I wanted to and I accepted graciously without hesitation.

And that night I slept the most peaceful, relaxing sleep I had ever had. No insomnia. No insanity in my head. No worries on my mind. I slept and for the first time since I could remember, I felt a smile spread across my face.

Chapter Ten

Collecting Myself

Moving into the Williams was exactly what I needed. I had only been there for a week but already I felt like I was breathing fresh air for the first time in a long time. A tremendous burden had been lifted from me and a streak of light had pierced through my grey clouds, offering me hope.

It was late in May and there was only a month and a bit left before the school year would end and once again the summer would approach. I spent the rest of the school year doing my best to enjoy my time with friends and thanks to my new living situation, I was able to bring all my grades back up to a passing level. Some of them I even managed to bring up to an A or B. I was grateful to finally be getting myself together again, grateful for this time to collect myself and recover from the insanity I had been bombarded with for all these months before.

As I had begun to start feeling significantly better and my meetings with Dave had become more of us discussing politics and less of us working on my depression, I told him that I appreciated everything he had done but I felt that it was no longer necessary for us to meet. After a fond farewell I bid Dave goodbye and felt like I had made serious progress in the stability of my mind. It seemed I was finally getting things together.

The Williams had two daughters, Sarah and Michelle. Sarah was a grade ahead of me in school but was only one month older than me. Michelle was exactly one year younger than me and so all three of us were able to communicate on pretty much the same level. Although I enjoyed hanging out with Sarah and we never had any disagreements, for some reason I felt Michelle and me had more in common.

So as the school year came to an end once again, I was excited and grateful to be spending the summer at the Williams and not at Rebecca's. I hadn't talked to Jake since I left and I had no intention of doing so. I wanted to stay as far away from the Jennings as possible. I wanted to forget that part of my life entirely.

During the summer Michelle and I bonded quite a bit. We went for walks, we stayed in on rainy days and played board games, or if we were feeling adventurous, we'd go splash around in the rain like little kids. It seemed almost like Michelle and I were developing a deeper connection, something almost romantic. I pondered that idea for a while but couldn't bring myself to date any one. The wound Amy had left in my heart was far from healed and I wasn't ready to move on to someone else.

Although my insomnia had virtually disappeared, I was often restless at night and since I had nothing else to do, I would stay out all night seeking adventure and

excitement. I'd take my guitar and walk all over town. I'd go to this all-night diner and for $2.00 I could enjoy a bottomless coffee. It wasn't long before the staff at the diner and I became good friends.

Most of my summer evenings were spent out and I loved every second of it. As the end of the summer approached however, I grew tired of having virtually no money so I figured getting a job would be a half decent idea.

There was a pizza shop not far from where the Williams lived and it turned out that Sarah had worked there just a few months prior to me moving in. She said she'd put in a good word if I applied so that's exactly what I did. I dropped off my resume numerous times over the course of several weeks and eventually got called in for an interview. I was nervous as I met with one of the managers who were going to interview me. I had never been through an interview process like this at the go-cart track or the gas station, so this was entirely new for me. Luckily the manger who was interviewing me seemed like a good guy and so I did my best to be relaxed and outgoing as he conducted the interview. His name was Mike and in many ways, I saw a part of myself in him. The words he used, the way he talked, his personality—a lot like me. Perhaps this was the reason the interview went so well because when we had finished, he seemed excited to congratulate and welcome me to the team. With a big smile on my face I shook his hand and expressed my thanks for the job. He said to come in the next day and he'd get me started.

Walking home I was pretty excited. Sarah had told me that working at this pizza shop was a lot of fun and the people who worked there were all good friends.

Along with getting the job at the pizza shop I had also just gotten my driver's license and after my first paycheck, I bought my first car. It was a red 1989 Ford Escort LX Hatchback. I had no idea what that meant, but it was a nice little red car and it only cost me $500.00. I picked it up, and the drive home was incredible. I sat there in my own car with the window rolled down, cruising down the road with a cool breeze rushing in, soothing my face from the heat outside (since there was no air conditioning).

I thought about how far I had come this summer. How I went from being completely miserable with nothing, to feeling half decent with my own car and a good job that I didn't mind. Things were continuing to look up.

I got the hang of making pizzas in no time. Turns out it was much easier than I thought and after getting tossed into the insanity of kitchen life right away, I memorized how to make everything on the menu in no time.

On top of that I had come to make some good friends at work. Mike and I were especially bonding. He was a really awesome guy and before long I looked up to him like an older brother, plus, we had much in common. He was four years older than me but to him that didn't seem to matter, so it didn't matter to me.

As the summer came to an end, a familiar feeling began to come back to me. Despite the fact that I was no longer living in the hellish environment that the Jennings provided me with, I was starting to feel that "grey" feeling again. I could feel the depression creeping back towards me, and couldn't shake it.

During the course of that summer I had rekindled my friendship with my long time friends Ryan, whom I had been friends with since the fifth grade, and Aaron who I had been friends with since the seventh. We all got our driver's license around the same time and ended up hanging out a lot. Probably the biggest thing that glued Ryan, Aaron, and I together was our love for music. We all played several instruments and had been in musical projects all throughout middle and high school. Aside from that though we generally just got along really well as friends and would frequently get together and hang out.

Although I considered all my friends equal, Ryan and I had been friends for a long time. He'd been by my side since the fifth grade. He was with me when my dad passed. He was there when my mom went off to rehab. Ryan had always been there to support me through all the obstacles I faced in my life. My friendship with him couldn't be compared to the ones I had with others because I didn't share that kind of history with anyone else.

Although Ryan had spent his grade eleven year at another school and in a sense I had lost touch with him in that regard, he was coming back to finish his grade twelve year with me and the rest of our class that we had grown up with at our tiny Christian school. I was glad to be seeing him on a regular basis again. It was our time spent together in that last year of high school that really sealed the deal for our friendship and although I didn't know it yet, Ryan and I would continue to play an active role in each other's lives for years to come.

Although my circumstances in life at that point in time didn't seem half bad, it didn't matter to me. I'd decline hangouts to be alone with my thoughts and leave early at get-togethers to think and smoke. As a result of my depression creeping back into my life, the school year started off a little shaky. I was in grade 12 now, the final year in my high school career. This year would be quite significant and full of surprises. Unfortunately though, none of them would be good surprises. But of course, I didn't know that at the time.

School started in early September and by the time October had come around I was getting anxious at the Williams. When we had originally talked about me living there, it was more of a temporary solution than a long term one. Since I had been there about five months already, I felt like I was crossing the line from temporary to long term. Despite the fact that the Williams insisted it was fine that I stay as long as I'd like, I still felt like I was getting in the way and part of me also wanted to move on to new things.

It was around this time when Sarah had mentioned to me she had a friend named Andrew who was looking for a roommate. I had been wanting to live on my own since my family split for the second time, and this seemed like a perfect opportunity for me to experience the freedom that I wanted.

At Rebecca's my freedom was very limited. Although I could do anything I wanted outside the house, inside I had no freedom. The Williams took on somewhat of a parenting role over me, which I appreciated, but I felt I was too old to be parented. Plus I hadn't had a "parent" tell me what I could and could not do in quite some time. This chance to live on my own seemed like my chance at ultimate freedom, at independence. No one to tell me what to do, no one to rain on my parade. Of course this is another prime example of how naïve I used to be. It's true, I was mature and experienced in some ways, but in so many others, I was just a kid.

Sarah gave me Andrew's contact information and after a couple days I managed to get in touch with him. He brought me up to see the place. The house was in the same neighborhood I grew up in; it was also the same neighborhood where my dad passed away, a bizarre coincidence. I had seen this house countless times driving to school as a kid and now here I was about to live in it.

Andrew rented out the basement from the guy who lived on the upstairs floor. After meeting with both of them they seemed like good guys and since I was eager to taste freedom, I told Andrew to count me in. I moved in and for the first time in my life I was independent. Food, laundry, cleaning, hygiene—these were all now my sole responsibility.

It didn't take long though for the excitement of living on my own to be replaced with my growing depression. In fact, after spending many nights alone in my new place I realized that living on your own was quite a lonely experience and at times I would regret leaving the family atmosphere that I took for granted at the Williams.

As my depression worsened my ability to interact with my peers in social situations declined. Due to both the way I was feeling and the fact that most of the people at my job smoked, my habit went from two cigarettes a week to five a day. At this same time I had run for school president as it was something I had wanted to do for several years and seeing how this was my grade 12 year, I figured this was my last chance to make it happen.

Students were not allowed to smoke at my school though, let alone the school president, whose job it was to be a role model for younger students. I had always been on good terms with my teachers at school, and I was close with the high school Principal Mr. Reid. I'm not sure what brought the two of us together. Perhaps he saw potential in me that I wasn't using. Perhaps I thought he was down to earth enough that I could talk to him about things. Whatever the reason, he became an active mentor in my life and next to Mark, he was the closest thing I had to a father figure. When Mr. Reid had found out I was smoking after I was elected school president, he pretty much lost it on me.

The Parent Teacher Committee didn't want a smoker to be the president of the school and on several occasions I was threatened with the loss of my presidency if I didn't quit.

Although I wanted to quit smoking, it was the only thing in my life that I was able to take pleasure from. I wanted to be a good leader on the student council and make my teachers proud but I was in such a troublesome state that I couldn't fulfill my duties as the school president. After a while rumors got to my ears from other students that I was a crappy president. It didn't feel good to hear that but I knew they were right. I wasn't being the best I could be. I wanted to with everything in me but every day I awoke to misery and once again in my life, it would take everything I had just to get out of bed in the morning.

Being in grade twelve brought a whole new wave of emotions upon me. My school had been the one thing that had remained constant in my life when everything else had changed. When I lost my family my school remained. When I lost my best friend my school remained. When I lost the girl I loved, my school remained. The thought that this was my last year with the people I had grown up with really contributed to my depression. I felt like I had taken my school for granted and now it was about to be stripped from me. The school had become like my family and without seeing these people every day, I didn't know how I was going to make it. I didn't know what I was going to do after I graduated. I didn't know who I was going to be friends with and who I wasn't. There were so many thoughts and fears that went through my head they ended up driving me completely mental.

Often times I'd stay out all night, just driving aimlessly around trying to figure life out. Almost every night I'd drive to my school and spend at least a couple hours just sitting in the parking lot, drinking coffee, smoking cigarettes, and just reminiscing. Then I'd spend a couple more just moping around, depressed that after grade twelve, all of this would be gone.

I didn't want to leave this place behind. I hated change. I hated how I was never able to control it. Life just changed arbitrarily and there was nothing I could do about it. I couldn't get over how at one point life was so good for me and now everything had been stripped away. My family, my love, and my life—I didn't know who I was anymore. I wasn't able to move with life and its ever changing state. I hung for dear life on to the past and so as time continued to move forward, I got left behind. I was dreaming of a reality that no longer existed. I tried to recreate that reality somehow in my head but all it did was allow for me to fall further and further behind. While my friends were making plans for their future, I was making plans for my past. The depression that begun while living at the Jennings was starting to look like nothing compared to the way I was feeling at this point. I felt like I was in the bottom of a hole, covered in quicksand. I couldn't move, I couldn't breathe, and I couldn't get out.

In this last year of high school I bonded with one person more than any other. Somehow Jake's sister Amanda and I had formed a strong friendship. Amanda had started smoking around the same time I had, so often times we'd leave the school together to go for a smoke break. After a while other kids in the school who secretly smoked found out about our little gatherings at lunch and in between classes and before we knew it, we had a small group of smokers who met up a few times a day.

For some reason it seemed that Amanda understood me better than anyone else. In fact the two of us were very similar people. Perhaps this is the reason we became so close. When I talked to her about my depression, she could relate. Maybe not on the same level or same intensity that I was feeling, but she could relate and that brought me comfort. It made me feel like I wasn't alone, which was the way I felt most of the time.

Despite how much time had passed since my relationship with Amy had ended, I had not recovered. The outcome of my relationship with her was also one of the biggest contributing factors in my depression. For some reason I just could not accept what had happened. I was still hurt and overwhelmed with the pain of losing my first love. I had put everything into the way I felt for Amy and when our relationship ended, I lost everything.

But time went on. My teachers thought I was trying to a badass or rebellious by smoking when really I was just trying to relieve this feeling of despair hence, I was misunderstood. My friendship with Amanda continued to grow as we in a sense, fed off of each other's depression and by doing that grew closer, maybe not in the healthiest way. My social life—aside from hanging out with Amanda—was virtually non existent. I was even finding it difficult to work. If I could hardly get out of bed in the morning, how on earth was I going to make pizzas for eight hours? Juggling an almost full time job and high school was hard enough on its own. But once again things were going to change. I was about to be reacquainted with an old friend.

During the course of the past month or so I had become reacquainted with my old friend Jake. Although we never discussed the reason why we had a falling out after I left his place, it was evident that we both knew.

Since we had started hanging out again, Jake refrained from any touchy feely things and I refrained from calling him gay. Since we now had an unspoken understanding, we were able to resume where we left off and just spent time hanging out and driving aimlessly around town. Since Jake had just got a decent job and I was still at the pizza place, we talked about getting a place together. Since I didn't really enjoy living in the house I was at now and I really didn't know Andrew at all, I figured that Jake and I getting a place was a good idea. So after giving my notice to Andrew, Jake and I found a basement suite and moved in January of that year.

Things started off pretty good. It was a little pricey, and our rent plus the cost of food, car insurance, and gas took a toll on the old checkbook. Money was tight on my end. To compensate

I had to work overtime at the pizza shop while juggling high school and everything that came with it. So on top this monstrous depression was added financial difficulties and not a whole lot of free time. It was a good thing in a sense though because when I had free time, that's when I felt the worst. At school and work, my mind was focused on other things and therefore distracted me, even if just a little, from my depression.

Shortly before moving into this place with Jake, Brian had thrown a new year's party at his place. Somewhere along the line in the past year, Brian and I had made mutual peace with each other. Although I had no desire to be good friends with him, I was able to put away my resentment and was able to somewhat enjoy his company from time to time. Jake, Brian, and I would hang out sometimes, almost like the old days.

That new years party at Brian's was the first party I had ever attended and the first time I learned what being drunk meant. I had been against drinking, as I had also been against smoking, for most of my life, but my recently discovered new attitude was "I feel like shit so I don't give a shit," played a decent role in changing what I viewed to be right or wrong. As in this instance, was the case for drinking.

Being a newbie in the whole party scene must have been entertaining for others who were experienced veterans at the party. I remember pulling up to the liquor store with Jake and a few others who were old enough to buy booze for us younger guys and asking Jake for his advice on what to get. His immediate response was vodka. He said you got to love the vodka before you can love anything else. Since I didn't know there were other liquors than vodka, it seemed like a good choice. So I handed our driver my thirty bucks and he returned a few minutes later with my first two-six of vodka.

Upon arriving at the party and after making my first drink I realized that when you mixed vodka with orange juice, it wasn't half bad. This of course led to me making several mixed drinks, which also led to me vomiting. Although unexpected and unpleasant, when I had finished I was somehow back in party mode. That didn't last long as I vaguely recall making one last drink, taking a sip or two and then laying it to rest on top of the fridge. The next thing I remember after that is making out with some girl (which is something I had never done and did not know how to do), in the front yard. I remember it was very sloppy and probably looked ridiculous to anyone watching. I didn't know where I was or what was going on. Next thing I knew I was pissing in the front yard and passed out on the lawn shortly afterwards. The following morning I awoke in my bed trying to figure out how the hell I got home.

That experience, although somewhat unpleasant gave me a new understanding of booze that I didn't have before. My whole life I was told to stay away from alcohol and that it was in no way good. After this experience I could see why but the feeling of being intoxicated justified everything else.

So as the rest of the school year progressed I drank almost every weekend. Jake and I would throw parties at the house ever so often. Our landlord didn't like it one bit. She was a young single mom and thinking back to it now, it was quite rude of us to be so loud all night long. She was pretty good though most of the time. She almost felt like an older sister at times as she was only a few years older than Jake and me. She was always giving me advice and telling me I was being a dumb ass by getting drunk all the time. I knew she was right but I didn't care. I didn't care about anything.

At this point in my life I also began to notice a deep longing for female companionship. I was eighteen now and as far as I was concerned I was virtually a full grown man. My heart was still broken from Amy and I hadn't felt that way for anyone else since then. I was older now and in many ways my old ideals of what I thought a relationship was had vastly changed. Romance and chivalry were dead in my opinion. I learned from older guys and at parties that girls just wanted to have fun. There was nothing special about relationships and that was just the way it was.

When I was drunk I felt confident and outgoing. I was outspoken, which often got me into trouble. I was also a complete mess. I would throw myself at random girls at parties in an attempt to hook up. More often than not I did but the next morning I would always kick myself for being such a fool.

Often times I forgot I was still in school. Skipping class and not showing up at all were not uncommon. Some times Mr. Reid would come to my house when I didn't show up for school and bang on the door until I woke up. He'd ring me out for not showing up, remind me of my duties as the school president and basically try and knock some sense into me. I knew he meant well but I'd always argue his point of view by saying that he didn't understand what was going on in my life.

It was actually quite true though to say that he didn't understand. In fact no one did. Hell, I didn't even understand.

When I did go to school I was absolutely miserable. Focusing on my studies was nearly impossible let alone my duties as the school president. All I could think about was how terrible I felt.

I would often leave the school campus at random times throughout the day to smoke at what become my designated spot at this park across the street from the school. I'd usually go by myself, not alerting any members of our smoking posse.

I'd just sit there, on these concrete steps chain smoking one cigarette after another, listening to depressing music and feeling so miserable all I could do was smoke and cry.

I didn't know how to tell anyone how I felt. I wanted to go up to someone and be like "Hey, you don't know this, but I am currently extremely fucked up and dealing with emotions I never knew existed. I feel on the verge of insanity and if something magical doesn't come along to save me, I have a feeling I'm going to end my own life." Of course how would someone handle that kind of information? Even the closest of my friends or mentors wouldn't know how to react.

It was true though. I was reaching a point in my depression where suicide became an actively debated topic in my head. It seemed like the only solution out this mess.

I deemed the situation hopeless and gave up. I was finally at a point where I was willing to let it all go. I was ready to die.

Being stuck in this mentality made it difficult to perform even the simplest day to day activities and concluding that I couldn't work because of this feeling, I called the pizza shop one day at lunch and told them I quit.

My boss was choked. He had done a lot for me and I felt terrible about just quitting on the spot. But to me, it felt like I had no choice. I couldn't work in this condition. I couldn't even live in this condition.

It was also around this same time that I had randomly gotten a phone call in the middle of class. Upon seeing that it was an out of area number, something inside me told me this was it. This was the phone call I been waiting almost nine months for. When I answered, my suspicions were correct. It was my mom. After almost a year she had finally called me.

Talking to her for the first time in so long was an emotional experience. I immediately walked out of my class, left the school grounds, and headed to the park across the street when I realized it was her calling. I needed a smoke for this conversation. We talked for a long while. I let out my anger, frustration, sadness, and concern and she expressed her unending remorse and guilt for abandoning me and my siblings. When our conversation ended I made her promise to call me again soon. She gave her word but as fate would have it, we would not speak again for a while.

That phone call had assured me that my mom was still alive but the pain of her absence felt stronger now than ever. I hadn't heard from my mom in so long, the pain of losing her was slowly healing by the flow of time. When she finally did call, it felt like the scab had been picked off and the wound reopened. So I continued on in misery, grateful that my mom was alive, but fearful that fact might change.

One day after school I went straight home and while making dinner, I wrote a note to each person in my life who meant something to me telling them everything I loved about them. I apologized for what was going to happen but told them it was for the greater good and that I would finally be at peace. After eating, I put on my best clothes, did my hair, and got into my car to drive up to a mountain top that I had used to climb as a kid. I knew the spot well. I had spent many hours on the top of this mountain when I was younger and I knew it would be the perfect spot. At the mountain's edge was a huge drop. Jumping off pretty much guaranteed your death. If you didn't die from height of the fall, the jagged collection of rocks that sat on the bottom would surely welcome your head or back when you hit the bottom.

For three hours I sat on the ledge of this mountain that viewed the city below. I sat there and reminisced of younger days and everything that had happened in life so far. I remembered coming up here as kid, as an explorer looking for adventure. I was so care free. Now here I was up here again only this time I wasn't here to explore. I wasn't here for adventure. I was here to end my life and the very thought of that seemed so messed up.

Convinced however that this was the only solution to my problems, I continued to sit and prepare myself for what needed to be done as the sun slowly set in a colorful array of orange and red.

"It's actually quite poetic," I remember thinking. "The sunset, the nice clothes that I'm wearing . . . it's almost perfect."

As I sat there I knew that I would have to get this over with sooner than later. I figured still that I would take just a few more minutes to ready myself. It was more difficult to just throw myself off the mountain than I had originally thought.

It was then that I noticed several small rocks sitting not to far from me. Deep in thought I wasn't even conscious when I picked a few up and started throwing them at a nearby fence post. It was in this moment that something occurred to me.

I was throwing rocks at a fence post that I was aiming for. This meant that I had a target or a goal and by throwing a few rocks, I would eventually hit that target. It was then that I realized that I still had a purpose. If I could throw a rock at a target that I aimed for, then I could hammer a nail into a piece of wood. I could shovel dirt. I could flip burgers at a fast food restaurant. When I thought about it, I could actually do anything I wanted.

This newly discovered concept brought my thoughts from the extreme low that they were sitting in just a moment ago to a point where I actually started to make some sense out of things. I talked it over with God, saying that I still might have a purpose. I also told Him though that I couldn't continue to live with this depression so something needed to change.

Some of our school's students were about to head down to Mexico for a mission's trip where we would be helping out at a school for disabled children in less than a week. I had intended to kill myself before the trip but with this newfound idea in my head, I decided to make other arrangements. I told God that I would go on this trip, which happened to be a month long, in hopes that I would return refreshed and renewed. I was hoping that an escape from my problems back home in western society was just what I needed. A vacation in a sense was exactly what it was. The more I thought about it the more I liked the idea. By the end of it, it seemed I had made a deal with God. I would go on this trip but if I returned in a state no different from my current one, I would come back up to this mountain and finish what I started.

God was probably laughing at me from above. I knew in my heart He cared about me and that suicide was not His desire for my life. He and I both knew that if I held on for just a little longer, things would change. And He was right; things would be changing very soon.

About four days before we were going to be leaving for Mexico Mr. Reid and I had gone for coffee just to chat about life. He was concerned about me and was trying to understand why I wasn't living up to all this potential he saw in me. I tried to explain how I was feeling but didn't get through to him. It wasn't until we arrived outside my house to end the night when I decided to throw everything I had at him. He was clearly confused about everything I had said earlier so I knew I needed to make my point simple and blunt.

"Mr. Reid," I began, letting out a hefty sigh. "Two days ago I went up to a steep mountain top with the intention of throwing myself off." Mr. Reid just kind of looked at me like I was joking. "I'm dead serious," I said trying to prove that statement with the expression on my face. "I am ready to die. I am at the end of my rope. I've spent endless nights thinking of an alternative, but I realized that this is the only option I have left. I would prefer death over living with these feelings that engulf my life every day."

Mr. Reid sat there in silence for a few moments. It was clear that I had made my point and it was also clear that he did not know my situation was this critical.

We talked for a while after that outside my house. I told him how the thought of my mom out there on the streets in a big city made me fear for her life every day. I told him that Amy had broken my heart and I couldn't get over it. I told him that I couldn't accept this ever changing world, that I couldn't let this school go, that I wasn't ready to graduate.

After a little while longer I knew Mr. Reid and I were on the same page. I told him that I thought Mexico might be the thing to save me and he said it could be just what I needed. After some encouragement and wise words from Mr. Reid, we parted ways for the night. I was glad to have finally been able to make someone understand what I was going through. Even that thought that I was now not entirely alone brought me comfort. For the time being, it would be enough comfort to get me to Mexico. What happened after that was anyone's guess.

My time spent in Mexico was just what I needed. I left most of my worries back home and miraculously enough, I even managed to quit smoking for the first two weeks we were there. My depression let up enough to give me some breathing room and so for one month I had a chance to gather some strength.

When we got back from Mexico I felt rejuvenated. It seemed that God had held up His end of the deal so I didn't end up going back up to the mountain top.

The weeks flew by when we got back and before I could think twice the day I had been loathing arrived. Everyone looked fantastic and all dressed up. The night was spent with laughter and reminiscing of younger days. It was evident that our graduating class of twelve students had been close over the years. Everyone talked about their plans for the future and we all agreed to keep in touch. Everyone just seemed so happy. I hated the fact that I was so miserable.

I just couldn't let these kids go. I had gone to school with some of my classmates since the second grade. These people meant more to me than anyone else I knew. They were the closest thing I had to a family.

In my despair of anticipating this day I had written a song that described how I felt towards this whole occasion. I was glad to be able to perform this song in front of my class and our guests at our grad banquet, although I found it difficult to keep myself together.

Graduation

(vs1)
I know we've all been waiting
But I've been secretly hating this thing we call graduating, its
    excruciating
But look at all of you
All dressed in your best with black vests
Red dresses I'm certainly impressed

Brandon Krogel

And when tonight ends
When life sends us on our way I wish I could stay, for one last
    day
One last time to talk
One last time to walk around the school grounds,
Just listening to all the sounds

(bridge)
And time is terrible
It can only kill
And the thought is unbearable
Knowing it won't stand still
And this is a parable
Explaining what it will
I don't do so well with goodbyes

(chs)
Twelve years of memories
It's taken eleven for me to see
How much this means to me
You're not my friends
You're my family

(vs2)
Remember younger days
Trying to find ways to raise our age, and fit in with the older
    grades
But now were are the oldest
And I swear we were the closest ones
But the end draws near, our time here is done

(bridge)
And time is terrible
It can only kill
And the thought is unbearable
Knowing it won't stand still
And this is a parable
Explaining what it will
I don't do so well with goodbyes

(chs)
Take everything that I have
I'd trade it for just one more chance
To be with you, see life through your eyes
I cannot exist without all of you by my side

The rest of the night carried on and I tried my best to enjoy what was most likely the last gathering of our entire class in a single setting. When the night had ended we bid our farewells and promised to hang out again soon. I knew we all meant well but I also knew that keeping in touch wasn't going to be as easy as that.

Things back home had gotten a little strange between Jake and me. He was hanging out with a new group of friends and it just seemed like we were heading in two different directions for the time being. Shortly after graduating our land lady had told us that she was selling the house so we'd need to find new living arrangements in about a month. Since Jake and I were already moving in different directions, we figured rooming together again wouldn't be in our best interests.

So as my life in high school ended so did my living situation with Jake. He was moving back home to live with Rebecca and Amanda until he figured something else out and I had yet to find a place to move in to. In fact as the deadline approached for us to be out of the house I grew increasing concerned as I hadn't found a place to live yet.

It was at this time when Mr. Reid and I got in touch in the late summer and I mentioned to him that I was looking for a place to live. He told me his parents had a basement suite and would probably be willing to rent it out to me at an affordable price. He said he'd talk to them and get back to me and over the course of the next few days I waited anxiously for a response. Luckily enough his parents had agreed to let me move in and they had been very generous in the amount of rent they wanted me to pay.

September rolled around and it was time to yet again leave one phase of life behind and begin another. Jake helped me move my stuff into my new place and with a solid hug we agreed it had been good living with each other and we'd be spending some time together soon.

After Jake left I spent the rest of the day getting settled into my new place. It wasn't a big suite, but for just one person being there, it had plenty of room. I was actually quite excited to have my own place. I had lived with roommates since I had left the Williams and this was the first place that just belonged to me.

Just after we had gotten back from Mexico a few months ago, I, along with my good friends Ryan and Aaron, happened to get a job at an emerging computer company that designed flash games for kids. For the three of us this was a dream job for just getting out of high school. The pay was way above average and the work load was minimal. Our duties could be summed up as simply customer service and moderating the games. It was the most money I had ever made at a job and it involved virtually no physical labor. The whole shift was spent on a computer. Needless to say, I was quite happy with my current employment situation and not only that, I also got to continue to see Ryan and Aaron frequently after high school.

One day I was riding my skateboard to work from the upper part of town to the city center where my job was located, as my car was in the shop for repairs that day. Despite arguments with myself that taking back roads instead of following the main highway through the city would get me to work faster, I continued to travel down the main road. I was about eight minutes away from work, skateboarding down this sidewalk when I spotted someone on a bicycle approaching me head on. I paid little attention to the rider but moved to the side to give us both enough room to pass. It was after we had passed each other that I heard my name called and upon turning around, I was surprised to see Mike, my old manager from the pizza shop standing before me. It had been about six months since I had last seen Mike, and I was glad to see him. When I thought about it, I wondered why I hadn't kept in touch with him all this time.

His car was also in the shop that day and he was biking to work in the upper part of town from downtown. We both considered it quite a coincidence that both our cars were in the shop and we were using different modes of transportation to get to work. He was heading uptown and I was heading downtown. We concluded it was fate that had brought upon this meeting.

We chatted for a few minutes about what was new in each others lives. I asked him if he was still at the pizza place and he said that he unfortunately was. He said he hated working there and after three years he was still only making minimum wage. I told him that I had secured a great new job and that we were hiring at the moment. I told him with his customer service and manager experience he would be perfect for the job and that I'd give him a referral as soon as I got into work.

Mike seemed very appreciative of what I had said and after getting each other's current contact information we wished each other a good day and both headed off to work.

When I arrived at my job I immediately went into my boss's office and asked if we were still hiring. When he said we were I told him that I knew a guy who would make an excellent addition to the team and that I would even recommend him over myself. It was a little extreme to say but I think my boss got the point because he told me to tell Mike to drop off a resume in the next couple days, and he'd see what he could do.

I called Mike right after I left the office and told him the good news. So the next day he dropped off a resume and only a few days later he was hired. To say I was excited to work with Mike again was an understatement. For some reason this guy had always felt like the older brother I never had and I looked up to him in many ways.

On Mike's first day I was eager to introduce him to all my friends at work as I had told them stories of our glory days back at the pizza shop. As I hoped, everyone got along right away and before long, Mike was our new best friend.

As the weeks went by, we started to have frequent hang outs at Mike's place. Since he was a couple years older than Ryan, myself, and the rest of our group, he always had a story to tell or something interesting to share. Everyone enjoyed hearing of his adventures and whenever he talked, we'd listen.

At around the same time I got Mike the job, Ryan had also referred a friend who ended up getting hired. Mike along with Ryan's friend Matt were hired at close to the same time, so they were both looking for people to bond with at their new job. Since Ryan and I were best friends already, I brought Mike into our group and Ryan brought Matt in. Amanda also started hanging out with us and in no time, we had our own little posse going on. Almost everyday after that, we'd get off work, get some beer and all go down to Mike's to hang out and play video games.

Since Ryan, Matt, Amanda and myself were all still not legal age, Mike was usually the one who'd boot for us but he didn't mind. We'd hang out frequently and it wasn't long before we had all become close friends. It was at this point in time when things were going relatively good, that they would make a sudden turn for the worst.

Living on my own had become a lonely experience. Jake would stop by every once in a while to hang out but most of the time, I tried to stay away from my house for as long as possible and would only come home to sleep.

It was during one lonely night at my place where I was just relaxing and playing some video games when I got a phone call from the Williams. My mom was supposed to be arriving at the bus depot that night at midnight and they felt that I should know. I thanked them for informing me and after hanging up the phone I had a million and one thoughts racing through my head. I hadn't seen my mom for nearly two years. To find out that she was coming into town that night brought a wave of emotions that made it difficult for me to organize my thoughts. I went out for a smoke.

My depression had certainly not left. In fact it probably would've been much worse if it hadn't been for this job and the amount of money I was making. That cash bought some happiness and comfort. I knew that seeing my mom again would be difficult, but I wanted to see her. I decided to pick her up from the bus depot.

When midnight rolled around I was waiting just outside the bus depot. The front doors were made of glass and if you looked through them you could see people getting off and on the bus. Not wanting to yet make my presence known I watched and waited for my mom's bus to arrive and unload from afar. When I caught a glimpse of her getting off the bus, my heart broke. I barely recognized her. She was moving about appearing not fully in tune with her surroundings. Her luggage consisted of several garbage bags and a beat up old duffle bag. She hadn't noticed me standing by the doors as I continued to watch her move about.

The makeup under her eyes was running, it was evident she had been crying. Her face and body were so thin I could make out the distinct shape of the bones in her body. When she had collected her belongings she made her way to the payphone and after several failed attempts due to her constant twitching, she inserted the quarter into the machine. By this point I had walked up behind her and waited for her to turn around.

"Sure are a lot of crack heads around here," I heard a guy say to his friend who were both standing just a few feet away from my mom. They were staring her down with disgust. I wanted to beat the shit out of them.

My mom's hair was ragged, tangled, and in dire need of a cut. Her clothes looked like they had been found in a dumpster in a back alley. Her fingers were black as night and as she held the phone by her ear as she picked her nails which were extremely long. Her legs moved back and forth as she stood there, almost like they had a mind of their own. Although I had never seen anything like this before, I knew she was probably going through withdrawal and I knew she was calling a drug dealer on that pay phone. Before I gave the phone a chance to ring, I put my hand on my moms shoulder and doing my best not to cry when she turned around said "Hi mom. Let's get your things."

"Hi hunney," she replied quietly not looking up to meet my gaze. It was clear she was ashamed that I was seeing her like this. "I'm going to take you back to my place okay?" I said as I grabbed her bags and motioned for her to follow me out to the car.

When we got in the car I offered her a smoke and lit one up myself. I put on some soft music as we pulled out of the parking lot and headed back to my place. The drive was spent mostly in silence. I think both of us were just soaking up that moment. It was difficult to speak.

She asked me how I'd been and I told her I was good and that I really missed her. I gave her a minor update about what Lisa and Eric were up to these days. She tried to acknowledge what I was saying but it was clear she was quite incoherent due to her withdrawal. It must have been so fucked up for her to be sitting in that car with me in the condition she was in. I know it was for me. Words cannot express the strange, uncomfortable, unpleasant, bizarre feeling that I'm sure both of us shared as we drove back to my place.

When we got back my place I showed her the spare bedroom and said she should go to sleep and that we'd take care of things in the morning. After she had lain down I went for another smoke, overwhelmed with emotions.

It was difficult to see her like this. I had this image in my head of what my mom looked like and this person did not meet that description. I couldn't believe how terrible she looked and I tried not to think about what horrors she had experienced living on the streets for nearly two years.

I was afraid that she might try and leave that night to get a fix so I barricaded the front door with furniture and slept in the living room to make sure she didn't leave. Luckily when I awoke in the morning after virtually no sleep, I opened the spare bedroom to find her still there.

Since I had no idea what to do I called the Williams and told them that my mom was with me and I was pretty sure she was withdrawing from the drugs. Mrs. Williams, who also happened to be a nurse, said she would come by and take my mom down to the hospital.

After hanging up the phone my mom came into the living room and asked if she could have a smoke. I gave her one and we didn't say much as we just stood outside and puffed. She was sweating now, profusely. Her legs were shaking and moving much more intensely than they had the previous night. Her nervous fidgeting was something I had seen addicts do before when I had walked in the sketchiest parts of downtown. She did not look well.

When Mrs. Williams arrived I was relieved. I didn't know how to handle this kind of situation and I was glad that I wasn't doing this on my own. Since I had to work in a few hours I couldn't join them as they went down to the hospital but Mrs. Williams assured me that she'd take my mom there and get things in order. She said she'd give me a call later and let me know how things were going. I thanked her for her help and as they left for the hospital, I sat on my front steps, lit another smoke and wept.

Later that night I got a call from Mrs. Williams saying that she had checked my mom into the hospital and then left for a couple hours to attend to her own agenda. When she returned the nurse informed her that my mom had left the hospital and had most likely hit the streets.

I was devastated. All this energy I had spent in the last twenty-four hours had been for nothing. Once again I was reminded of the power that this addiction had over her. I tried to distract myself after getting off work that night by heading down to Mike's with the guys and having a few beers. It would be a while before I'd hear from my mom again. I took little comfort in knowing that she was at least in the same city as me and not somewhere far away.

I had been at this computer job for about four months when the company began to expand. This in turn I knew would provide for more advancement opportunities to staff that had been there a while, as the company would be hiring new team members. In an attempt to show the company what I was capable of in order to win their recognition, I designed a fan website based around one of their games that had become quite popular.

When I revealed what I had done to my boss he said he wasn't sure what the company's policy was on something like this so he said that for the time being it was fine however, I may be asked to take it down. I replied by emphasizing that this website was merely an attempt to prove my worth and that I valued my job over anything. I said if there were any problems with the website to let me know and I would take it down immediately. My boss assured me that things would be fine for now and if something did come up, he'd inform me.

A few days had passed since I showed my boss the website and upon coming in to work shortly after, I was called into a meeting with my boss and his boss, who was one of the three owners of the company.

When I arrived in his office I felt privileged to be there. Few of the staff had actually been in this guy's office so it was kind of a big deal. I sat down with my two superiors and was expecting them to either applaud me for my skill on my website or they were going to ask me to take it down but when I heard the head boss speak, it was not what I expected to hear. "We're letting you go Brandon," he said calmly. I just looked at him with a neutral grin on my face like I hadn't heard what he just said. I continued to stare at my head boss with a smile as my brain desperately tried to understand what was going on.

"If you would be willing to sign these contracts that state you will stay away from the company, its sponsors and affiliates for an entire year, we are willing to give you eight weeks of severance pay," my head boss said as he handed me some papers.

It was when I held this bundle of documents in my hand that I finally understood what was happening. I was being fired. I asked if this was about the website but my head boss wouldn't elaborate on any specifics. I reminded him that my other boss, who was still in the room, said it was fine for the time being and he'd notify me if there were any problems. Upon saying that, my other boss stood up and immediately denied ever saying those words, and so in that moment I knew that I had no allies in this situation.

"How long do I have to make a decision about these contracts?" I asked nervously. The head boss cleared his throat and looked at me. "We'll give you to the end of the week." With my head hung dejectedly I left the building through a different entrance that I had entered from. I wasn't allowed to speak to any of the staff on my way out.

I took the contracts to a lawyer who said I was fired for being a business threat to the company and said that my best bet would be to sign the contracts and get what money I could. Upon hearing that I thought "How does an eighteen-year old kid with no post secondary education or particular skills become a business threat to a multi-million dollar company?" It didn't make sense to me, but I had no choice but to accept that I was no longer working at my dream job, and that thought destroyed me. Because without this job, my depression could overtake my life and soon enough, that would be the case.

Just like that my job had been stripped from me. One month after getting Mike the job, I had lost mine. When asked what I was going to do next I told my friends and coworkers I was going to take the severance pay and move to another city. I claimed there was nothing left in this town for me and so a few nights later I drove nine hours through the mountains, in the middle of winter, to the next big city east of the one I was leaving.

I couldn't deny there were things in my town that would've made it difficult to leave. It's where I grew up. My family, friends, and life were here. Despite these few things, in my mind at the time they seemed insignificant to the bigger picture. I knew my siblings were safe and I knew one day they might even leave this town. My mother was here . . . somewhere, but because I wasn't in touch with her it felt as though that reason didn't apply. My friends had all went their separate ways. If it wasn't for this job that I just got fired from, I'm not even sure if I would've kept in touch with Ryan or Aaron after high school. In the end I concluded I needed a fresh start and I felt I couldn't achieve that here.

Brian just so happened to be going to school in that particular city so I managed to hook up accommodation with him and his roommate for a couple days while I scoped out a place to live. It was weird hanging out with just Brian. I hadn't really seen him since we graduated and honestly after we did, I didn't think I would at all. We got along well considering. It was clear we had both left the past in the past when we were together and in some small ways, it felt just like old times.

Unfortunately though I was unable to find a place to rent and was forced to come back home empty handed. The downside was that I had already told my landlords (Mr. Reid's parents), that I would be moving at the end of the month. Since I wasn't able to take that notice back, I was starting to panic about where I was going to live. It was one night when I was hanging out with Mike at his place and told him my worries about a place to live that he offered his place to me. He said he and his girlfriend Kristy wouldn't mind if I moved in and he even had an extra bedroom for me.

To hear him say that made me overjoyed. Living with Mike sounded like the best idea I had heard in a long time. Since I was there most of the time anyways, it didn't seem like things would be much different.

So as the end of the month approached I thanked Mr. Reid's parents for letting me stay in their suite and with some help from a few friends, moved into Mike's.

Little did I know that this move, which may have seemed insignificant at the time, would spark the next chapter in my life. I could have never imagined in my wildest dreams that, the one fateful day when I had ran into Mike on my way to work would lead to this. It was the dawn of a new age in my life and what was about to unfold would be the most extraordinary times of my life. I would live, then die, and live again before this next chapter that was beginning, would conclude. It was the beginning of what would come to be known as 1814. A number I would not soon forget.

Chapter Eleven

A New Era

Mike's house had always fascinated me since the first time I had stopped by. He lived downtown and only a five-minute walk away from the beach. The house was older but it was a full out house. Since I was used to living in duplexes and basement suites, this was a big deal. Mike and Kristy were renting the main floor and the basement while two other tenants were renting the attic suite on the upper floor.

Unlike any place I had lived in thus far on my own, Mike had given his house a very warm and relaxed feeling. The sweet scent of a particular incense would linger about in the air. The TV spoke gently as Mike almost always had something playing in the background. Truth be told when I was at Mike's house I felt like I was at home. None of my own places ever had this vibe and I was eager to learn all I could from him, and how to achieve this peacefulness that his house glowed of.

After a few weeks, the money I had received as severance for losing my job was thinning quickly. I had been trying to present myself the same as I had while working for this computer company. I didn't want people to think I was any different because I lost my job. During my time of employment with this company, Ryan, Aaron, and I would, every Tuesday after work, get a bunch of the staff together and go to this restaurant to take advantage of their specials on pasta. We called it pasta bowl Tuesdays. Just prior to me getting fired, out little Tuesday get-togethers were at record numbers. What started off as just Ryan, Aaron and I taking advantage of some cheap pasta had turned into a group of twenty people taking advantage of some cheap pasta and a few drinks.

When I was fired I tried desperately to remain in touch with the same crowd I had just been forced to seclude myself from. Because this computer company had taken off so rabidly, the staff had tripled in just a few short months. Since the company did most of their hiring through referrals (if you knew someone who already worked for the company that was basically your only ticket in), the staff had become a very tight click.

It seemed that before long everybody in town had heard about this company and their exceptional pay and benefits to their employees. This in turn possessed every single person I knew to apply for a job there and many of my friends did in fact get hired. This was the problem though.

Since all my current friends still worked at this company, I had to remain a part of it in some way or I was going to be one friendless individual. Both Ryan and Aaron, who were the only two friends that I really kept in touch with from high school, still worked there. I had just gotten Mike the job there and in no way did he want to go back to the pizza shop so it seemed like he was there to stay. So basically at that point, virtually every one of my friends worked for this company. And I did not.

Pasta bowl Tuesdays continued and I would attend almost every one in an effort to remain connected to this group of peers. After a couple weeks though, finances had taken their toll and I was virtually out of money.

Going out every Tuesday became increasingly more stressful. All everyone talked about was work and how great it was. The new innovative stuff the company was doing, the benefits, the pay raises, all I ever heard about from these people was how great their jobs were and every time I heard this, I was reminded that I no longer had that job.

I foolishly wasted what little money I had left on pasta and beer. I was trying so hard to present myself to others as just fine. That even though I had lost my job I could attend these weekly meetings and still talk to this whole crowd of people I used to work with. Trying to uphold this image became expensive and soon I was flat broke. I knew I needed to get another job if I wanted to continue to do things like pasta bowl Tuesdays. But where would I work?

I was in a certain mentality that working for this company had brought me. My head was up in the clouds and I was cocky. After making such a great wage, working for a company that had great benefits and also whose workload was minimal, finding a job that paid minimal wage with hard labor was not something I could humble myself to do. Ryan and Aaron had progressed in life since high school and to me it was unfair that I had to take a step back. It was difficult for me to swallow these facts.

It was during one pasta bowl Tuesday that Mike and I ran into an old co-worker from the pizza shop. When I had worked with her, she was a waitress. She told me that the old manager had quit and she had taken over the place in his stead. I figured it was now or never and I approached her before we left the restaurant and asked if she needed any help in the kitchen. We had already worked together in the past, and she felt that an interview wasn't necessary. If I wanted the job, I could start the next day. I was grateful for the work and in some small way, a little excited. Whatever excitement I had in me though, was drained quickly in the coming days.

After less than two weeks of working back at the pizza place, I had once again quit on the spot. My boss was furious; she had made me promise that if she hired me, I wouldn't quit suddenly like I had back when I was in high school.

Although it may have appeared to everyone else that I was being rude and completely ridiculous by rejecting a job that was just handed to me, there was much more to it. I could just not humble myself. I was so bitter at getting fired. All that went through my head was how it seemed I had traded places with Mike. That one day we had met had changed both of our fates completely. I had saved him from his miserable life at the pizza shop, and now our roles had been completely reversed. Now I was the miserable one still working at the pizza shop and he was the happy one working for this company.

I often wondered if I would've still had my job if I hadn't met Mike again that one fateful day. It was on his computer that I created that fan website that got me fired, as I didn't have my own at the time. If we had never met again, that website might not have come to pass and my life would not be as miserable as it was right now.

Regardless of how I felt and my own justification of things, Mike was upset when he found out I had quit the pizza shop. It was evident but he refrained from making a big deal out of it, as difficult as that might have been. I assured him that I would find a job in less than a week and there would be nothing to worry about.

For the next few days all I heard was the ramblings of Kristy who would relentlessly remind that I needed to get a job whether I liked it or not. I found it completely senseless and frustrating coming from her as she was also unemployed. The woman seriously drove me nuts. I had no idea what Mike saw in her.

I knew I had run out of options. I couldn't jeopardize my living situation or my friendship with Mike and I was losing it being at home all day with Kristy's unfailing babbling. It was time to go back to the beginning. Although I most certainly did not want to, I didn't have a choice. I had to go back to the gas station.

The thought of me going back to work at the gas station was embarrassing so I figured I'd apply at the same company, only at a different location. Luckily my old boss from back when I was fifteen and myself had ended my employment on good terms. I gave my full two weeks and always worked hard. It was nice to hear when I was hired by my new boss that my previous one had given me an exceptional reference.

I went home that night to inform Mike about my new employment situation and eager to tell Kristy to fuck off if she gave me any more unwanted advice about getting a job. Mike was glad to hear the news, and I assured him that I wouldn't quit this time. So for awhile, things were okay, or at least as okay as they could be considering.

Ryan, Matt, Amanda, Mike, myself, and, unfortunately, Kristy, continued to get together frequently and party. I thought I had partied in my last year of high school but that was nothing compared to how much we were partying now. I enjoyed getting drunk with my friends and that was really about the only thing I enjoyed at that time of my life.

My depression was worsening. Since I had been extremely depressed for several years now, I had become accustomed to the feeling so to speak. I knew what to expect. I knew people didn't want to hear that you were depressed. I had become quite good at wearing a smile by this point as well, although it was getting difficult to keep it for longer than a few minutes.

Still my heart was broken from Amy and still I could not accept the fact that I had graduated. I couldn't accept any change and it was really making things worse. I hadn't heard from my mom since the morning after the bus depot. Although I was working somewhere, I still couldn't accept that I had been fired from my dream job and this only contributed to my depression. The bitterness and anger of losing my job, which was the only thing I had going for me then, was pure anguish. To have to see and hear this and that about the company from every single person I knew was infuriating and frustrating. Being outside the circle of this company did make me ask myself some important questions. Was I like these people before? Was all I talked about work and how great my life was because of this job? Did I sound this annoying? Was I this clicky? I was about to share these same questions with someone else, as it turns out I wasn't the only one the company was trying to make an example out of.

It was my day off from the gas station and I was sitting at home doing my best to avoid direct eye contact with Kristy who was also at home, when I got a phone call from Ryan. He sounded distressed. He had just gone to work to find out he had also been let go from the company due to an instant messaging conversation that he had online with a co-worker. Our conversation on the phone was brief. He said he was coming by and that we were definitely getting drunk tonight. I couldn't say no to that so I waited at the house for his arrival. About 20 minutes later he showed up and the two of us drank the night away.

During this period of unemployment I had struggled to find out the true reason I had gotten fired from the computer company. I was determined to find out. I began to devise a business plan in my head, a way to get back at and compete with the company. "Yes, I would show them what I could've done for them. They fired me for being a business threat so a business threat I would become."

The weeks went on and our get-togethers at Mike's remained frequent. Mike and Kristy had gotten in a huge fight shortly after Ryan got fired and after a bunch of screaming that echoed from Mike's lips and an assortment of strange sounds that Kristy made between sobs, it seemed that the relationship between the two of them had ended. And I honestly couldn't have been happier. Kristy moved out a few days later and Mike seemed like a happier man.

Unfortunately though this meant that there were now just two of us living in this house, which increased my rent by quite a bit. I did not make very much at the gas station, and I had trouble paying my share of things. I'd either have no money after paying rent or a just a few bucks to get groceries. Needless to say I wasn't eating like I used to.

Going to work everyday at the gas station was a struggle. I was never, even for just a moment, not miserable. I hated my job. I hated how I was back at the gas station. After Ryan got fired, Aaron was promoted to a position that Ryan and I had been considered for. Since Aaron was the only one of us three that remained employed by this company, he got the promotion. This only added to the bitterness that had rooted itself inside of me.

At the gas station there was this kid who was about a year or two older than me who would frequently come in to buy smokes and usually, a significant amount of munchies. He told us to call him J.R. I learned why his visits were so frequent after only a short time working there. Every day he'd come into the store without fail and ask me and whoever else was on shift if we wanted to buy some weed. Although some of my co-workers smoked pot, I had never tried it and had no intention of ever trying it so I always replied with a simple "I'm good man, thanks."

I knew that Mike used to smoke pot for a couple years and he'd often tell stories of his adventures living with his roommates out by the coast before he moved to our town. Although Mike no longer smoked pot, he in many ways suggested by the way he talked about it that marijuana was not as big of a deal as most people were brought to believe. I didn't give this idea much thought; I would never use drugs because of what it did to my family and from my understanding, pot was a drug.

As the weeks continued to pass my situation did not improve. I was always broke. It was at a point where I couldn't even bring a lunch to work because I didn't have any lunch to bring. I continued to be bitter and refused to humble myself as I rallied myself up more and more every shift saying that I was too good for this place. My growing depression as well as my ideals that I couldn't work at this gas station anymore because it was embarrassing and demeaning, eventually brought me to one night that I probably knew was coming.

I was working late shift and closing the store that night when I had finally just got fed up. I hated my job. I hated my life. And the "not caring" attitude that led me to abandon my ideals to smoke cigarettes and to drink alcohol instead was about to give me some more food for thought.

The store had been fairly quiet that night and in that particular moment, it was completely empty. I was going to be closing up in about an hour or so and I had already decided that tonight, I was quitting. I had written my boss a note apologizing for the inconvenience stating that there was just too much going on in my life and that I couldn't work here any longer.

Shortly before closing that night, J.R. had stopped in for some smokes and a bag of chips. As usual he asked if I wanted to buy any pot and as I was just about to say "No, I'm good," for the millionth time, I didn't and instead, for some reason, asked him what the cheapest amount of pot I could get was. He told me that I could get a dime bag for ten bucks and that was one gram of weed. For a moment I paused, contemplating what I should do. "I'm on shift right now man, and there's cameras everywhere. I don't think I could pull off buying anything from you right now."

J.R. looked around and then back to me. "Just give me the washroom key and I'll leave a bag in there for you. Slip me the cash with my change for the smokes." I thought about it for a moment. It seemed like a plausible strategy. "Alright dude, sounds good I guess." With that I gave the washroom key to J.R. and he returned a few moments later.

"You're good to go," J.R. said with a big grin on his face. "Cool, uh thanks," I replied a little awkwardly. It was clear that I had never bought or smoked weed before. So I slipped an additional ten bucks in with his change from the smokes and he thanked me for the business and then headed out the door. I hesitated for a moment and then made my way to the washroom to pick up my first bag of weed.

I went into the restroom and found the little bag sitting on top of the paper towel dispenser. Inside was a decent sized nug of this green stuff. I had never seen pot up close like this, I had only smelt it in the air or on someone. It actually looked quite interesting.

"So this is weed," I said to myself. "I wonder why this stuff is illegal. It just comes from a plant right?" Without asking any more questions I put the bag in my pocket, bought a packet of rolling papers, closed up the store and left my notice on the till.

After locking everything up, Mike arrived to give me a ride home. Since cash was tight, I couldn't afford insurance or gas so driving my car was out of the question. Not only that but the heater had broke shortly after I got fired from the computer company and that made driving around in the winter an embarrassing and freezing adventure.

I didn't tell Mike that I had quit the gas station right away. I told myself that I would find a way to pay rent without having to let him know that I was unemployed. Unfortunately that would be very unrealistic. On top of that, my life was about to get a little greener.

When Mike and I had arrived home that night, I pulled out my dime bag and tossed it on the table with a grin on my face. "Dude, did you buy pot tonight?" Mike asked surprised. "It would seem so," I replied. "The only problem is that I have no idea what to do with this stuff. Wondering if you might be able to help me out?" Mike looked at me almost laughing. "I think I might remember a thing or two."

When I said I had never smoke pot before, that wasn't entirely correct. A week or two before I had moved into Mike's, I had gotten drunk with this girl that I was debating whether I had feelings for or not. I was just hammered that night, a complete mess. She had brought over some pot and when I saw it in her purse I suggested that we smoke some. She asked if I had ever smoked pot before and I replied instantly that I hadn't but I was drunk and was willing to give it a try in this moment. She mentioned that if I hadn't smoked before, combing it with alcohol might not be the best idea. Not really taking what she said into consideration I assured her it was fine and that we should give it a try.

She had her pipe with her so we went outside and she loaded a bowl. After a quick debriefing of how to smoke a pipe I gave it a shot. I lit the first bowl, inhaled and then exhaled to realize that pot smoke was a little harsher on the lungs than I imagined. After recovering from a minor coughing fit, I lit the bowl again for round two as I didn't feel the effects right away.

After the second hoot though, it kicked in and I burst out laughing for no apparent reason. She must've thought I was losing it and I was actually quite embarrassed because I couldn't stop. Something was ridiculously funny in my head, but I had no idea what it was. When we got back inside, that sensation quickly changed and I understood what she meant about not smoking pot when you're hammered. Suddenly I felt extremely nauseous and so not wanting to hurl on the carpet, I made my way to the kitchen sink and spent the next half hour vomiting profusely, a collection of beer and chicken wings from earlier that night. Yum!

After that I sat on the couch next to her completely zombified. I had no idea what was going on. I was slipping in and out of consciousness. We put on a movie and the next thing I knew, it was over. My vision was blurred and I couldn't speak. I felt like a pile of mush, unable to communicate or move.

After that experience I had, in my mind, been educated as to the nature of marijuana. Upon telling Mike my experience with weed a few days later, he had an interesting thing to say. "Man, I don't want to encourage you to smoke pot but you should know that your first weed experience was not really your first weed experience." I looked at Mike a little confused. "Okay...?" "If you're drunk and smoke, the chances of your night ending miserably just increased by a million percent. You don't feel high as much as you just feel fucked. If you really want to form an opinion about weed, smoke it when you're sober."

I suppose that comment had been lingering in the back of my mind when I bought that dime bag off J.R. and tonight, I was going to take Mike's advice so to speak, and try smoking the stuff soberly.

Since we didn't have anything other than rolling papers to work with, Mike suggested the best way to smoke this bag that I had just bought was to roll a joint.

I had no idea how to roll a joint but Mike offered to teach me the concept. He hadn't smoked in over a year but you'd never know it as he worked carefully to cut up the bud into small pieces and roll it in the paper. I was impressed. When it was finished he held it up in the air to approve the final product. After concluding that it was satisfactory he handed it to me and said "Here you go. It's a nice little pinner." I took the rolled paper from his hand. "Pinner?" I asked wondering. "A pinner is a thin joint," Mike explained slightly amused by my innocence.

I held it in my hand for a moment, analyzing this marijuana cigarette. I found it bizarre that I was about to smoke a joint. This was something I did not ever see myself doing. "Do you want me to start it?" Mike asked. "If you want to, sure man," I replied. With a slight hesitation Mike brought the joint to his lips, took a lighter out of his pocket and lit it up. Once burning, he put the lighter down and took a decent sized toke. I remember watching him as he sat back in his chair with his head tilted back, gracefully exhaling the smoke in his lungs. It was a picture I'd never forget.

"It's been a long time since I did a hoot", Mike said half enjoying half regretting his decision to puff. "Your turn," he said grinning as he passed me the joint. That was the only time in my life that I have ever seen Mike smoke.

I mimicked his movements, put the joint to my lips and began to inhale. After a few puffs I got the hang of it. Not wanting to overdo it and not sure what to expect from smoking this joint, I only smoked part of it and put the roach back in the bag. Not sure what to do, I sat on the couch and watched TV.

"I actually already feel it from that tiny puff," Mike said in my direction. "How are you feeling?" I looked over at him from the couch. "I'm not sure man. I don't really feel much and it's not a particularly enjoyable sensation." I said slightly disappointed. "I don't know dude, if this is all smoking pot is like then I don't think I'm going to smoke it again." Of course looking back now I was most definitely not stoned. I had only smoked a little because I didn't know how intense the feeling of being high was going to be.

The next day I had told Amanda that I smoked pot the previous night. She was a little upset at first but after explaining to her that it was overrated and I had no idea why it was illegal or why everyone had always made such a big deal about it, she calmed down. I told her I was probably going to just smoke the rest of my bag that night to be rid of it since it seemed useless. She said she wanted to try it with me before that happened, so I went up town to pick her up in my uninsured, heatless car that miraculously enough had enough gas to get me there and back home again.

Matt had also stopped by that night and when he found out Amanda and I were going to be smoking, he asked to join in. Matt had smoked pot occasionally when he was in high school but at that point, he hadn't smoked in awhile.

It was actually a funny picture with the four of us all huddled around in a big circle in the living room. With this many people smoking, Mike suggested that a pipe could be fun. Since we didn't have one, he improvised and after a few minutes, he had managed to turn a beer can into a pipe, which I thought was just incredible.

So there we were passing around our homemade beer can pipe. Mike just watched Amanda, Matt, and I pass around the can, amused at how we were reacting to the weed. Although I cannot recall the details of this night in particular, I do remember feeling high and at one point, I recall all of us eating ice cream somewhere. This night was significant for me as it showed me that the previous night, I was not high. Tonight, I was definitely stoned and to be honest, I enjoyed the sensation. So what I thought was me quitting smoking pot before I had even really started, turned out to be just the beginning of a new habit, and the very next day, Amanda and I met J.R. to get another dime bag.

As the days continued, it was becoming increasingly difficult for me to fake that I was going to work every day. I would have to leave the house at the usual time I used to leave for work and spend most of the day out and about to fill the time. This concept was working at first but Mike had stopped at the gas station to fill up during one of my supposed "shifts" only to discover that I was not there. After speaking with my boss he learned that I had quit on the spot some time ago. He was not only choked that I had quit my job but that I hadn't told him. I apologized and said that I had intended to have my financial situation back in order before it even mattered because I didn't want to stress him out. The only problem was that I hadn't got things in order. In fact things were far from orderly and now with my newly discovered enjoyment for the smoking of marijuana, they weren't going to get any better.

Amanda and I started to get stoned every night. After a while we'd end up smoking a dime bag in a single sitting and had to resort to buying two dime bags to make the night last. As I started to become comfortable smoking pot, I became fascinated by the sensation of being high.

Often times I felt like I was reliving childhood emotions and commonly recalled events from my childhood that I had completely forgotten. At times I was even recalling dreams that I had when I was younger that I completely forgot about. I was always analyzing things and a lot of the time, I would over-analyze things. Smoking weed just made me think. The entire process of being high took place solely in my brain so my mind was the one thing I was constantly exploring. It was intriguing. I pondered whether I could discover why I felt so miserable all the time just by smoking weed. If I was constantly exploring my mind and if my depression was rooted in my mind, then perhaps I could discover an answer. In many ways I did gain understanding about things I didn't before.

In recent years I had developed a strong relationship with my brother. When our family had split for the second time and my brother and sister had gone to live with the Scotts, while I went to the Jennings, I would have the opportunity to visit my siblings ever so often. Usually once very couple of weeks. During these visits Eric and I seemed to communicate on a deeper level than we ever had before. For some reason all of our childhood differences no longer applied and we were able to speak and communicate with the maturity of adults. As a result of our ability to talk to each other without any conflict or argument, we truly started to become brothers. As time continued to move on, our relationship as brothers grew stronger and not long after, Eric had become someone I could count on to talk to and get advice from.

One day after only about a week or two of smoking pot, I had shown up at my old school where Eric was attending classes in the tenth grade. School had just gotten out and I had parked purposely away from the crowd and hustle that occurs when the 3:00 p.m. bell rings. I saw Eric off in the distance and after getting his attention, beckoned him over to the car.

"Hey bro!" I said enthusiastically. "Hey man, how's it going?" Eric replied. "Ah not too bad," I said as I lit up a smoke. "How was school?" Eric let out a deep sigh. "Gay." I couldn't help but laugh. "Same as always, eh?" My brother let his backpack drop to the ground and kneeling down began to rummage through it.

"I seriously can't wait until I'm graduated. I fricken hate school." I felt another chuckle escape my lips. "Well man, soon enough you'll be out there making things happen. For now just keep working hard and before you know it, you'll be working nine to five Monday to Friday," I sarcastically reassured him. "Not exactly the vision I had in my head," Eric smirked. "So why are you here anyways?"

Motioning for Eric to come over to where I was standing, I leaned in and reached into the car. "Check it out dude!" I said excitedly as I pulled out a small bag of weed from the glove compartment.

My brother looked shocked. At first his expression seemed like he thought I was joking but when he looked closer at the green stuff in the bag, he freaked out. "What the hell man!" Eric was clearly not impressed. "Relax dude, it's just a little bit of dope," I tried to calm him down. "You're smoking weed!?" Eric half asked half accused. "Yeah man but it's not a big deal, seriously, hear me out on this one." Eric looked choked as I tried to explain to him that pot wasn't that big of a deal. I don't think he was really listening. I don't think he really cared for any justification I could offer him at that moment.

"You're going to end up just like mom!" I stopped talking for a moment when I heard those words come out of Eric's mouth.

Angry and offended of ever being compared to my mom in regards to addictions, the tone in my voice changed. "Whatever man. Clearly you're not mature enough to understand what I'm trying to say to you."

And with that I got into the car, angrily slammed the door and drove away without saying a word, all the while my rear view mirror reflecting the expression on Eric's face. He seemed confused, upset, and sad. He looked hurt and as I drove off into the distance, I slammed my fist on the dashboard, now feeling like shit for forcing my brother to emit this expression that he was now wearing.

After a couple days we had both calmed down and I picked Eric up from school. I told him I was sorry and that I didn't want something like pot to come between us. As we sat in the car, not going anywhere, I asked Eric if we would at least hear me out about what I had to say in regards to smoking weed. He agreed so I spent the next half hour telling him my thoughts on the whole thing.

I believe the reason why I was so eager to reveal my findings of pot out to my brother is because I knew if he tried it, he'd see things in the same light as me. In my opinion pot was not a big deal. Its effects were minimal along with its consequences. No one ever died from smoking pot. No one ever killed themselves when they were high on weed. This "drug" didn't relate to the rest of the substances that it was categorized with. Acid made people go insane. Cocaine broke apart families. Crystal Meth destroyed lives and ecstasy damaged your nervous system. Smoking pot had none of these affects. The only bad thing I could think about it was that it's probably not healthy to inhale any kind of smoke. Other than that, I couldn't find any problems with weed.

After relating this information to my brother, he seemed to have understood most of what I was saying. I was trying to get him out of the mentality of taking the words of other people as fact. I was trying to get him to think for himself and make informed decisions. My whole life I had been told to stay away from weed but now after smoking it and experiencing its effects, I wondered what the big deal was.

"Look man, I'm telling you right now that weed is not a big deal. I've honestly racked my brain trying to figure out why people have gone a-wall over this stuff and I've come up with nothing." Eric sat there as I continued to explain myself. "I mean, it's a fricken plant! It's not made with chemicals found under your sink, it doesn't have highly addictive properties—you grow it in dirt, you pick off the bud, you put it in a pipe and then you smoke it. Easy as pie. It's probably even healthier than pie," I joked. I watched Eric laugh out loud at that last one. "Seriously dude, I'm not trying to pressure you or anything but I just want you to understand that pot is not as big of deal as its been made out to seem. But the only way you're going to realize that is if you try it for yourself."

Eric continued to sit as I continued to talk. It was obvious he was weighing out everything I had just said.

I felt bad in a way for offering my brother a chance to smoke pot. Mostly I just wanted him to see what I was seeing and to experience what I was experiencing, which ultimately was the fact that in my opinion, pot had been wrongfully labeled and it was enjoyable to smoke.

Its true Eric was a few years younger than me but in my mind, we were on equal levels in regards to maturity. If I didn't have a problem with it, I couldn't see him having a problem with it. So that day in the car, I asked him if he wanted to come over and smoke with Amanda and me. I told him if he didn't like it—whatever, he tried it, no big deal and now he could form an accurate opinion about the stuff. After giving it a few moments of thought, he decided to give it a go.

As we drove back down to my place, I continued to reassure him that there was nothing wrong with smoking pot and it was likely that he'd enjoy himself.

A few hours later, we met up with Amanda and sitting in my car, parked at the house, we brought out the old can pipe and loaded it up. I took the first hoot and Amanda the second. When it came around to Eric he looked at us with nervous excitement and double checked that this wasn't going to mess him up. We assured him he'd be fine and the only way to truly know how he would feel about marijuana was for him to try it himself.

So I sat there as I watched my little brother take his first inhale of pot smoke. He coughed but not much and recovered quickly to find himself with a grin on his face. "It has an interesting taste," he said licking his lips as Amanda and I chuckled in the background.

The can was passed around a few more times and the smoke in the car amplified things until we decided it was time to get out and go for a walk.

Upon getting out the car, the effects of the smoke had clearly hit us all. After examining each others eyes and in between laughter expressing how red everyone's were, we managed to pull ourselves together to start walking.

We decided to head to the beach as it seemed like the only worthwhile walk we could think of. Eric seemed convinced that he was conducting a marching band as we walked down the street. I had never see Eric with that much energy, especially in the last few years. His movements and the sounds coming out his mouth were already a give away, but at that moment, he was conducting a marching band and it was awesome.

The next day I had talked to my brother and asked what he though of the previous night's adventure. He said his eyes had been opened and he couldn't believe that his whole life, everyone had made pot out to be this terrible thing when really, it wasn't.

I was glad that Eric shared my view on weed but at the same time, I was disappointed in myself for having gotten him into this. I often wondered if I should have just let Eric discover pot on his own, if he even ever did. Right now, I could directly be blamed for introducing him to weed. I felt like a shitty role model for him and didn't believe I was setting the best example.

We got together a few times again that week and smoked, but the whole time, I felt pulled in two directions. One where my brother and I shared a unique and entertaining experience, which is many ways, was bringing us closer. The other was where I felt terrible for introducing Eric to dope and the whole time we were high, I would be miserable at that thought.

Talking with Eric recently I asked him if he resented me for introducing him to pot. He said it was likely he probably would've tried it at one point in time or another regardless but he was glad to have his first experiences with me. He said he looked back fondly on the times of us smoking up in the car, listening to good music, and just driving around. I was relieved to hear him say that.

At around this time Amanda had gotten into a huge fight with her mother, which resulted in her mother apparently kicking her out of the house. So one night I got a call from Amanda asking if she could spend the night because she had nowhere to go. Of course I said yes and so she took the bus down to the house.

There was really nowhere for her to sleep though as the couch in the living room was often used. Not really having any other options, I offered my room and bed to her for the night.

My room was quite small, really only about the size of a somewhat large bathroom. There was just enough room for my dresser and bed, nothing else. Having two people sleep in a double bed was cramped as well. I was grateful that this was only a one night thing. However, I would soon discover that my gratitude was premature; Amanda was unable to secure alternative living arrangements. She was my best friend, and I couldn't just kick her out so after talking with Mike, it was decided that she could stay.

So we now had two people living in a room and sharing a bed, that were both barely suitable for one person to begin with. Needless to say, things got cramped really fast. Along with that

I wasn't particularly happy to be sharing my bed with Amanda. I knew it wasn't a good idea. I knew how she felt about me and I knew that us sharing a bed wasn't going to help anything. Regardless I couldn't find it in me to tell her to leave and so as a result, my stress level continued to rise and more often than not, Amanda was the one I'd take it out on.

I was still a depressed mess and hadn't found any work. This in turn meant I had no money, which also meant that I couldn't pay my rent or buy food. I was already behind on my rent and it was clear that Mike had grown tired of paying for my half the past two months. Luckily Amanda had a part time job and made enough cash to buy us a small amount of food a couple of times a month.

Matt and Mike had grown particular close as friends at that time and so that along with me being behind in rent, led me to not be surprised when Mike talked to me about Matt moving in. Of course I was fine with that, in fact I thought it was a great idea. I in no way wanted to burden Mike with my financial problems, but I just couldn't get myself together. Having another roommate would help with the money situation around the house.

At around this same time Mike's cousin Kevin came to live with us for a while so during a very short time, the number of people living in this house jumped from two people to five people. Since the house was only two bedrooms, this made things interesting.

Matt had managed to turn a storage room in the basement into his bedroom, which I thought was quite impressive. Kevin had claimed the rest of the basement as his own domain for the time he would be living here. In an effort to make things cozier, he painted the whole place midnight black and crimson blood red. Every time I was down there, I felt like I was on a set for a horror movie.

With five people living in this house and Ryan coming over virtually every day, there was never a dull moment. Only for a few hours each night were things actually quiet but as soon as someone woke up, the house came alive again. Having all these people living here also brought a wide circle of acquaintances. My

friends, Matt's friends, Amanda's friends, Mike's friends, K
friends, and even Ryan's friends would all stop by. By the end of
it, we had quite a large group of mutual friends. So it came as no
surprise when we decided to invite a few people over for a new
year's party and instead got a huge mob of guests.

This community of people, these friends and roommates,
was the essence of what we called 1814. 1814 Abbott Street
was our house address. When we'd invite people over, we'd say
come down to 1814. When people arrived we'd welcome them
to 1814. After a while, people just started calling everyone who
lived at the house the 1814 crew. I believe that 1814 in itself was
the manifestation of an idea that I had drilled into my head. It
was a concept that I had romanticized. It was a desire to relive
the experiences and stories of another person. That person was
Mike.

Mike was always a good story-teller and he actually had
quite a few to tell. Before moving out here, Mike had lived on
the west coast with two roommates, Tom and James. I had met
James through Mike. He had moved out here shortly after Mike
did and before 1814, they were rooming together. Both Mike and
James referred to their time spent at the coast as "The Times"
and I was always eager to hear Mike and James talk about their
experiences. They were living in a party house, drinking every
night and smoking weed all day. At the time, Mike and James
were both just out of high school and had road tripped it out
to the coast, from their home in Saskatchewan. They had been
eager for adventure and had found it.

They were all big stoners and so smoking weed was a frequent
endeavor out there. When Mike would tell me about it I'd always
imagine how it was in my head. All they did was just live and have
fun. Out of high school, on their own, seeking adventure, and
finding their own truth about themselves and life. That concept
thrilled me.

Mike would tell me about their drinking adventures and all
the insanity that came with it. He'd talk about the long nights
and the crazy parties, the good times they had with friends, the

joints they rolled and the bongs they smoked. The more I listened the more my desire to live "The Times" grew. When Mike would show me pictures of him and James out by the coast, I got to see firsthand some of the adventures they had shared. Behind every picture there was story and I listened infatuated, as Mike would tell it. I told myself from this moment on, I too would document all of our good times with pictures and video footage so I could look back on them one day as Mike did now.

I remember asking Mike one night when he was telling me about some of their adventures, if he ever missed "The Times" and what made him stop living them. He paused a moment, thinking of how to word his answer and than calmly replied. "Man, The Times were an amazing part of my life that I will never forget," Mike began to explain. "It was phase though, a part of my life that I look back upon fondly but also a part of my life I have no desire to live again. Those days were fun and I'll always remember the good times I had out there but I'm older now, I've changed and it really was "The Times" themselves that changed me and brought me out here. I grew tired of smoking dope all day long and drinking every night. I started to crave something more in life. Partying was losing its appeal to me. I didn't even like getting stoned anymore. So I left "The Times" behind to move on with life. Something that we all have to do again and again."

I couldn't grasp the concept of living those times and then just moving on. It seemed like it should be so much more complex than that. I struggled with that thought for so long. Perhaps it was just in my head where that question needed an answer. I still hadn't let go of my high school. I couldn't accept change. Maybe that's why I couldn't accept Mike's change from "The Times" to now. Regardless though, Mike had lit a spark inside of me and I vowed that I would also live "The Times" and understand for myself everything Mike had told me.

For a long time after I was convinced that I needed to move to another city like Mike did to live "The Times". It took me a while, but one day I realized that I was living "The Times" for myself here at 1814. Upon understanding that, I tried my best to soak in everything that happened around the house and party as much as possible. Unfortunately my ever growing depression didn't allow me to fully enjoy myself as much as I wanted to. Although I knew that I was living "The Times," I was miserable and flat broke, which made soaking in the experience somewhat difficult.

I had stopped drinking for six months, as after playing my first game of "quarters" with Ryan and Kevin, I had gotten completely hammered and mouthed off Mike when he came into the kitchen to tell me to keep it down because I was being extremely loud. Feeling bad the next day, I apologized to Mike and he said all was "well." I decided after that, I would take a break from drinking. So for six months I did not drink and instead, I smoked pot all day every day.

After six months of not drinking, I finally got drunk. The circumstances were foggy as to why I started again but regardless, I made an interesting discovery that night. Being intoxicated I would bask in my depression and reach such a low that I would actually get high. The concept is strange but true. I was extremely depressed and when I got drunk and focused on this, really soaked myself in misery, I would reach a certain high. To enhance the sensation I often spent my period of intoxication alone in my car, listening to music that triggered sad thoughts and memories, while everyone else would be partying inside. In these moments alone I would cry tears of pain, sadness, and confusion, and after a while, I started to drink just to reach this point because it gave me a sense of control over my life. I was so low, so utterly and completely depressed that I felt like I could jump in front of a car, off a bridge or into pool of rapidly rotating saw blades with no worries or concern. The fact that I felt like I could do anything in that moment without thinking twice, made me feel like I was once again in control of my body, mind, and the way I felt. Hence reaching such an extreme low brought on a "high" like sensation.

After my dad passed I told myself I would be strong and so since that day I never cried from physical pain. At this point in time though, crying became a release and an outlet. I didn't care about being strong anymore, I just wanted to feel better. After a good crying session that only alcohol and a strict focus on my depression could bring about, I would always feel better. Hence, drunken weeping became my new favorite past time. Like many other things in my life, this was short lived as after a while I could not achieve the same stage or point I had been reaching before. For some reason, I just couldn't get there, into that mindset. So instead I'd often over drink and spend the night puking in the bathroom or outside. I gave up trying and continued with my daily life just like I had the six months prior to this. The only difference was this time around, I was drinking much more often.

Things had started to get more miserable than I could've imagined. I felt like a zombie, a creature who had no emotion or control over its body. I felt hollow, like there was nothing inside of me. My brain felt like mush combined with an intricate tangled web of wires that were broken, sparking, and not connected properly. Since cigarettes were my only relief and the main reason I argued with myself of why I could delay killing myself as long as I had my smokes, I was now smoking a pack a day.

Of course I was flat broke and had no money for food and rent let alone cigarettes. So where did I get the cash to smoke? Honestly I have no idea how I was always able to have a cigarette but I was. Unfortunately I have to say that I was so addicted to smoking (I literally told myself if I couldn't smoke I'd kill myself right then and there), that I would frequently steal change from Matt's room when he wasn't home and continue to rack up my debt to Eric.

The thought and understanding of what I was doing made me feel even worse. I was stealing from my friend and I was borrowing money from my little brother for shit. It was his hard earned money; he should be the one to spend it. Here I was not even working and I racked up a $650 tab to him. My life was so miserable in my eyes that it took everything I had to stay alive. Desperate times call for desperate measures and for me that meant going against what my heart told me by lying and stealing.

During the course of the last seven or eight months I had for the first time in my life begun to experience what I found were called panic attacks. An experience that occurs when the mind has an anxiety overload and the body can't keep up so as a release, you begin to freak out and your body starts shaking. From afar you look completely messed up and most people will stay the hell away from you. It lasts a few minutes and then it's done. While you're experiencing one, you're pretty much convinced that you're dying and you either make your peace with God or just flip out and loose it. When it's finished, you feel relieved, like vomiting after getting food poisoning. You feel like you've forced something out of your body that shouldn't have been there in the first place.

Having anxiety attacks was never fun, but having one of these experiences when I was stoned was even worse. You feel dizzy and disorientated. Sound and noise becomes muted and you can't hear anything. Your vision is blurry and you don't know whether to lay down on the ground or continue to stand up. You worry that lying down is a way of surrendering, of accepting that you're going to die, so despite your desire to fall to the ground, you do everything you can to stand. Needless to say, my body was trying to tell me something and I was pretty sure I got the message.

It was the summer of the first year that I had moved into 1814. The miserable winter had finally passed and although I was more miserable now than ever, the sunlight brought a tiny shred of light and comfort to the dark world in my head.

Kristy had moved back in, which I had seen coming. Mike had never been without a girlfriend for more than a few months throughout the years. In many ways it seemed that he needed a girl to complete him. Regardless, I was impressed to have seen him without Kristy for as long as I did, but this story was nothing new. Mike and Kristy had been on and off since they had met. I knew Mike did care for Kristy but I also knew that he didn't truly love her and she was his temporary solution until he could find someone else. Unfortunately this temporary solution was lasting longer than he probably imagined. It certainly was for me.

With Kristy moving back in, we had six people living in the house. To say the house was ever clean would be a lie. The dishes pilled up while you were washing them. It was insane. On the flip side through, having so many colorful people in the house made things interesting and eventful.

Being already as messed up as I was, having Kristy around again didn't make things any better. My depression had worsened significantly since the fall when she had lived here last and if I couldn't stand her then, I didn't know how I was going to stand her now. Ryan, Matt, and Amanda weren't particular excited to hear the Kristy had moved back in either but everybody put on a smile and took an oath of mutual tolerance.

After not hearing from my mother for the longest time, it had come time for life to arrange an encounter between the two of us. I had run into my mom on the streets downtown once that past winter. She looked like hell.

I had brought her back to 1814 as Mike had gone back to Saskatchewan for the Christmas holidays. Matt, Kevin, and Amanda had not moved in yet and Kristy had moved out a month prior to this. I told her that I had the house to myself for six days and if she was willing, she could detox here. She amazingly agreed and so my Christmas Eve and day of that year were spent watching TV in the living room as my mother lay restless in my bed, sweating, vomiting, in pain, overtaken with nightmares as her body tried to push the drugs out of her system.

Since I knew nothing about how someone detoxes, I looked it up online. Upon doing so I discovered that it can be very dangerous for someone to withdrawal from drugs without proper care and medicine to assist them. When I read that I had called the Williams and asked them what to do.

No Face

Mrs. Williams gave me a couple of recommendations that I followed carefully and told me to call her if the situation changed. I set out to follow the directions she had given me. I was paranoid that my mom was going to sneak out of the house when I wasn't looking so I got virtually no sleep for three days. On the fourth day my mom seemed to be doing a little better and I took some small comfort in that.

The Williams had called that day and suggested I get out of the house and they'd take over watching my mom for a night. It just so happened that a good friend of mine was getting married that night, so I gladly and gratefully took the chance to clear my mind, relax a little and pass on my best wishes to the newlyweds.

Halfway through the night, as I was enjoying the wedding, Mrs. Williams called and said that my mom got a second wind and was actually able to get up and walk around. Upon hearing my mom walking around the kitchen Mr. and Mrs. Williams entered the room to see her standing there with her jacket and bags, ready to head out the door.

When asked what she was doing my mom claimed that she needed to go out and get some belated Christmas presents for my siblings and me. The Williams obviously seeing right through her attempt to get back on the streets said they had promised me that they would keep her here.

Feeling pressured and panicked my mom tried to make a run for it out the door, but Mr. Williams stepped in to physically restrain her. Upon doing so my mom started screaming at him which in turn alerted our upstairs neighbors who decided to call the police. A few moments later the cops had shown up and busted down the front door and upon the Williams explaining to them what the situation was, they arrested my mom.

I was devastated. "Of course this would happen," I told myself. "Just when I left the house for a few hours after being stuck in there for four fucking days, this happens." I was choked at my mom for attempting to leave and I was skeptical if physical restraint was actually necessary on Mr. Williams's behalf. You can't force an addict to get better; that just makes things worse. If she had her mind made up on leaving, they should've tried to talk her out of it but not physically restrained her.

After hanging up the phone I sat there for a few minutes and had a smoke. When it was done I went back inside to take advantage of the abundance of free wine and got pleasantly drunk, letting my mind forget my own feelings and instead borrowed some joy from this lovely wedding.

I had not seen or heard from my mom since this incident in the winter that had just passed. It was the summer now and I was hoping a new season would turn over a new leaf.

After bumping into my mom downtown, I made arrangements to meet her at a convenience store that wasn't far from my house. As I waited for her I did nothing but chain smoke. She was late.

It was so dysfunctional with the two of us together in that moment and it probably looked that way from afar. My mom who was clearly high in front of me was trying to talk to me like a normal person. I was so fucked in the head at this point that I couldn't even speak. She'd ask me what was wrong and I'd try to relate to her how extremely depressed I was and this fucked up experience we were both having right now wasn't helping.

She tried to console me like a mother would. It made things even more messed up. Realizing how awkward this moment was she said she was going to go for a bit and she'd call me in half an hour and stop by the house. Since I was feeling so shitty I could hardly speak and she took my mumbled failed attempt at forming a sentence as a thumbs up. She left and I got back on this incredibly shitty bike I was using as my mode of transportation and headed home. Neither of us really knowing why we were heading in opposite directions, but we both knew that the experience we just lived was incredibly messed up.

When I did hear from my mom, she had called my house two hours later. Luckily no one was home because I was about lose my mind. "Hi hunney," I heard my mom say as I answered the ringing phone. I paused a moment before saying anything. "Mom . . . you said you'd call in half an hour . . . that was over two hours ago!" Turns out she had a good excuse. "Oh I was just chatting with my friend George here . . ." My thoughts interrupted what she was saying. "Every single fucking time . . ." I thought to myself, feeling more and more agitated. "Every time it's a new guy. Oh I'm just hanging out with Frank! Oh I'm just hanging out with Joe! No! You're fucking hanging around drug and disease infested addicts in some run down crack shack! Don't try to pass these individuals off as good people!" My thoughts calmed down enough for me to hear the rest of what she was saying.

"I told George you're good with computers and um, he's being having some trouble with his laptop. If we bring it by, could you take a look at it?" I paused for a moment, perplexed at what she was asking me. "Could you use a laptop computer Brandon? George might have an extra one around here somewhere."

It took me a moment to register what she was saying. Was she serious? Why would she ask that kind of a question at a time like this? This guy didn't have an extra laptop lying around and even if he did I sure as hell didn't want it. No I was not going to do repairs on this random laptop. I knew she was fucked on something and I didn't know how much more of this ludicrous I could take.

Something broke or snapped in my brain. I had never experienced anything like it. I screamed into the phone savagely like someone who had completely lost their sanity. I felt like I had damaged my brain. People always wondered if when you're insane—do you know you're insane? I'm not sure but I do know that you are conscious of your transition from sanity to insanity because I'm convinced that's exactly what happened to me.

Screaming and yelling into the phone unleashing a fury of anger, hurt, anxiety, and border line insanity. I vented at my mother how ridiculous she was. I screamed she was insane and had no idea what she was talking about. I yelled into the phone with such ferocity that I scared myself, saying she knew nothing about my life and the way I was feeling. Scared of my own reaction, I hung up the phone and stood hunched over, shaking. Although I've never been able to explain this to myself, for some reason as I stood there hunched over, shaking, looking completely fucked, I let out a hearty chuckle that most certainly didn't sound healthy. Afraid that I was transitioning into craziness like a werewolf transitions when the moon comes out, I collected myself as best as I could just as Amanda walked into the living room.

I didn't know she was home, but she had heard the whole thing and when she asked me with fear in her eyes if I was alright, I said nothing as I went to the back porch to have a smoke.

Dealing with my mother in her condition and with my depression, was always a bizarre experience. Putting even the sanest individuals in this situation would turn many of them crazy. To describe what that experience was like could never be done. I wish the overwhelming feelings, emotions, and anxiety during that phone call with my mother on no one. If you have experienced an instance where you have lost your mind, even just for a moment then you know what I am talking about and I am sorry that you had to experience that.

Fearful that I would lose myself after that one day, I became very afraid of going insane and this fear only added to everything else that was on my plate.

In an effort to improve my situation I decided to stop smoking weed. It wasn't easy because I enjoyed getting high. It brought me a euphoric relaxed state that still remained as one of the few things I took pleasure from in those days. Regardless I decided it was for the best.

On the third day of not smoking, I'm not sure whether as a direct result from smoking or not smoking pot or simply just another fucked up experience that I was seeming to have more and more of these days, I woke up after a bizarre night, feeling completely fucked. I had woken up that morning after getting virtually no sleep. The night had been filled with bizarre thoughts and images constantly running through my brain and due to my active mind, these things had prevented my body from sleeping. It had been only a few days since I had smoked pot and I decided to blame this experience on that although, it possible that dope wasn't responsible because I was generally fucked either way regardless of what I did.

When I opened my eyes that morning, I was instantly awake. Not a shred of drowsiness remained. I sat up in my bed right away as though I had never been asleep at all and stood up as quickly as possible. For some reason, without even thinking, I walked right out to the back porch with the intensity and speed of someone trying to get to the toilet before throwing up. As I hurriedly made my way to the deck I knew something was very wrong but I had no idea what.

Grabbing a smoke from my pack on the table outside, I lit it immediately and waited. I had never in my life woken up and had a cigarette before doing anything else before. I knew something was coming and so I waited. I waited like someone who's waiting to throw up. You know its coming and so all you can do is wait for whatever is in your stomach to be forced out. Then, my body began to convulse as my eyes poured out tears like someone would pour out their stomach over the toilet.

For several minutes I wept profusely, unable to stop. I felt like I was vomiting tears out of my eyes. It was one of the most fucked up experiences I ever had. Just as it was ending Kevin came outside and upon seeing my face, asked me if I was alright. Not knowing how to explain what had just happened to me, I told him I was fine and went back inside shaking, trying to decipher what had just happened.

My relationship with Mike was reaching a dangerous point by this time. It was mid summer and I was five months behind in my rent. I knew Mike didn't want to but I suspected that he was going to kick me out. Fearing that I would have no where to

Brandon Krogel

live on top of the mess that was currently my life, I decided that I could not let that happen. It came time for me to muster the strength to get a job.

A nationwide cable company was hiring for telemarketers. This job was definitely not something I wanted to do nor did I believe that telemarketing was a good thing, but seeing as how it was my only option, I gave it a try. Luckily I managed to get hired thanks to an exceptional reference from Mike. The first week of work was spent in a classroom setting where we learned about the company and just exactly what it was we'd be doing.

One person in my training group stood out to me. Her name was Melissa and apparently my skills at discretion weren't the best, since it was evident she had caught me throwing too many glances her way throughout the day. Luckily for me, she returned them with a smile. After the first day was done, I found the courage to approach her. She, obviously knowing that I had been staring at her all day, was kind enough to indulge in some conversation. After a little while she had to take off and for some reason, as I watched her drive away, I felt something I had not felt in a long time. I felt attracted to this girl.

A few weeks had gone by and the classroom training was done. We were on the floor now making calls and trying to sell people cable and although I didn't agree with what I was doing, it was alright at first. Melissa and I had become friends with a hint of something more and for the first time since I could remember, I started to feel a little bit more alive than before. I talked to her about my problems and she gave me sound advice for many things. She detested smoking and encouraged me to quit. I knew she was right but of course, I still couldn't let go of the one thing that in my mind, had kept me alive for the past couple years.

When I was with her, I felt free. In a sense I almost felt like she was taking care of me. Here I was, this messed up guy who couldn't get his life in order, and here she was, someone who did have their life in order helping me piece mine back together. I felt bad that I had entered into that role. At times I wondered if she was hanging out with me because she felt sorry for me.

When I was with Melissa I was alright but as soon as I was alone again, my misery would come back and with a vengeance for briefly escaping it. One day, which I believe to be the pinnacle of my depression, I died in some way. It was the most depressing day of my life and a point that I never thought I'd get to.

Amanda wasn't home that day. Kevin and Matt were both out, and Mike was in the living room doing something on his computer. Kristy was in the kitchen engulfing Chinese food into her mouth by the fork load. There was a window by the kitchen sink that over looked the back porch for the most part, except for the corner where I happened to be sitting on a very uncomfortable chair. Although Kristy couldn't see me, I could see her and I watched with disgust as this woman, who had clearly never missed a meal in her life, chowed down on an enormous plate of Chinese food. I felt bitterness swell inside of me, which, other than misery, was the only emotion I was feeling that day. I had woken up late that morning and it was now late afternoon, and I had not left the chair all day. I hadn't even gotten up to use the washroom. My energy level was lower than it had ever been before. The reason being was that I was extremely malnourished. For the past two months I had eaten virtually nothing. I had been running off cigarettes and coffee for nearly sixty days. Because I had no money for rent, I had no money for food. So as a result of that, I simply could not afford to eat. I had lost forty pounds and was thinner than I had ever been in my life. I had gone to the beach with my sister Lisa the week before to spend some time with her and upon taking off my shirt, she started crying after seeing the bones poking out of my skin.

Not being able to eat made working difficult. I had no breakfast, no lunch to take to work and no dinner when I arrived at home so concentrating on my work was difficult. Often I resorted to stealing whatever food was sitting in the staff refrigerator.

I remember biking to work just a few days before. After riding for about five minutes I had for some reason, stopped peddling and fell off my bike. Lying on the ground bruised and scratched I wondered what the hell just happened. One minute I was peddling the bike the next thing I knew I had simply stopped and the bike just fell on its side with me on top. After that had happened I was concerned as to why I had just had this experience. I picked up the pathetic excuse for a bike that I was riding (it honestly amazed me that it could even be ridden before I fell off it), and walked to the doctor's office. I knew I was going to be late for work but I was hoping the doctor would give me a note excusing me.

After seeing the doctor he told me that the reason I most likely fell off was because my body didn't have enough energy to sustain the movements of peddling. He said I was incredibly malnourished and hadn't seen anybody in North America look like this for the majority of his career and told me to go home, eat, and wait a week before I went back to work so my body could get the nutrients it needed. I thanked him and left. When I arrived back at home, I realized I had forgotten to get a note so when I called into work explaining why I couldn't make my shift that day, my boss probably thought I was out of my mind. For most people in western society, to hear something as ridiculous as what I explained over the phone would seem like a joke. Truth is, I was a starving kid. I wasn't far off from those commercials you see for world vision, no joke!

Sitting in that chair watching Kristy destroy that plate of Chinese food was difficult to watch. All I wanted was something to eat, I was always so hungry. Here she was, someone who didn't need to shovel two massive plates of Chinese food into her stomach, and here I was, starving, skinny, and wishing I could enjoy the simple pleasure of eating a meal. I had noticed that my head had been hanging down for most of the day and I was starting to feel some serious neck pain. It took everything I had to lift it up.

I sat in that chair wishing for death, smoking cigarette after cigarette when suddenly a bizarre idea entered into my head. In fact it wasn't even an idea it was something that I was going to do no matter what. Without even thinking, feeling as if someone else was controlling my body, I went into the basement and found an exacto knife. Removing one of the razor blades I put it in my pocket, walked back upstairs, and back onto the deck to the little chair that had become my new home.

I sat there with the razorblade in one hand and a cigarette in the other. "What was I doing?" I wondered, perplexed at what was happening. For some reason I just knew, and I don't know how, but I knew if I cut my arm I would somehow feel better.

I struggled with that thought for a moment. I had never done anything like that in my life. I knew people in high school who did that and I never understood it. I'd get mad at them saying that cutting yourself was the stupidest, most pointless thing anyone could do. Now here I was in this moment about to cut my own arm. It was then that I understood. As I drew the first slit down my arm and watched the blood pour out I felt something unexpected. I felt relieved. I felt like I was draining a toxin from my body. Continuing to watch myself make marks with this blade up and down my arm I couldn't help but feel sheer despair. Although relieving, it was incredibly fucked up for me to be doing this and I despised the act immediately. Yet I could not stop.

As Kristy ate her Chinese food in the kitchen, I sat like a dead man in this uncomfortable chair, cutting my arm and watching the blood flow out in terror and amazement. I wonder what the theme song to that scene might sound like.

Overwhelmed with how messed up I felt, I needed something to help me cope with this experience. After stealing enough change from Matt's room, I got on my bike and slowly made my way to the liquor store hoping that a bottle of southern comfort would hold true to its name.

When I got back to the house I was exhausted from spending the energy that I did not have, that I used to get to the liquor store and back. Sitting down on the chair I chugged half the micky and waited a moment. Lit a smoke and when it was done, for some reason, the dirty wooden floor of the back porch seemed comforting and inviting so I laid down and went to sleep.

When I awoke the sun had set and it was early evening, the sky not fully black, as the sun gave the last of its glow of the day to illuminate a dark blue sky. The reason why I had awoken is because Ryan had just pulled up in the back carport and had found me on the deck. When he asked me what the hell happened, the desperation in me lurched out and I told him the events of earlier that day.

Not knowing what to do and not knowing how serious my condition was until now, Ryan desperately tried his best to offer me advice and comfort. As I finished the rest of mine, he asked if I wanted another bottle. Already a little buzzed, I couldn't pass up on some free booze.

Later that night, everyone had a couple drinks and was mingling about much like we always did. Since I was decently drunk I had the courage to joke about my situation. While everyone was gathered around Mike's computer watching something online, I took off my shirt and said "Hey guys check it out. You can see my ribcage poking through my skin."

At that moment everyone had stopped what they were doing as they watched with eyes wide open, me with my shirt off and my bones clearly defined along with freshly made slit marks on my arm that was holding up my shirt. I think everyone understood that I was not well and after Mike went off for several minutes about how he couldn't believe I was that skinny, he reached into his wallet and gave me $80.00 to go get some food.

After that, Amanda and I walked to the nearest grocery store and when we got home, I made the best pasta I had ever made in my life. It probably didn't taste all that well considering I had never made it before but to me, this precious food was glorious. When I had finished eating I felt sick and remained that way for a few hours. I hadn't put this much food into my stomach in such a long time and my body was having trouble adapting.

The $80.00 for food lasted only a few days as I ate every last item of food I had purchased like a madman. I was so afraid of going hungry again that all I did was eat. Soon it was gone and for a few days it was painful as my body again readjusted to not having any food in it.

It was the end of the summer and Mike and Kristy had made arrangements to move out. It was clear this place wasn't meant to house six people. Since the house was in Mike's name, everybody had to leave. Kevin was going back to Saskatchewan at the end of the month and Amanda and Matt were trying to make their own arrangements. I of course wanted to keep the house but it seemed like there was definitely no way I was going to be able to pull that off.

The computer company I had worked for had just gotten bought out by Disney which was big news in our small city. As a gift to all the staff, the company had decided to give each staff member $15,000.00. The thought that if I had still been at this company I may have never endured the hardships that I had faced from then until now, and now I would have $15,000.00 to follow my dreams, was incredibly depressing to say the least. Ryan was equally as choked. We of course did our best to be happy for Mike and Matt as they told us about the whole thing.

That night Ryan and I got drunk and let off some steam. We talked about how crazy it was that I had gotten Mike the job with the company and Ryan had gotten Matt the job. It seemed like the effort we made to help out our friends turned around and kicked us in the ass.

The one good thing that I received from Mike getting that cash was that he forgave my debt, which had now totaled more than a thousand dollars for months of missed rent among other things. I was very grateful to no longer be in such extreme debt to Mike but the bitterness of the thought that said "That could've been me," made if difficult for me to fully appreciate what he had done.

Horribly depressed, bitter, angry, starving, and with an arm covered in slit marks, I sat on the back porch one night and contemplated what I was going to do with my life. 1814 and everything that came with it was about to end. I had no money, no motivation, no nothing. I had absolutely nothing. Most of my socks were ripped beyond repair, my single pair of pants was ripped and tattered and I had to improvise a belt to hold them up as I had lost significant weight since I had bought them. The three pairs of boxers I owned were ripped, it was probably better to wear nothing underneath my jeans. After thinking about it long and hard I was trying to figure out what exactly I was living for.

Was I waiting for a savior that was never going to come? Was I waiting for a break? For someone to throw me a bone? Was I waiting for money to rain down from the heavens and save me from myself? I started laughing when I thought about it. It made perfect sense. "I'm not supposed to be alive," I chuckled to myself slightly hysterically. Perhaps something had gone wrong in the grand scheme of things and life had accidentally forgot to kill me when it took everything else away. Concluding with all my heart and soul, with conviction I had never felt before, I made preparations for the end.

The next day I called my work and said I was too fucked up and had to quit and I apologized for any inconvenience. A few days later Melissa called me and asked what was going on. She said she found out I quit from our boss and was upset that I didn't tell her. I said I was sorry and that I had found something else that seemed more promising and that I'd keep her posted on how things went. That was the last time I ever talked to Melissa.

I had made all the arrangements and for the first time in the past few years I was ready. In fact I was more than ready. Before I didn't have the courage, then I didn't have the energy, but now, I finally had the resolve and the will. It was over. My life was over and since life had been cruel enough to forget to kill me, I decided I had to take things into my own hands. I had picked a day and with every thing in me, I had committed myself to ending my own life. Suicide was about to become my solution. I was going to throw myself off this bridge that wasn't to far from the house. I was finally going to be at peace.

The day was set. I planned that Friday afternoon, which was two days away, I would bring a dramatic ending to 1814 and my life. The most fucked up part about the whole thing was that I waited in anticipation for Friday to arrive like a child waits for Christmas morning.

Little did I know however that by some divine intervention, my plans would be thwarted, my ship spun around and a new course in my life would be set. Of course as I lay in my bed Wednesday night I didn't know that and upon waking up the next morning, the day before I would kill myself, my life would dramatically change.

When I awoke Thursday morning, I was calm and quiet, silently reflecting on my life. Since I had convinced myself that I was indeed going to kill myself, my mind took it as the real deal and so for most of that day my life flashed before my eyes, slowly but surely. There were so many terrible times and memories yet, hidden beneath the surface, there were so many good ones as well.

I wondered if suicide was indeed the only solution to my problems. What if there was another way? If there was, I couldn't find it. "It wasn't like I just pulled this idea out of nowhere," I thought. This was a decision that as far as I was concerned, I was forced to take. I couldn't continue to live in this agony that I'd been wallowing around in for as long as I could remember. The only way to stop this feeling was to stop all feelings altogether.

My roommates had all found out I had quit my job and were trying to relate to me the fact that 1814 was disbanding and I had no money and quitting my job might not be the wisest of decisions. Mike didn't even say a word about it. He had seen this story to many times before. It was nothing new. He had lost hope in me in some way and was ready to just let me do my own thing.

Like every other time before, I knew it was foolish to quit my job like that but it's hard to work when you're starving. It's hard to work when every paycheck you get is instantly devoured by the bank and other collectors the second it goes in your account.

Forget about paying your rent that you're months upon months behind in, let alone food to keep you alive. Every company and person you owe money to waits eagerly for your debt to be repaid. Making it through two weeks of work starving, depressed with absolutely no resources takes an immense amount of dedication and effort. When pay day arrives and you have not a cent to show for that, not a fucking cent! Well, if you weren't motivated before, you definitely aren't now.

That wasn't the only reason. I knew it didn't matter whether I had a job or not since from what I gathered, employment wasn't required in the afterlife. Many Christians claim that to kill oneself is the same as murdering someone else and therefore upon doing so, cannot pass into Heaven when they die. I don't know how Christians know these details but I believed that God would sympathize with what I was doing, that He would see my heart and my pain. I told Him that I didn't want to end my life but there seemed to be no other option. I told Him I didn't want to upset Him and I just wanted to come home. I prayed He would see my heart and grant me peace.

As I tried to explain to God that I needed to end my life to achieve peace and that I couldn't carry on like this, He was trying to explain to me that He knew that and was about to step in. Drowning in my own emotions and problems though, I couldn't hear Him talking to me. It was that evening when God would intervene in my life and throw me a life preserver telling me to hold on for just a while longer.

That night I got a phone call from a man named Jeff. Jeff was an older guy, in his 50's, although he had the strength, charm, and charisma of someone who was 25. He was from Poland and Mike and I had worked with him back in our days at the pizza shop. Jeff was trying to launch his own business. He had hired Mike and I to do some graphic and website design work for him. He promised us rewards of wealth and power in the future if we helped him for free for the time being. We tried to take him seriously but it wasn't easy. Mostly I felt that we were just humoring him. Although he thought his business would one day make him billions, we thought he was out to lunch. But to be good friends, we did what he requested and thanked him every time he promised us unimaginable riches.

We hadn't heard from Jeff in a while so I was a little surprised when he called out of the blue and wanted to talk solely to me for some reason. When I answered the phone my surprise changed to utter shock when I heard him speak.

"Hello Brandon!?" Jeff asked enthusiastically with his thick polish accent. "Hey Jeff, how are yah? I asked out of routine phone etiquette. "I am good chief! How are you?" Jeff always called me chief. I never knew why. "I'm good," I said trying to sound convincing. Jeff cleared his throat before he spoke again.

"Look, Brandon, I am painting for a man named Edward. I told him about your business plan and he wants to talk to you about it. He may want to invest in your idea." It took me a moment to process what Jeff had just said. I retraced the steps in my head. "Okay, Jeff does exterior painting for his day job," I reviewed. "And one of his clients is interested in hearing my business plan? Was this what Jeff was telling me?"

I couldn't speak as Jeff continued to talk through the phone. It was true that I had written and completed a business plan but I had abandoned the project months ago after concluding that getting the funds to start it were completely impossible. Finding out that someone was actually interested in seeing it blew my mind!

Jeff explained that Edward wanted to meet with me sooner rather than later and was hoping we could get together the next day, Friday, which was the day I had planned to kill myself. I told Jeff that I was most definitely able to meet with him and Edward tomorrow at any time and so Jeff made the arrangements and said he'd pick me up the next day at noon. After hanging up the phone, I desperately tried to comprehend what had just happened.

I told myself not to get too excited. I reminded myself that Edward was interested in hearing about the business plan and wasn't sold on the idea. It was incredibly unlikely that he would truly be interested in investing in this project. Still, I found it difficult to contain my excitement as this was literally, the best news I had heard all year.

In an effort to present my business plan well I reread the whole thing that night to refresh my mind of just exactly what it was that I'd be doing.

The concept was fairly simple. I had created this business plan after being let go by the computer company all those months ago. In an effort to understand why and how I was a business threat to that company, which lead to the termination of my employment, I had come up with this idea which I thought was somehow ironic.

I chuckled when I thought about it. Here I was. I got fried for being a business threat which was the farthest thing from my intentions at the time. Now, as a result of getting fired, I just might end up becoming that threat that the company was clearly so afraid of. They did it. They created their own threat which manifested in me. I was the product of their actions.

My business plan was to compete with what was, at the time, a very weak merchandising department that the computer company had launched. Since one of the company's flash games became so popular, it made sense for them to start printing t-shirts, hats, and other paraphernalia with pictures and logos of the company, the game and the characters that were apart of it.

Before Disney had bought them out, their merchandising department was weak. They only had a few concepts of available merchandise and most of it didn't look that good. My goal was to create a copycat of their department that would target the same market.

The company had created a market with millions of users who played their game. This was a market that the company created and profited from 100%. There were no competitors. I figured that if I made my own characters that closely resembled the ones the company had, only with a more attractive design, their market would buy my merchandise over theirs. The goal was to mimic their characters concept closely enough that we could in a sense "pass off" as the company's characters while still avoiding the very thin legal line of copyright infringement.

The company was raking in millions of dollars every month before Disney bought them out and it was evident that they were making even more now. I hoped to launch my business undetected and I didn't think they would mind too much if I sold a few t-shirts to their fans here and there.

I had met up with a graphics designer back when I had originally finished the business plan to come up with some concepts for our own characters. We had actually come up with quite a few clever designs and I was excited to see what we might be able to accomplish.

I was trying to become the Mega Blocks of this company. If you ever played Lego as a kid and your family knew about it, often times you'd get a box of Mega Blocks for your Birthday or Christmas. To someone who didn't play Lego, Mega Blocks look virtually identical. The only way to tell if you were holding a piece of Lego or a Mega Block in your hand was to try and fit them together with other pieces.

The Mega Blocks would never fit as good and it was clear that the quality of plastic they were composed of was not as good as the Lego pieces. Despite this though, Mega Blocks had seen how big of a market there was and the amount of money Lego was making off these little plastic pieces, so they decided to start their own. Like Coke and Pepsi and so many others, this was the concept I was aiming for.

The next day I awoke with more energy than I had in a long time. After having five cups of coffee and a few smokes (which was usually my meal for the day), noon arrived and Jeff showed up at the house to pick me up.

During the drive there Jeff explained more to me about Edward. He had spent his life in the US military as a jet fighter pilot. When he retired a few years ago he moved up to Canada to our town, which was quite a popular place for tourism and rich retired people. Since I was going to be dealing with a military man I did my best to recall everything I had learned in Army Cadets when I was 15 but upon meeting Edward it was clear that he wasn't as strict as the movies portrayed retired military men to be. In fact, he was quite the opposite.

We sat down on some chairs and a table that was set up on Edwards's front porch as we all introduced ourselves. Edward lived in one of the nicest neighborhoods in our city and it was a little uncomfortable for me to be surrounded by such wealth.

Edward spoke gently and there was kindness in his voice. I could tell he was wise and experienced. Before I could ask him about his, he asked about my life and who I was. I told him everything in a summed up version. How my father had passed and how my mother got addicted to drugs. I told him about my time in high school and everything that happened in that era. Finally I told him about 1814 and how I had lost my job from the company. How I was miserable for the longest time and how I didn't understand why I was let go. I told him that it was after getting fired that the concept for this business plan came to life.

He seemed saddened to hear about my life and offered words of hope and wisdom. When he asked about the business I presented him the plan, but he didn't want to read it; he wanted to hear the ideas from my own mouth. So I told him about my idea, how the company's merchandising department was weak, how I felt I could effectively compete, and how I thought there was big profit potential in it.

Edward asked a lot of questions and luckily I had an answer for each one. After about an hour and a half of talking he said he was interested in funding the project and asked how much I needed. I told him I needed $17,000.00 to prepare, launch, and support the company in its early stages. He reminded me that that kind of money was substantial and that with money comes responsibility. I assured him that I was aware of that and felt confident I could handle that responsibility. After a little more chatting Edward had made a decision.

"Well Brandon, I'd like to give you a shot. I'm interested in this project and I'd like to see you have a chance at success,"

Edward said with a smile on his face. "I uh don't know what to say sir . . ." I tried to find words but nothing came out of my mouth. "Please, call me Edward," he asked kindly. "I want you to give this your best shot and it sounds like you know what you're doing. Just remember, your life is in your hands. What you choose to do with it is up to you."

I thought about it for a moment. It was true. Really it was common sense. How strange that it sounded so uncommon.

Edward said that he wanted to give me a chance because he believed I never got one. He said he didn't know me but he felt like he could trust me. After listening to his reasoning he finished by saying that he would indeed fund this business in return for 20% of all company profits. In a blur of craziness in my head I shook his hand and said it was a deal.

Edward said that we would meet together for lunch downtown on Monday and at which point he would have a certified check for the funds. I thanked him profusely and assured him his investment would not go without reward as Jeff and I headed back to the car.

When I got home I was in a blur of somewhere between excitement and insanity. When I told everyone what happened and that on Monday I would be getting a check for $17,000.00, no one could believe what they were hearing. Hell, I couldn't even believe what I was hearing.

So that night, the night I was supposed to die, I lived. I was reborn with new energy. My situation went from nothing to everything in the blink of an eye and come Monday, my life would change drastically, and I knew it would be for the better. Suddenly I had a reason to live. Suddenly I had a purpose.

When Monday rolled around I was hysterical, but tried to present myself as calm and confident when I met with Edward for lunch. As per his request and I also agreed, I had written up some contracts over the weekend stating our roles in the company and who was entitled to what in regards to company profits. After reading the documents Edward seemed satisfied as he signed his name at the bottom of the page. I did the same.

When we finished lunch Edward looked me in the eyes to state one last point.

"You know my wife thinks I'm crazy for doing this," he stated perhaps curious as to what my response would be. I wasn't sure what to say. "She does not support this decision. I have kids who could use this money but I feel like I'm supposed to invest in you." I heard a nervous gulp escape my mouth before I said "You don't have to do this you know. Your wife thinks your crazy? Hell, I think you're crazy!" I half joked. "I just ask Brandon, that you remember what an enormous responsibility this is." He looked me dead in the eye when he said that and I felt a little intimidated. "I understand Edward," I assured him. "You can trust me."

So we left the restaurant and headed to the bank where he got a certified check for $17,000.00. When he came out of the bank, he held out the check and it took me a few moments to take it from his hand. I stared at this little piece of paper in disbelief and calmly took the check from his hand. With another thanks and a few more words assuring him things would be fine, we shook hands, gave each other a solid nod and then parted ways.

I had told Edward that I would contact him every two weeks informing him of the progress of the business. He said he didn't want to do anything in the company; he just wanted to be the investor. He said the rest was up to me.

Edward had mentioned that if the company failed, he would not desire for me to pay him back but would instead be satisfied that we tried our best. Hearing that brought me great peace but also reminded me of the incredible responsibility this was. I contemplated these things as I walked to my bank which was a few blocks away.

When I arrived at my bank and approached the teller, she smiled politely as she asked what she could do for me today. I told her that I need to deposit this check into my account but I would need $2,000 in cash. She seemed a little puzzled upon hearing that as I was not dressed like someone who would be making those kinds of demands. Her face looked even more puzzled when I handed her the check for seventeen grand. As soon as she saw the amount the check was for, she quickly excused herself and went over to her boss. They talked for a few minutes analyzing the check. The teller kept pointing back at me and it was clear they must have thought the check was fake, despite the fact that it was certified. After making a call to Edward's bank, the teller came back to me and with an awkward smile on her face confirmed my request.

"So you want $2,000 in cash and the rest deposited in your account?" I nodded at her calmly saying "Yes, that's correct." She smiled nervously as she said "Okay I'll be right back with your money sir."

"Sir," I chuckled to myself. "Am I a sir now?" The teller returned quickly and counted out $2,000 before me, informed me that the remaining funds had been deposited into my account and after giving me a receipt, wished me a very good day.

When I got outside the bank I could do nothing but stare at this piece of paper that told me I had $15,000 in my bank account that just a few moments earlier had been overdrawn $750.00. I now had a chance at life. My day of death had turned out to be a day of life. I would no longer starve. I may no longer be miserable. God must have seen how serious I was to end my life and stepped in at what couldn't be any later to save me. He was the lifeboat and I was the drowning victim. He had pulled me out of the water to give me a second chance at life and He had done that through Edward.

As I walked home I still couldn't believe everything that had happened in just a few short days. It boggled my mind beyond anything else. And so as I continued to walk I decided that I would make my first business purchase. I went to a nearby restaurant and for the first time in a long time, I ate delicious food until I was full.

Chapter Twelve

"The Times"

That night I gathered all the roommates along with Ryan and Eric and bought enough beer for everyone to have a good time. I had bummed off these people for so long and I was eager to show them how much I appreciated everything they had done for me.

I had somehow convinced the landlord of 1814 that I was the best candidate to take over the lease after Mike and Kristy left. He was reluctant at first but after discovering that the amount of people interested in the place was low due to the condition of the house, he granted me the lease.

Matt and Amanda didn't want to go back home to live with their parents so Matt agreed to share the lease with me. After all, he now had thousands of dollars in bonus money in the bank. So just before the end of August we met with the landlord to sign a year's lease in both of our names. After that, 1814 was officially ours.

Mike and Kristy moved out a few days later. Kevin was heading out too at the end of the week. Since we didn't know the next time we were going to see him, we decided to throw him a going away bash, and after inviting as many people as we could think of, we had the biggest party we had ever had in the house.

I also paid Eric what I owed him, left $100 in Matt's change jar to make up for the money I'd taken from him over time, and went shopping for clothes, socks, and boxers. It felt incredibly strange spending money and wearing new clothes. I also managed to buy a car (as I had sold my other one months ago for a measly 50 bucks).

Not having to worry about food, rent, and other things that revolve around money, lifted an immense burden off my shoulders. My depression however continued to be a problem. Having money meant that I had the ability to distract myself from it more efficiently. Alcohol was my medicine, and boy did I ever pound that shit back. I was getting hammered every night. I'd take care of business stuff during the day and as soon as the sun would set I'd hit the liquor. Ever so often I'd drink too much and spend the rest of the night puking in the bathroom, eventually falling asleep with my face pressed against the toilet. There was always a good chance that I would get super depressed while I was drunk and spend hours in my car listening to sad music and crying profusely. When company showed up randomly and saw me in that state, I was usually too drunk to care.

One night I had drank a micky of whiskey in shots in just shy of half an hour, the whole time listening to the saddest music I owned. I remember just standing by the kitchen stove, sobbing like a child as I brought each shot of whiskey to my lips. After the bottle was finished I went outside for a smoke and the next thing I remember after that was waking up at 6:00 a.m. hugging the toilet in the bathroom with the taste of vomit still fresh in my mouth.

Often times I'd be the only one home and since the sun had set it was time to drink. I'd take a shower and dress in my new best clothes, head into the kitchen and decide between the liquor in the cupboard or the beer in the fridge. After making a decision I'd grab a challenging cup and play the drinking game of quarters with myself. The game is usually played with at least two people. You bounce the quarter into the cup and if you get it in, you hand out a sip to another player. That person then has to take the sip and can't take their turn until doing so. The only way to leave the game is to forfeit, which requires the player to chug the rest of their drink regardless of how full it is. If you fall over, loose your ability to speak, or throw up you become disqualified. Whoever remains wins. This was the game that Ryan and Kevin had taught me back when Mike was still here. The game that had gotten me so drunk I mouthed off Mike. The game that had made me stop drinking for six months. Since I had lost miserably before, I decided to improve my skill with or without an opponent.

My rule was every time I bounced the quarter into the cup, I didn't have to drink, but every time I missed, I had to take one sip of whatever I was drinking. At first this game would generally get me pretty drunk but after a while I became quite good at bouncing the quarter into the cup and eventually even Ryan refused to play against me when I'd offer him a challenge.

As time went on 1814 began to develop a large circle of friends and it wasn't long before the term "1814" became popular around town. We'd show up at parties and people would shout out when we arrived "Hey, the 1814 crew is here!" When we'd throw parties at the house people would refer to Matt, Amanda, and I as 1814, a single collective under that name.

Along with Matt and Amanda we had also recruited another roommate. Peter was also someone I had become friends with while working at the pizza shop back in the day. Peter had just moved into town after spending the past year traveling across Canada. Upon arriving back in our town, he had nowhere to stay so Mike sent him our way. We told him he could live with us for cheap and since his options were few, he gratefully accepted.

Peter was a cool guy. A little nerdy but then again, we all were. He was 27 and Matt, Amanda, and I were all still 19 or 20. He didn't drink and hadn't smoked pot in years so he wasn't much of a partier. I knew that although we were all good friends, Peter didn't particularly want to live with a bunch of pot smoking, alcoholic kids. He had already had his party phase and at this time in his life, he was seeking a more relaxed living situation. It was evident that the frequent smell of lingering marijuana smoke in the house bothered him, although he never spoke about it. Regardless, we had all put up a mutual tolerance for each other's differences. Without that, life would've been quite stressful.

At around the same time Matt and I took over the house, new neighbors had moved into the attic suite upstairs. Eager to make peace with our new neighbors, as we were quite loud through all hours of the night and day, we introduced ourselves.

Luckily for us our new neighbors were a young couple, only a few years older than us. Leah and Jack enjoyed partying just as much as we did and both of them smoked weed. However, Leah was in school and could only party on weekends while Jack worked as a framer and generally never got too crazy. He loved the weed more than the booze and more often than not, we'd all get together and have a session.

It was actually pretty cool. It seemed like even though Jack and Leah were our upstairs neighbors, we were all living in the same house with similar lifestyles. Leah and Jack would come down to our level sometimes together, sometimes individually and often times we'd go upstairs to chill out either as a group or individually. It was clear 1814 had become quite the party house.

I remember getting baked one night and contemplating my life. It seemed so crazy, so many things had happened. I often thought about "The Times" that Mike used to tell me about. This was it. This was my Times. I wanted to experience the same things Mike and James did and here I was doing it. In a sense, I had set a goal for myself and was now achieving it. In some strange way it felt really good.

I often thought about what 1814 really was. To me it was an entity of something. It was the concept of community and friendship that brought people together. It was all about finding yourself and your own truth. Most of us were just out of high school and all we wanted to do was party and have a good time. Amidst that though was the search for self and meaning in our own lives and among the parties there were also quiet times of deep philosophical debate and questions of life and death, truth and lies, why, how, where, and what—we sought to find our own identity and the meaning of our lives.

1814 represented community and friendship. That was the core of it. Our house became a haven at any hour of the day or night for any of our friends to come by and unwind. We'd have friends who were having trouble at home who just wanted to relax and have a beer and talk with some people. We had friends who were out partying downtown but didn't want to walk home because of the weirdo's on the streets so they'd come chill and crash at our place. 1814 became a place that was open 24/7 and if you needed anything, anything at all, we'd do our best to accommodate you. Whether it was food, a friend, or a place to stay, if you came down to 1814 in need, we'd do our best to meet those needs.

The popularity of our parties was revealed when that New Year's Eve we threw the biggest party we had yet. It was nuts. There were so many people in the house you couldn't move around without touching shoulders with someone. The kitchen was full of the people who wanted to be loud—drinking, dancing, and shouting amidst the music. The living room was full of the people who wanted to be more social and laid back, smoking weed and chilling on the couches and chairs. The bedrooms were occupied with people who had snuck off to make out or explore the house. The bathroom was packed with people in an attempt to create the most badass Hawaiian hot box (having the shower running with hot water so the steam could open your lungs and allow for more smoke to be inhaled that was in the air). The basement was for the adventurous people. Some had migrated down there to make out or get dirty, others went down there to smoke a bowl and philosophize. The back and front deck harbored all the cigarette smokers who mingled with each other with drinks in hand. It was unreal. I didn't even know that I knew this many people yet somehow I did. It was probably the craziest party we ever had at that house and I had a blast that night.

The next day everyone was too hung over to clean but it was evident that the previous night had been one hell of a party. Everything seemed in order and nothing was stolen. There was no damage to the house that we could tell. On the plus side of things, we did have a small fortune in refundable beer cans and bottles.

A few weeks before that New Year's, Matt, Amanda, and I completed what was one of the most insane 24 hours of my life. Although extremely unhealthy, it was quite a lot of fun.

I had gotten drunk (as usual), by myself earlier in the night. It was 4:00 a.m. and Matt, Amanda, and I were all hanging out in the kitchen. I was sobering up and was planning to go to bed right away when Matt made me a ridiculous offer. It didn't help that Amanda said she'd match Matt's offer if I actually did this.

There was a micky of brandy that had been unopened in the cupboard for a few weeks now. Jeff had given it to me some weeks ago when I wasn't feeling well. He said to pour some brandy into tea and it would make me feel better. Apparently it was an old European technique. I was pretty sure that despite how you were feeling, you'd feel better if you put brandy in anything but I took the alcohol gratefully.

Basically Matt and Amanda had each offered to pay me $10 if I drank the whole micky right at that moment. It was 4:00 a.m. and I was still sobering up from my adventures earlier. Even for me, the last thing I wanted to do right now was drink more booze. I could use the money for something though and hell, it might even be funny, so I ended up agreeing to their proposal.

I was miserable drinking the stuff. After only a few swigs I already found the drunk in me coming back to life. Matt and Amanda filmed the night: At several points I was completely hilarious (and ridiculous). By the time 9:00 a.m. rolled around I was starting to sober up again but was still decently drunk. Matt and Amanda had been with me the whole night so they hadn't slept a wink either. I guess after watching me they wanted to join in on the fun so at 9:00 a.m. when the liquor store opened we arrived to be the first customers of the day. Matt bought a bunch of booze and when we got home we each made a drink.

Feeling creative and adventurous I took every cushion, mattress, pillow, blanket, and any other comfortable material I could find in the house and threw it in a big pile in my room. My bedroom had been transformed into a giant cushion-pillow paradise. So for the entire day we drank and smoked weed among the collection of comfortable accessories. When we finally did go to bed that night around midnight, we were exhausted and I ended up sleeping for the better part of the next day.

When we did all get up we reminisced about the previous day and all the craziness that came with it. The more we talked about it the more we got pumped on how incredibly awesome 1814 was. Feeling that 1814 meant something more to us than just a house address Amanda said she wanted to get it tattooed on her arm and she was going to do it the next day.

Matt liked the idea and said he'd get it done with her. I was skeptical about it. I wasn't sure if I wanted to get my house address permanently inked on my arm but after imagining what it would be like if Matt and Amanda got it done and I didn't, I decided that I had no choice but to join them. Once we got it done, I was glad that I had decided to go through with it. And so from that day on Matt, Amanda, and I all had 1814 tattooed on the same spot on each of our arms. I knew now that 1814 would be with me for the rest of my life, no matter what happened.

Despite how I might have presented myself, I was drinking everyday for deeper reasons than just wanting to have fun, and I had spent far too much money that should've been used for the company on random bullshit. The cost of my drinking every night was racking up a fortune and the more I realized I wasn't going to have enough money to actually launch this business, the more I drank to forget that fact, getting deeper and deeper into the bottom of the barrel that was my finances. Eventually I had reached a point where I only had a few hundred dollars in the bank and I knew I had to tell Edward the business would not be launched.

I loathed this inevitable conversation. He had put his trust in me, given me a chance and I had foolishly spent that opportunity. He had saved me from killing myself, and in return, I had abused his generosity. I emailed him the bad news, and he wrote me back.

February 8, 2008 9:34:41 AM

Just moments ago I was able to open the attachments . . .to say I'm in shock would be an understatement . . . I am leaving for Alberta to deal with some family issues and will return next Friday. I obviously will need time to digest what you have said. Your letter's contents have taken my breath away. I am seldom lost for words but today I am.

You must understand one thing . . . when bad things happen it's not the person who's bad it's the actions of that person and my response will be about that and not who you are as a individual. We all make mistakes, the worse the mistake the larger the consequence. You must be prepared for that. It's about being a man and doing what is right. We will see. You are to be commended for being honest. That in itself is a huge step.

I'll be in touch when I get back.

Brandon Krogel

March 4, 2008 11:33:42 AM

Hello Brandon

I have been tardy in getting back to you but have had the flu for a couple weeks.

I've thought a lot about what has happened and decided to keep this response short. There is no point in making things worse than they are. Only one point you failed to mention in you letter about the money. Don't forget you conned me out of another 1500 as well. You now owe me $18,500.

Just one thing I need to say to you. As long as you see yourself as a victim in life nothing will ever change. Victims always have an excuse and therefore no reason to change. You need to pull yourself through the hole of self pity and get on with it. I could tell you hundreds of stories of people I know—including myself—who have done just that. Suffice to say, it's up to you . . . I wish you all the best and if you are able to pay the money you owe me I would at least know you have done what it takes to step up to the plate and be a man. To be honest, I would expect nothing less from you.

Pulling for you

Edward

Edward took the news better than I thought he would. As a military man I thought he might send someone out to kill me but luckily Edward's personality proved him to be understanding—even when the situation was not in his favor.

I thought long and hard about his words: "*As long as you see yourself as a victim in life nothing will ever change. Victims always have an excuse and therefore no reason to change. You need to pull yourself through the hole of self pity and get on with it.*"

Perhaps he was right and so from that day on I tried not to think of myself as a victim in this life. I abused that chance to make something of myself and the trust Edward had put in me still eats me up everyday and I have every intention of paying him back no matter how long it takes. I felt like a failure and I was. Now I had no money, no business, and no idea what to do next. So as I waited to develop a game plan, I passed the time by drinking away the rest of the money I had in the bank. Depressed, failed, and broke I sat on the kitchen floor as haggard as could be, with a bottle of whiskey in my hand and a joint behind my ear, doing everything I could to forget about the reality I was now stuck in.

Amanda's Birthday was only a few days after New Year's Eve, so we didn't even have a chance to recover from that night before her birthday was upon us. Needless to say, it was a complete repeat of New Year's. Another full house with so many people that you felt like you were in the middle of a mosh pit. It was the day after Amanda's birthday when Matt, her, and I were walking to this all night diner in the middle of the night, still drunk but sobering up.

In the midst of our conversation Matt suddenly blurted out an outrageous yet invigorating idea. My first impression was to laugh and be like "Oh yeah that would be fun if we could actually pull it off," but after letting out a hearty chuckle at the idea I noticed that Matt seemed a little more serious than I thought.

Matt had just had his heart broken by this girl who had pretty much just been leading him on for the past few months. He wasn't happy at work and often expressed that he was at a stalemate in his life. For the most part, Matt was more of an introvert which in many ways was common ground for him and me to grow as friends.

After this girl ditched Matt, he became increasingly troubled to the point where I wasn't the only one who was now depressed. He went to see a doctor and the meathead wrote him a prescription for some anti-depressants. After a couple days of taking them, Matt seemed more depressed than ever and I knew those drugs were to blame. He bought a sixty of vodka and drank the whole thing. He was wrecked for 24 hours straight. It was intense. He missed work. He didn't eat. His dad even had to come by to try and talk to him.

Matt had recovered enough to be functional in his day to day activities but it was clear he needed a break or some kind of escape. When he suggested that we should just get in the car and start driving somewhere, it didn't matter where, I could see where he was coming from. I also had some things on my plate and maybe a short vacation was something we all could benefit from. One thing in particular I felt I needed some time to weigh out was a relationship I had just ended with this girl I was seeing for several months.

Although Matt cared for this girl he was interested in, my girlfriend Missy was a different case. When we first met at a poker game at Brian's a few months back, she seemed like a nice girl and since I was "rich" at the time, I had the confidence that money brought to approach her (which was something I hadn't done in a long time). After getting to know her however it was evident that she had some problems (as did I) and it turned out to be quite a dysfunctional relationship.

She had slept with so many guys she had lost count and she got tested weekly for sexually transmitted diseases. Since I was inexperienced in that regard, I wasn't too excited to contract a disease, especially since she was one of the first girls I ever really messed around with.

I was drunk virtually every time we were together. When she'd want to come over I'd dread the idea and wished that I had my single life back. We spoke to each other like we were trying to create something out of nothing. It took enough effort for us to hold up a conversation let alone a relationship. Since the first day we were officially "dating," I knew that this relationship was pointless. So when I finally decided I had enough, I gave her a call and told her how I was feeling. Needless to say, neither of us was surprised when we decided to call the whole thing off and the feeling was mutual. In the end it had been a waste of time and money, but I suppose I learned a few lessons along the way.

Matt's crazy idea turned out to be more insane yet adventurous than I originally thought. He basically wanted to get in the car, just go, and drive east until we found an oasis of serenity and happiness. The idea, although exciting, seemed completely unrealistic. First of all, it was the middle of winter, which from what I knew wasn't the best time to drive all the way across the country. Second, I was flat broke and Amanda had hardly any cash. Third, my car was uninsured because I couldn't pay for it and it was in need of at least $500 for repairs and snow tires if we were to make it out of the city let alone across the country.

Matt replied to all the problems I listed with one answer. He said he'd pay for the whole thing. At first I wondered what on earth he was talking about and then I remembered that he still had around $9,000 in the bank. I thought about it for a moment. I didn't really want Matt paying for all of this, it would cost a small fortune but I couldn't help but entertain the idea. I did want to get out of this town for awhile. Maybe an 1814 road trip was just what I needed. Maybe it was what we all needed.

Amanda and I repeatedly asked Matt if he was sure he wanted to do this and reminded him that he'd have to pay for car repairs, food, and accommodation the whole time we were gone for all three of us, rent for all of us at the house while we were gone, gas, insurance, and probably a decent amount of other miscellaneous things. He assured us he was ready to pay for it all as long as we could get out of this town. When we talked about when we should leave, Matt blurted out "Tomorrow!" and so the very next day we got the car repairs done in the morning, got *packed and prepared in the afternoon and managed to get out of the house at 7:00 p.m. that night.*

We left the house in an absolute mess (we hadn't cleaned from Amanda's birthday two nights before), and we told no one that we were leaving until we were on the road. I wrote Peter a note apologizing for the messy house and informing him that we'd be gone until God knows when. I also mentioned that I'd give him a call when I got a chance and he could follow us on Facebook as we had started a group for the event. The first entry I wrote for the occasion on the group page is below.

Amanda, Matt, and Brandon, 3 of the 4 roommates living at 1814 are about to embark on the craziest adventure of all time. After a solid week of partying, the spontaneous decision was made to go through with this outrageous plan. It's the 1814 road trip. On January 8th, Amanda, Matt, and Brandon will leave 1814 to travel across Canada in Brandon's car. They will travel until they reach the Eastern ocean shores of Canada. No one knows what possessed these people to go through with such an insane plan in the middle of the winter but they're going to do it. They don't know when they'll be back. It could be few weeks, it could be a few months. Only time will tell. During the trip, pictures, videos, and other forms of updating will be posted here so if you actually care, you can see what's going down. Wish us luck. We already miss you.

PETER:

Sorry we left the house so messy dude. We were going to clean it . . . but then . . . we didn't. We'll make it up to you when we get back. Promise. Don't forget to feed Diego and check the mail (cat food is in the closet). If a UPS guy comes delivering a package for me (Brandon), just leave it in my room. Oh and if Jeff comes by, tell him I'm no longer his "Chief" cause his damn website is pissing me off and I'll never be able to finish it now. Also check the basement for flooding. There's some buckets down there that will need to be emptied every so often. Thanks man.

The trip began with enthusiasm and uncertainty. No one was sure what was going to happen along the way or where we were even going. Since we left at around 7:00 p.m. we only ended up driving for a few hours before finding lodging for the night.

Already I felt free and relieved despite the fact that we had only been driving for a few hours. I knew this trip would give me time to think and reflect. So much had happened. I had been poor, depressed, on the verge of suicide and then to have $17,000 in my bank account, which I blew mostly on alcohol. Now here I was with my two roommates, my two best friends on a random road trip. There was so much to process. What did this all mean? What was next? I hoped this trip would give me some insight.

We started off in our town, which was a few hours away from the west coast and we were heading east. The farther east we got, the colder it became and the road conditions worsened. It took a lot more skill and focus to drive in those conditions than I had imagined. Being stoned virtually the whole time didn't help either.

The first place we decided to stop in was Saskatchewan to see Kevin. We had gotten in touch with Mike's dad whom Amanda and I had bonded with the previous summer. He had come down from Saskatchewan to visit Mike for a good week and during that time, we all spent a lot of time together smoking weed and cigarettes on the back deck of 1814. Mike's dad had worked on the oil rigs up north some years ago when he had gotten into an accident. A pipe was about to fall on one of his co-workers. Seeing that this guy didn't notice what was about to happen, it was up to him to act and so just like a scene out of the movies, he pushed the guy out of the way and the pipe ended up falling on him instead, crushing his back.

After that he was told he couldn't work for the rest of his life and had permanent damage to his back. Not wanting to pump his body full of pharmaceutical drugs, a friend introduced him into smoking weed to help relive his pain. He found the herb quite helpful. So when he had come out to stay with us at 1814 and Amanda and I found out he smoked pot, we were eager to invite him to our little smoker's domain on the back deck. It wasn't every day you got to smoke pot with your best friend's dad. He was a cool guy, very relaxed, friendly, and kind. He had even taken Amanda and I out for dinner a few times.

When we called him and asked if we could crash at his place for a night when we got into town, he welcomed us over. The plan was to stay with Mike's dad for a night in Saskatoon and then head over to the next city the following day where Kevin lived. Kevin agreed to bus down to Saskatoon so he could ride with us and give us directions back to Prince Albert. He said he'd meet with us the next day.

We had been driving out of Alberta and through Saskatchewan for most of the day and I was so tired I could barely keep my eyes open. If you've ever driven through flatlands like Saskatchewan than you can relate to how difficult it is to stay awake at the wheel.

When we finally pulled into Saskatoon, our destination for the night, we were all relieved to be able to rest up. We were about a block away from Mike's dad's house when the cops pulled us over for a random license and registration check.

"Oh great," I muttered. I had never been pulled over once in my several years of driving and I had a clean record but that didn't stop the wavering uncertainty that was running through my head. I could see Matt and Amanda look around nervously. I couldn't help but feel a little nervous myself. Upon seeing the female officer approach, I rolled down my window and politely asked "What can I do for you offi-" She interrupted me before I could finish. "License and registration." I smiled politely as I reached for the glove compartment. "Of course," I replied.

Upon handing her my insurance papers, the officer jumped back and put her hand on the hilt of her gun, clearly upset by something. "You're under arrest for the smell of marijuana!" she barked. I sat there thinking she was joking. "The smell of marijuana? Are you kidding me?" Seeing how it was taking a few moments for me to comply she yelled: "Slowly get out of the car with your hands on your head!" I couldn't believe what was happening.

"Do you have any marijuana on you?" she asked demanding that we comply. Amanda and Matt exchanged a nervous glance. I knew it was up to me to do the talking. "Uh we have this ashtray of roaches," I said doing my best to correspond to the officers demands. "Is that all?" she asked intensely as she used her flashlight to quickly search the vehicle. Before I could reply, her partner got out of the squad car and came over. He was a bigger guy, more brawn then brains I bet. He walked over just as I was finishing getting out the car, spun me around and handcuffed me. "Get out of the car," he snapped at Matt and Amanda. Without saying a word they got out of the car.

My mind was racing. I still hadn't registered the fact that I was being arrested and for the "smell" of pot of all things. I'm from British Columbia, there's more pot than trees up there. There's even pot growing off of trees up here! Okay well maybe not growing off trees but everywhere you go you'll catch a whiff of someone smoking in the air. It's so common; the cops are apathetic to the stuff. I was learning quickly that things were done differently once you started heading east.

I was trying to think about how in the world this cop smelt dope in the car when she pulled us over. Then I remembered. We had smoked a joint in the car as we were driving when we were about an hour and a half away from the city. I never thought the smell would still linger so strongly after that time but clearly this cop had her heart set on treating us like we were transporting 50 kilos of cocaine or something.

Matt and I were cuffed and thrown into the back seat of the squad car where we just sat and watched quietly as the two officers rummaged through our stuff. The female officer continued to search the vehicle as the male cop walked back to the car and got in. He had our bag of dope in his hand. I watched confused as he opened the bag and began smelling it, picking up the pieces of bud and squishing it around between his fingers. Suddenly out of nowhere he turned back to face Matt and I and started screaming.

"You got ganji on my hands you fucking fucks!" Matt and I looked at each other trying to figure out what this guy's problem was. Obviously he got "ganji" on his own hands. "Is that what you call this? Ganji?" he demanded that we answer. "Uh . . . I believe they call it ganja," I tried to explain. "Get the fuck out of the car!" he yelled at Matt completely changing the subject. Matt looked at him perplexed. "Uh the door is locked form the outside . . . I can't get ou-" The cop cut him off. "I fucking know that!" he freaked as he got out of the car and went over to open Matt's door.

He took Matt out of the car and brought him to where Amanda was standing with the female cop. Once there she lined Matt and Amanda up and told them not to move. I watched as the male officer made his way back to the squad car. When he got in, he closed the door and let out hefty sigh.

"Clearly this guy has some problems," I remembered thinking in that moment. "You can help out your friends you know," he turned around and spoke to me. I paused for a moment, wondering what this maniac was going to say next. "If you take full responsibility for the bag of marijuana, your friends can go. If you don't, you'll all go back to the station."

I thought about it for a moment. It wasn't my bag of weed, it was Matt's but I knew that out of the three of us, I'd probably be able to handle spending some time in a cell better than Amanda or Matt would. It was my turn to let out a sigh as I said "Yeah alright, that was my bag of weed. I take full responsibility." The male cop let an eerie smile creep across his face. "You're a good man." With that he got out of the car, opened my door and brought me over to where the female cop was standing. "It was his bag," the male officer stated. "Is that true," she asked looking right into my eyes. "Yeah it was mine. I take full responsibility." She looked over at Amanda and Matt and then back to me. "Okay, you two can go," she said as she went over and removed the cuffs from Amanda and Matt. "Is there anything you need to say before we go?" she asked. I paused for a moment. There wasn't much to say. "How long will I be gone for?" She shrugged her shoulders, "Probably just overnight." I paused for another moment. "Can I bring my smokes?" I asked hoping I would get a chance to smoke one before this was done. "That's fine," she stated. "But you'll have to wait until you get out to have one."

I was sad to be deprived of one thing I could really go for right now but reluctantly I nodded my head as Amanda brought me my cigarettes. And with that they escorted me back to the squad car. I bid Matt and Amanda farewell as I got in the back seat, then we drove off to the station.

Amanda and Matt couldn't drive my car because neither of them had their license, so they just ended up walking to Mike's dad's house. From there they got in touch with Kevin, who ended up coming down to drive my car back to his dad's place that was here in town.

As I watched Amanda and Matt fade off into the distance from the back window of the squad car, I tired to process everything that was happening. This whole thing was utterly ridiculous. A waste of time, money, and effort. As a taxpayer I wasn't pleased to know my tax dollars were going to such bullshit arrests. I wasn't a criminal. I was a traveler from British Columbia, where someone was smoking dope on the corner of every block. Smoking weed wasn't a crime. The fact that this was happening and that I was being treated as a criminal enraged me. In my mind I had done nothing wrong.

After I got let out of the holding cells at the police station the next morning I met up with Amanda, Matt, and Kevin and went back to Kevin's dad's place. That late afternoon we drove out to Prince Albert to stay with another friend of ours. When we got there I wrote an entry on the Facebook group about everything that had happened so far.

January 11th, 2008

Oh my goodness, were in Prince Albert Saskatchewan. So much has happened in just the few days that we've been gone, I don't even know where to begin. We left town and got to Revelstoke and decided to spend the night there due to terrible road conditions. We woke up the next morning, hit up Tim Hortons and headed onward for Calgary. The weather wasn't to bad the rest of the way there and in a few hours we found ourselves staring at the bright city lights of Calgary. We spent the night there, at another dirty motel but before that, we decided to hit up the Casino. Amanda and Matt both won 40 bucks off slot machines, which was nuts. I lost 60 dollars at poker . . . which sucked but we didn't let that dampen our spirits and decided to spend the money we did win, on drinks and more slots (yes, all of the money we won was gone very quickly). On the way to Saskatoon, we had a good time (despite the never-ending long long long long straight roads that go from Alberta right into Saskatchewan). I almost fell asleep while driving but thanks to a burger from A&W and another coffee from Timmy's, we were able to make it into Saskatoon alright. We had just got into Saskatoon and were looking for our good friend Kevin who was part of the 1814 crew last spring and summer the cops pulled us over.

THIS PART IS WHERE IT GETS CRAZY

I was asked to step out of the vehicle, cuffed, and arrested. Our car was searched and I was sent to jail for the night. Those who know us well know our habits, and that's what got us in trouble. The cuffs were tight and I had never been arrested before. I could feel the circulation to my hands being cut off and when they were finally taken off, I had crazy red marks around my wrist. I was brought into the cop shop through an entrance that only the cops had access to. Everything on me was taken away, even just a single penny I had in my pocket. They also took my shoes and left me in just my jeans, t-shirt and socks. I was searched by the biggest dude I had ever seen so instead of fighting back, I just decided to take it easy (joke). I was led to my individual cell (I was thankful that I didn't have to share it). Imagine a small concrete room no bigger than your average bathroom. There wasn't even enough room to lie on the floor and fully stretch my legs. There was a toilet in the room, which was just this dirty metal object, a mirror above the sink that dispensed water so gross tasting, I was pretty sure it was going to give me some crazy disease. The cell had three solid concrete walls and where jail bars might be, there was a clear see-through plexi-glass wall. The door to the cell was part of that wall. There was a security camera pointed directly at the cell. Anything you did in there was being watched by the cops at the security section and yes, if you wanted to use the washroom you were not alone.

The cell was cold and all they give you is a sheet to sleep with and some toilet paper. There was a roll out mattress similar to those blue mattresses that you can take with you camping. The mattress was so hard and uncomfortable I could've sworn the concrete floor would have been more comfortable. There was dried, old piss all over the floor along with various other disgusting substances and I could smell a strong scent of puked up liquor on the walls. There was no clock, no windows, and a single light that remained on all night, hidden behind a strong glass covering in the ceiling.

I did not know what time it was. I believe I got in there at around 11pm and I didn't have court until the next morning at 9:00 a.m. I lost track of time in that cell. I kept asking the guards for the time, but they never responded and instead just looked at me like a convicted serial killer. I tried to sleep because I was so exhausted but the cell was so uncomfortable and cold, I couldn't sleep. After lying there for a few hours though, I finally passed *out, if only for a little while only to awake not knowing where I was. When I remembered what had happened, I started to feel full of panic and paranoid that I had slept though my court meeting and I would have to remain in that cell even longer. I started pacing back and forth not knowing what to do and only just wanting to know the time, so I could know how much longer I had remain in that terrible place. I calmed down and lay down again, attempting to fall asleep but the screaming, yelling, and consistent profanity of all the other prisoners in their cells kept me up.*

I fell sleep again finally only to be woken up shortly after to a guard bringing the prisoners McDonald's for breakfast. I didn't want to eat for fear that I would have use the washroom. I was thirsty though, so I had a few sips of orange juice. Shortly after that, they took all the prisoners out of their cells and piled them all into a single concrete room with a huge steel door. The door could only be opened from the outside.

I stood silently as I watched everyone else in the room. Everyone looked like hell. One guy looked like someone beat the crap out of him. Another guy was withdrawing from cocaine and was shaking frantically. It was pretty intense.

The cops cuffed three of us together at a time and led us to a transport vehicle where we were locked in the back, trapped in a steel cage. They brought us to the courthouse and transported us from one concrete room to another. When it finally came time to go into the court room, I was so tired and messed up from everything that had happened, I could barely focus on what was going on.

The court session lasted about five minutes. The prosecutor explained to the judge why I was there and when she was finished, the defense attorney and the judge exchanged a few words. Finally I heard those amazing words. "Mr. Krogel, you have been granted absolute discharge." "Thank you your honor" I said as I made my way out of the court room.

My belongings were returned to me and I left the court house sleepy, dazed, and still trying to come to terms with everything that had just happened. I walked to the nearest place that served food, called up Amanda and Matt and got a ride to Kevin's house where I slept for most of the day. I woke up later on, took a shower and then we drove out to Prince Albert, where we are now.

The whole jail experience was one the craziest things that ever happened to me and even though I was only there for one night, I made a vow that I would never put myself in that situation again. Thank God for getting me out of there when He did.

Anyways though guys, rest assured everything is fine now and our journey continues. We will be staying here in Prince Albert for two days and then we continue driving east. Keep us in your thoughts and I will update again when I get a chance.

> *Love from 1814,*
> *-Brandon*

The whole experience was frightening. I knew I never wanted to be back in that situation again. In many ways I just wanted to head back to British Columbia.

We had been gone almost a week and a half and tensions were starting to rise. We spent most of our time in the car so everybody got a little cranky from time to time. The road conditions were worsening and our heater seemed to be failing. After making Amanda and Matt face the facts, we all agreed to head back home. Matt and Amanda wanted to carry on but I couldn't do it. It would've been foolish. Matt's money was running low as well. We had already spent nearly $4,000, it was bananas! We stopped in Medicine Hat, Alberta where I wrote the last entry for our trip.

Brandon Krogel

January 15th, 2008

Were in Medicine Hat, Alberta. This is our second night here. We decided to come home and this is our first stop on our way back. Were heading back because of the road conditions heading further east and because I have a ton of things I have to take care of back home. We're taking a different route back and were going to be heading up to Burnaby first before we come back (if the weather permits). Despite the fact that we didn't actually go all the way across the country, we had a good time. We got to hang out with some old friends and meet some new ones. We partied in a barn in Prince Albert with a bunch of huge, bearded, and tattooed metal heads. We drove through a snowstorm, we drove through intense winds, we drove during the day, and we drove during the night. Oh and let's not forget my little jail experience. My point is, this trip was a blast and even though we only made it as far as Saskatchewan, I ended up learning a lot of new things (and lessons) as well as reached a lot of conclusions about a lot of different things. Honestly, for some reason . . . I don't feel quite the same as I did when we left. Thanks for reading guys, hope it was somewhat entertaining. Looking forward to catching up with you guys when we get back.

-Brandon

After we left Medicine Hat we headed home with no stops. We decided since we didn't make it to the east coast, we'd at least go to the west one. We decided to treat our house like free accommodation for the night and then head out the following morning.

We got home and it was nice to be back. We caught up with Peter and he updated us on everything that happened while we were gone. The house was exactly as we had left it. Tired and burnt out, we headed to bed at a decent time and the next morning woke up and departed the house heading to the west coast, which was about four hours away.

When we arrived we met up with some of Matt's old friends and had a good time. We spent the night in a motel and then the next day it was time to end the trip and head back home. The drive back was fun. It was less than four or so hours and in many ways I think by this point we were all eager to get back home.

Although I don't believe Matt found what he was looking for, I think the experience was good for him as well as for Amanda and I. We talked about a lot of different things and in the periods of silence along the way, I knew everyone was working out their own questions.

It was true, when we got back to 1814 I felt like something had changed inside of me. I felt renewed with a new perspective. I was still depressed, that fact remained but I was sure that I had somehow found the answers to many questions that I didn't even know I had, along the way.

Once back at 1814, the old habits resumed. I don't know how we did it but Amanda and I continued to get hammered every night. About a month after we came back from the trip Matt's money had run dry and since I wasn't working, I knew this was going to be a problem.

It wasn't long before it became a struggle just to eat food everyday let alone pay for rent. I don't know how we did it but somehow we managed to pay our rent every month. It was literally nothing short of a miracle. In several instances it was our good friend Bret who literally saved our asses as he had given Matt and I rent money when we were broke.

As finances tightened tensions rose. Arguments were frequent. Alcohol brought out the worst in me at times. It was clear that things were getting messy and so much had changed since we had first taken over 1814 after Mike left. I knew the future was bringing something. I knew that my "Times," like Mike and James', wouldn't last forever. They couldn't last forever. In many ways I desired a change. I was beginning to understand all the questions I had about "The Times" and what led to the ending of those "Times" for Mike and James. Contemplating my life and the future in between drinks became a frequent pastime of mine as the months continued.

The spring was on its way and I felt something new the air. Shifting winds was what it was. It was true I was still in "The Times" that I had so greatly desired to live but I had a feeling, something was going to change. Perhaps it was my "Times" at 1814 that brought this change. Perhaps, if I were somewhere else it never would've happened.

What did end up happening was something I most definitely did not expect. It would be the end of the life I knew for so long and the beginning of something new. It would be the reason why I would come to write this book. It would be the first steps for a new life but it would come at the cost of an old one that I had grown accustomed to and in countless ways, very fond of.

Chapter Thirteen

Disbanded

It was late winter of that year and the road trip had faded into just a memory. Life had resumed where it left off when we got back. I continued to drink every night and smoke pot all day. Our financial situation around the house continued to worsen as neither Matt nor I had a job.

Around this time Amanda had gotten a job working at hotel doing housekeeping. The pay was above average and I knew I needed to also find some work before things got even worse. For the first time in a long time I felt like I could actually have the energy to work. After talking with Amanda about it she put in a good word for me and a week or two later I was hired for night laundry.

It wasn't bad. For most of the night it was just me in this big laundry room, folding sheets and pillow cases that seemed to be unending. The pay was good though and I was able to bring my CD's and listen to some music as I worked, so I really had little to complain about.

So for a couple months I worked for the first time in a long time. It felt a little strange to be back in the work force but it felt good to be making money again. While I was working, I could pay rent and afford to buy food but the rest of my money went to booze every night, sometimes even while I was still at work.

Luckily I never got caught, which would've gotten me fired immediately, but after a couple months there I quit because I refused to plunge a clogged up toilet in some rich guy's room.

It was after quitting this job that something miraculous happened. A month or two had passed since I worked at the hotel. All the money I did have was gone and spent. If it wasn't for Ryan stopping by everyday with a few cheeseburgers, we probably all would've starved to death.

Times were tough but whether that played a role in this or not is a mystery. The fact of that matter was that I was about to normalize. For the first time in years I was going to feel okay.

I remember it vividly. I had awoken one morning in my bed, slightly hung over but that wasn't anything new. I remember opening my eyes and staring at my ceiling, for some reason just wide awake. In that moment I knew something was different but for a few moments I couldn't figure out what. I felt clear and light, like a heavy burden had been lifted from me. My body felt like it had energy and a desire to move about. "Am I on drugs?" was my initial thought. Then I realized what was going on. I wasn't miserable. I didn't feel depressed. I felt fine, normal, alright. What a joyous feeling it was.

I rushed out of bed and started walking around, part of me unsure if this feeling was only temporary or if it was here to stay. Luckily it wasn't and as the rest of my day progressed I continued to feel "fine".

It was so bizarre. I couldn't figure it out. What happened? I went to bed feeling like garbage, drunk because I was miserable, and then I awoke less hung over than expected and for some reason transformed into an emotionally stable being. It didn't make any sense. Where does over three years of misery, sadness, and extreme depression just go? Why was I feeling fine now and not before? What had changed? I had so many questions and I still do.

My hopes in writing this book were to figure that out. My whole life I've always sought after an answer for the questions I had. This is one of the biggest questions I have ever had to ask myself. Where did my depression go? I couldn't accept that it just disappeared into thin air. It had to still be inside of me, somewhere. I didn't suffer in misery for three years to just have that misery leave like it was never there. That wasn't fair. I needed to know why this happened to me. Unfortunately I have still yet to answer that question.

At least something had changed though. Instead of drinking because I was depressed I was drinking, well really I was drinking just because. It had become routine to drink every night, I didn't know if I should stop just because I was feeling better. I suppose I couldn't accept that I was no longer depressed. For me, that depression made me. It was a part of me. It was who I was. Brandon Krogel was a very sad and depressed guy. That was me and that was the way I was used to feeling and used to presenting myself as. If someone were to say Brandon Krogel is a pretty happy guy I would know they were not talking about me but some other guy with the same name. Brandon Krogel, as far as I was concerned, had always been depressed and always would be. When that changed, I didn't know who I was anymore. So I drank and smoked to search for an identity. If I wasn't depressed than what was I? Who was I?

As the months went on I continued to struggle with the fact that I no longer lived in misery (as bizarre as that sounds). I realized that this time at 1814 had really given me a chance to think and reflect about my life. Perhaps I needed a good year of getting hammered, getting stoned, asking questions, and feeling messed up for my depression to go away. Perhaps this was what 1814 was supposed to do for me. Or perhaps not.

The months went on and I continued to ponder my newly discovered freedom from feeling shitty. Finances around the house didn't get any better though while I was contemplating life all day long, and everybody was cranky because everyone was hungry. Tensions started to build between Matt and me. I was tired of doing all the cleaning around the house and sharing what little food I had. He was probably equally as stressed in some manner or another. He had zero cash, which meant, he was in survival mode, living off only the bare necessities each day. Matt and I started arguing lots. We were beginning to disagree on almost everything. Our once pleasant friendship was slowly turning into nothing more than tolerance for each other every day, and our lack of finances was the source of our tension.

The late winter had changed to spring and then to early summer. Kevin had come out to live at 1814 for the summer and everyone was excited to have him back as part of the old 1814 crew. Just prior to Kevin coming back though, something had happened at the house. The community and the concept of 1814, the very essence of it, had been ripped in two from the source. I try to live my life with no regrets but this one terrible night is the only thing in my life I wish I could take back.

I had just managed to finally get another job working as a cook in a pub. The pay was excellent and the free meal at each shift was a huge bonus since I didn't have any food at home. I had just come home after finishing my first shift and was excited about my new job.

I felt a celebratory gesture was fitting so I borrowed some money from Leah upstairs and went and bought a two six of cheap whiskey. Matt was out at a friend's house so it was just Peter, Amanda, and me at the house. I had arrived at the liquor store only a few minutes before they closed and by the time I had gotten home and made my first drink it was around 11:30 p.m.

As I drank I began to discuss with Peter and Amanda the growing tensions between Matt and me and how I felt like he wasn't pulling his weight and I was sick of all the arguing. Peter and Amanda shared many of my concerns and their agreement only rallied me up further. I rambled on and on. I also continued to drink and before I knew it, the entire bottle was gone and I had even taken Amanda's drink (she was still on her first and I had finished the bottle), and drank that too.

The next thing I knew I had transformed into a monster. I was verbally assaulting every single person in the house. I was enraged, drunker than I've ever been in my life, and I was on a mission of destruction. For some reason that night I hated everyone.

I screamed at Amanda telling her that we were never friends, that she was always just Jake's little sister and that was it. I reamed her out saying she was annoying and I hated living with her. I told her I couldn't wait to move out and get away from her.

I cursed Jack who was upstairs at the time, uttering the most terrible insults I could come up with. Why on earth I was mad at him I'll never know. Ryan and Bret had stopped by and the moment they arrived they were greeted with insults that hit their mark and stung their hearts.

I am baffled at the words that I can remember saying. Every insult to each person was unique to them, fully customized, targeting the deepest insecurities they had confided in me. I had used their trust in me to attack them where it hurt the most. Even now I can recall in my blurred vision, the expression on the faces of my friends, as one by one I tore them down, destroying any bit of confidence they had, ripping away any joy or happiness.

Somehow I had saved the best for last and when Matt got home, I ripped him to shreds with my words. He wouldn't take it though and gave me a taste of my own medicine. Furious I stormed outside into the backyard with my baseball bat and started beating the shit out of random objects lying around.

When I got back to the back porch, Matt had locked me out of the house and honestly I don't blame him. By this point I was out of control and something needed to happen. Unfortunately there was no one there in that moment to intervene.

Shouting and banging on the door I yelled for Matt to let me in. When he finally did I approached him aggressively with the baseball bat in hand, making gestures implying that I might hit him with it. As I continued to verbally destroy Matt for locking me out of the house I noticed a hand reaching toward where I was holding the bat. When I looked down to see who it was, which turned out to be Peter trying to take the bat away from me, Matt saw an opportunity to knock some sense into me and sucker punched me in the face. It was a hard hit and knocked me to the ground but when I got up I was an enraged machine that felt no pain.

I took Matt down right away and relentlessly threw punches at his head. He resisted at first, but stopped resisting my attacks after only a few moments and it quickly turned from us fighting to me just beating him.

When I recall this terrible event I feel sick to my stomach. I despise alcohol and I despise myself. I'm not sure if I can ever forgive myself for the things I said and did that night. I hate myself for that; I was a piece of shit. I would rather die than ever do that to a friend again. I recall Matt's expression as I just stood over him punching him in the head repeatedly. Him just lying there not even fighting back. What had I become? What was this monster in me? My guilt to this day is overwhelming.

Seeing that things were clearly getting out of hand Peter stepped in with an old sword that he had in his room. His intentions were noble but his method unorthodox. He had placed the unsheathed sword in between Matt and me and yelled for us to break it up. His goal was to scare us with the sword in hopes that we'd stop fighting, but me being hammered out of my mind and all my attention focused on fighting Matt, I didn't see it.

It wasn't until Amanda screamed that there was blood on the wall that I stopped fighting and looked up. It was true there was blood on the wall. In fact, there was blood everywhere. The room looked like the Texas chainsaw massacre. Concerned that things had gotten more out of hand than I could've imagined and I had injured Matt to the point where he was bleeding, I frantically searched his body for signs of injury. It was then that I looked down to realize that the one who was bleeding was me.

Somehow when Peter had place the sword between Matt and me I had slit my hand on it and was spewing out blood like a fountain. A large piece of my hand was flapped over like someone turning a page in a book. Realizing that I was bleeding profusely and probably needed medical attention I rushed out the door, got on my bike and peddled, still drunk, to the hospital, which was luckily only about a ten minute ride away.

When I got there the nurse let me in right away and the doctors came in to take a look. I ended up needing fifteen stitches in my hand and four in my finger. A tendon had been severed which had temporarily made my ring finger on my left hand unable to function properly. The doctors suggested I press charges against Peter but I knew that was something I couldn't do.

Without Peter that fight could've worsened and it could have had even more severe consequences. In many ways I was grateful to him for breaking it up, even if his method was a little crazy. I knew I deserved far worse than this injury to my hand for what I had done that night.

When I got home it was around 7:00 a.m. and Peter and Amanda were waiting for me. Peter continuously expressed his apologizes for cutting me and I told him it was all good and that I was glad that he had managed to break up the fight. He seemed more shaken by the whole sword incident than I was.

I called my new job and told them my hand was sliced up so it was going to make cooking difficult. My boss said if it healed in a week I could still work there but if not, he needed to find someone else. I told him the doctor said at least a month and thanked him for the one day of employment.

Matt moved out the next day. It was sad. 1814 had been broken, The final straw was my alcoholism and rage. "The Times" that I wanted to live so badly were now about to end as a result of my actions. What I had created I had also destroyed.

Peter was shaken up about the whole event for days and I awoke one morning to find a note in the kitchen. Peter had decided to move out of town. I knew that whole incident with the sword played a big role in his decision to split as quickly as he did. He thanked me for letting him stay at 1814 and he cherished the good memories he had here. He said he was unable to take his stuff with him and felt bad for leaving it behind but said I could have or sell whatever he had left.

I remember reading that and realizing how much of a good friend Peter had really been to me. I was sad to know that he was gone and stood there wondering if I had taken him for granted as a friend, but I knew he was doing what was best for him. I also knew that this now meant the end of 1814 was at hand and everything we had created over this past year would be disbanded.

Matt had moved back in with his parents the day after the fight and Amanda had made plans to move back in with her mother at the end of the month. I had spoken with the Williams and they had agreed to let me stay with them until I could figure something else out.

Our lease was up at the end of the summer and it was obvious that we couldn't hold on to 1814 even if we wanted to. So Amanda and I remained at the house, just the two of us for the few remaining weeks we had left there. It was a little messed up. Luckily Kevin was there to help fill in the empty space. I was grateful he had come after that one night and not before so he didn't have to be exposed to my madness.

For the last few weeks at 1814 I did nothing but reflect and ponder everything that had happened. From getting that money to starting the business, to the 1814 road trip, to the big fight that ended it all, that year had been a crazy experience.

In many ways it seemed like everything had happened so fast. I knew that I never wanted to drink whiskey again and since that day I haven't touched it. I knew alcohol was what had destroyed "The Times," which ironically enough, had been an essential ingredient of it in the first place. Perhaps I had taken it too far. The money I got and that whole year went by in the blink of an eye. It's funny how much time flies when you're drunk virtually every night. I came to the conclusion that perhaps I didn't fully milk 1814 for everything it was worth because I was blinded by my need for booze. I knew, but wouldn't fully understand until after 1814 ended, that these "Times" were done. They could never be recreated. They were over, forever. My regret next to that one night would be that I was too drunk to enjoy them as much as I would've liked.

Before leaving 1814, we decided to throw one last party. Matt and I were able to talk just before the party and although I knew it would take a long time for forgiveness and healing to take place between us, I was grateful that I had a chance to apologize to him.

The party didn't have as good of a turnout as I was expecting. A lot of random people I didn't even know came to the house. Some of them were pretty sketchy. A bunch of stuff got stolen that night and at one point during the night I went outside for a smoke and realized this party was a failure and that nothing stays the same forever.

The next few days I contemplated the party and everything that had happened. It was clear the spirit of 1814 had changed and I didn't like where it was going. Perhaps it was time to let this place go but I knew that wouldn't be easy. In a sense though, it was already finished. The spirit of 1814 had passed on.

Although the majority of the time I was at 1814 I was miserable, it had been my home for two years. I had so many memories and so many things had happened. There was such a history here for me and by leaving it behind, I felt like I was leaving my whole life behind to start something completely new. All I had known was high school and then after that 1814. I had no idea what life would be like without 1814 and so in many ways I dreaded leaving, despite the voice in my head reminding me that it was necessary.

It was a sad, sad day when it came time to go. We had moved all of our stuff out thanks to some cash I got for selling my car that had just been sitting in the back car port for several months.

I remember walking through the empty house and saying goodbye to each room, remembering all the good times I shared in every corner of this house. Even though I was leaving a house behind, it felt like I was leaving a friend behind. It was emotional.

And so it came time to return the keys to the landlord and bid 1814 farewell. I knew that it would live on with me forever and I would take the lessons and memories with me for the rest of my life. On my right arm I had the tattoo symbolizing the community and friendship of 1814 and on my left hand I had the scars to remind me of that one night that led to its demise.

As I watched 1814 fade off into the distance as we drove away, my heart was heavy and I wondered if leaving was the right decision. I knew in my heart "The Times" were done but I questioned whether it was possible to save them or not.

When I got to the Williams the nostalgia was overwhelming. I got settled into my old room as best as I could and tried to come to terms with the fact that this was my new home . . . again.

Lying on my bed, I stared out my window into the night sky and wondered, if things hadn't gotten messed up somewhere along the way, what Matt, Amanda, Ryan, Bret, Peter, Leah, Jack, and Mike would all be doing if we were back at 1814 in this moment, still living "The Times".

Chapter Fourteen

Crossroads

The first initial weeks back at the Williams were incredibly difficult for me. The nostalgia was killing me, along with a billion thoughts and feelings that couldn't even be described.

Before leaving 1814, I had developed an attitude that said I was going to move on with life and make things happen because things were certainly not happening there. I was convinced I needed to move out of that house before I could make any progress in life. What I failed to realize is that progress can be made at anytime in life, regardless of where you live. I also failed to realize that I wasn't just going to walk out of 1814 and suddenly be a new person. So as I sat in my room at the Williams I became afraid. I was afraid that I had made a terrible mistake in leaving 1814. I thought life was going to be much better once I moved out but as it turns out, it was almost worse.

I couldn't recall the last time I had felt so alone. 1814 was home, my roommates and friends surrounded me night and day. Ryan and Matt lived on the complete opposite side of town, not that Matt would want to see me anyway. Peter was gone. Mike had left a long time ago. It felt like my circle of friends had evaporated into thin air. Luckily I had one familiar face to keep me going. Without her, I don't know what I would've done with myself.

Amanda had moved back into her mother's which just so happened to be in the same part of town I was living in. She was a twenty-five minute walk away or an eight-minute bike ride. With this being the case, we got together often, holding onto a fragment of our old life that we kept as friends, in this new scary world of uncertainty.

We'd talk about 1814 and how we missed it. We wondered whether it could have been saved or if its fate had been sealed before it even began. I was glad to have Amanda around to help me find an answer to these questions.

Although my depression had left several months ago, I was feeling depressed in a new, yet familiar way. Similar to one of the three biggest contributing factors to my depression before, I was now becoming depressed because I realized I didn't actually want to leave 1814. I had changed my mind. I regretted my decision.

After a few weeks of living at the Williams it was apparent that I needed to find a job. There was no room for excuses this time. Regardless of how I felt, I needed to work to pay my bills. Luckily because this looming depression I was now facing wasn't nearly as intense of the one before, I was able to hold myself together enough to work steadily at, guess where, yup the gas station.

Although I was feeling some new, strange, mutated version of my old depression, I had in many ways grown up in the past half a year or so. I felt like I had a new head on my shoulders and this new head was definitely better than my previous one. I felt like I had learned many lessons by the time 1814 ended. Of course these lessons required me to make plenty of mistakes but now, with this new perspective, I was determined not to repeat any of them. Regardless of this new found resolve though, emotions and feelings, much like they always had, ended up determining a large portion of my behaviour.

This in turn led to once again; my career at the gas station being short lived. I had worked there three times now (well three different locations). They say third times the charm. In this case, the first time was the charm. The other two didn't do much except piss off my boss unlike anything else. I never enjoyed screwing my employers over. To be honest I actually hated it. But desperate times call for desperate measures and my desperate time was then and my desperate measure was quitting this job, which was not a "good" thing for me in my own head.

Because of the way I felt, the real world was blocked out. I lived in my head. Not by choice but just because my emotions were so overwhelming that they were the only thing on my mind. To me, they were the only thing that mattered. For some reason while I was at the gas station, my emotions were too out of control for me to focus on what needed to be done in my life. So until I gained control of my feelings, it seemed I was doomed to be controlled by them.

Being unemployed again wasn't as freeing as I thought it was going to be. I was hoping to find some other means of making decent income without working a regular job. What I failed to comprehend is that you can't just hope something will come your way and then think its fine to just up and leave your place of employment. So now here I was without a job, waiting for something that wasn't going to happen. After a few months of not working, it was beginning to take its toll.

I never wanted to go the Williams because I knew I was significantly behind on my rent. I tried and tried to find work but there was nothing. I was beginning to reach a critical point in my finances. I knew if I didn't find a job or magically conjure up some cash that things were going to get messy. At one point during my desperation I had actually gone as far as to plan a robbery! It was insane. I was insane (or at least becoming). Luckily I didn't find the resolve to follow through with the idea but the fact that I was contemplating it on that level really made me wonder. If something didn't come my way soon, I didn't know what I was going to do. I was afraid that I'd end up just as depressed as before if I continued to be unemployed only this time, there wouldn't be a Polish guy calling me on the phone to inform me that his friend has $17,000 that he wants to invest in me with.

Amanda has just gotten a job working at liquor store in the area of town we lived in. While I was busy scheming robbery ideas she was happily working at this job which paid above average wage, had good benefits, and a pleasant staff. After hearing Amanda talk about how good her job was enough times, I implied that I needed to find a job soon or I was going to lose it. Luckily she was one step ahead of me and being the good friend she was, she had already asked her boss if they were hiring. Luckily again, they were.

So the next day I went to the store and dropped off a resume. The day after, I dropped off another. In the end it took nearly a month of pestering the head boss there with a few trees worth of resumes, a hundred phone calls, and several stop in visits to speak with her personally. She must have gotten the message that I desperately wanted the job because finally I got a phone call from her wanting to set up an interview. I was overjoyed. When I went in for the interview things went over smoothly and I was hired by the end of it and would start my first shift the very next day.

The job was good. The workload wasn't crazy and the pay was decent. I spent most of my time in the back of the store, stocking the cooler and unloading skids of beer and other alcoholic beverages.

Despite the fact that I now had a job, was making money and had no intention of quitting, working at a liquor store was probably not the best place for me to be. It was like a kid in a candy shop or in my case, a growing alcoholic in a liquor store.

Due to my relentless overwhelming emotions that I had yet to master, my decisions continued to be dictated by how I felt. Because booze was in my face all day at work, when I got off shift, it was all I could think about. I knew that despite how I was feeling, I wasn't depressed enough to justify drinking every night like I had before at 1814. At that point it seemed like I was drinking because I just didn't know what else to do. I guess old habits are hard to break.

After leaving 1814 I felt like I didn't have an identity. I wasn't a suicidal maniac anymore; my occupational title had now changed. But what was I than? I wasn't a high school student like I once was. I wasn't the school president like I once was. I wasn't part of the community of 1814 like I once was and now I wasn't depressed like I once was. I suppose if I had a title, you could've called me No Face. In many ways you could still call me that today.

No Face. A person without a face has no distinguishing features to separate them from everyone else. If we all didn't have a face, then we'd just be bodies walking around doing our thing. That image is a little scary but so was mine when I looked in the mirror. I saw myself as I knew myself but I didn't know just who it was that was looking back at me. I mean I recognized the guy. It was the same guy who had been staring back at me every time I looked in the mirror for the past twenty years. But this guy who was looking back at me now, well he didn't have a face, which meant I didn't have a face.

I figured that instead of dealing with the questions that were plaguing me like, "Who am I," and "What does it all mean?" I'd just drink and smoke pot and cigarettes all day until I found the answer (because that method seemed to work so well for me before). Regardless of how ridiculous it really was, I continued to stick with my traditional methods of healing while diligently following my never ending quest for an identity. So as things would have it, I once again crawled back into the bottle (although I don't think I ever left), and let my alcoholism continue to grow.

My life at the time consisted of six things: eating, sleeping, working, drinking, smoking weed, and smoking cigarettes. I woke up hung over every day, and I mean *every* day. I'd go to work and by the time I got off my hang over had faded enough that I could come home and get drunk all over again. Of course there was always a joint or rip off the bong throughout my day at least a couple times. Plus the cigarettes; usually one every two or three hours. I was not living by any means. I was simply surviving and I can't believe when I think back on it, how much abuse my body was able to take.

After a couple months at the liquor store I was able to mostly square up with the Williams and I felt relieved to no longer have that burden on my shoulders. However, even though I now felt more comfortable coming and going as I pleased, I didn't enjoy myself at all when I was there. I'd just sit in my room and think, jump on the computer or make plans to go out. I don't know why, I just didn't like being there . . . again. Things had changed so much since I was there last, but of course that's to be expected. Sarah had moved out and gotten married and Michelle had been in a long term relationship from pretty much the time I stopped living there at the beginning of my grade twelve year until now. I was hoping that Michelle and I would be able to reignite our old friendship but it seemed like we were now two completely different people. We didn't get along at all. I hated it.

On top of that, I continued to feel alone sitting in my tiny room in the basement. "How was this better than 1814?" I thought. "How was this worth leaving 1814 for?" Things might have been rough at 1814 but at least I was never this lonely. It was then that I recalled an old quote Mr. Reid used to say back in high school. "You never miss your water until your well runs dry." It was true. Perhaps I took my home for granted and now it had run dry. The most depressing part is that once it's gone it's gone. There was no going back.

While I continued to be plagued with all these thoughts and emotions, Amanda had secured new living arrangements. An old friend of hers named Ken had just bought his own apartment and Amanda had moved into the extra bedroom. Because she had been living with her mother, it wasn't like we could get together and drink and smoke at her place but now, it seemed like doors were opening for a new place to hang out.

I had met Ken on several occasions back at 1814 and always thought he was a good guy. He was a tad older than Amanda and I but his experiences in life only added to the livelihood we all enjoyed when he was around. Plus we'd always go to him if Amanda and I were having a disagreement on something because he generally had an answer to most of our questions.

I honestly hadn't seen or talked to Ken since 1814 but when Amanda moved in, it seemed like none of that mattered. We'd all get together and hang out frequently and the more we chilled, the more I'd come back for more. It reached a point where eventually I was spending every moment I wasn't at work, at Ken and Amanda's. After about a month of this, I started to contemplate whether I should ask Ken if I could move in. I mean, I was paying for rent and food at the Williams, but I was never there. I was hanging out at Ken's enough that I was surprised he wasn't charging me rent already.

The more I thought about it, the more the idea sounded appealing. I didn't like living at the Williams anyways. I appreciated everything they had done for me but the loneliness and growing tensions between Michelle and I were starting to get to me. The only downside was that I would once again have to share a room with Amanda. I loved Amanda as a friend, but nothing more. Amanda had romantic feelings for me in the past, and every time she brought that up, I would have to tell her nothing would ever come from it. It was always difficult to say because I could see the look in her eyes when I assured her nothing would ever happen. She'd be sad for a few days and then things would go back to normal between us, or as "normal" as they could be for us anyways. I knew working with Amanda, along with sharing a room with her, along with the fact that she was one of my best friends was eventually going to put a strain on our friendship. When you see someone that often without any breaks, well that in itself is enough to drive a wedge between any relationship. Regardless, it was a risk I was willing to take. Not only that, but it was taking an increasingly large amount of effort to sneak into the Williams every night drunk out of my mind, trying not to wake them up as I made my way to room.

So a few days later I talked to Ken and he agreed to the idea. He laughed when he said he saw it coming. I suppose I had been there enough lately to make my intentions clear. He said at the end of the month I could move in and so gratefully I thanked him and started developing a strategy with Amanda on how on earth we were going to fit two people in this bedroom.

I told the Williams that I would be leaving at the end of the month and once again thanked them for opening their house to me. They were concerned that moving into Ken's might not be the best idea. Although I agreed in a way, I assured them that everything would be fine.

The end of the month approached and coincidently enough, my birthday was just a few days away. Ken said I could move in the day before my birthday so we wouldn't have to deal with the aftermath of the party and the move at the same time. I was grateful.

Pretty much around the same time that I started coming by Ken and Amanda's, Matt, Ryan, and sometimes even Bret would all show up to hang out. I took these initial times together to do my best to continuously show Matt how sorry I really was for all the shit that had gone down back at 1814. It took some time but eventually him and I were able to put it behind us and I was glad to be hanging out with Matt just like we used to.

After I moved in our gatherings became even more frequent. Ryan and Matt would stop by often. Bret ended up finally getting his driver's license and after that we saw a lot more of him as well. My brother Eric also came by often to hang out. Even Mike would drop in from time to time. In a way I suppose we tried to plant another 1814 seed which seemed to be growing decently however, "The Times" were done and I knew trying to recreate them would only end in more misery.

As it turns out when you get older, hangovers seem to get worse and worse. I was reaching a point where every afternoon I'd wake up just utterly defeated from the previous night's adventures. Yet for some reason I continued to get completely smashed every night. Things felt like they were getting grim. I was beginning to feel like I was at a point where I couldn't even stop drinking if I wanted to. Now that thought was scary. I tried to escape it by drinking more but that didn't turn out so well.

I remember one night being totally hammered and miserable that no matter how much I drank and smoked, things would never go back to the way they once were and if they couldn't do that, then I was forced to find an identity whether I wanted to or not. Since I couldn't recreate 1814, I was out of options and no matter what substance I put into my body, nothing was satisfying anymore. So as I walked in from the balcony after finishing a dirty drunken cigarette, I stepped into the living room, fell to my knees and cried out to God to save me from myself because if He didn't, I was screwed. I felt better after a quick sob and knowing it would be too soon to notice if anything had really changed, I went to bed, and was out like a light in no time flat.

A couple of weeks passed since that night and I carried on with my regular routine. Despite the fact that I was still remaining in my destructive habits I felt something changing. Like the wind blowing away the leaves to reveal a patch of grass amongst the dirt that with, just some sunlight and some water, could grow and spread throughout the mud and change the dead ground into a field of life. I wasn't sure what was happening but something was, I knew that much. So I waited, watching to see what would be revealed.

It was late summer and I had been living with Ken and Amanda for nearly six months. One August morning I awoke to feel the change that I had been waiting for. The moment I opened my eyes I knew what had happened. It was just like before. So bizarre, so miraculous, and so confusing but it mattered not, because I knew God had answered my call. I awoke free from the alcoholism that was controlling my life. It cannot be explained. I just woke up and I knew that I wasn't going to drink anymore. That day I went to work and when I got home, for the first time in a very long time, I did not drink. It felt incredible and for almost a week, I didn't drink once. As time went on my drinking endeavors became less frequent and I saved having a few beers for the odd time when we'd all go out to the pub for a Wing Wednesday.

Shortly after my newly discovered freedom from drinking, perhaps coincidental or perhaps not, I was let go from the liquor store. It seemed my hangovers had finally taken their toll on my work ethic and I turned out not to be the outstanding employee I proclaimed myself to be back when I first started the job.

In a sense I was almost relieved to not be working there anymore as dealing with alcohol all day was a big temptation for me at the time. The only problem now was that I was out of a job and I remembered back to how much effort it had taken me to get this past one. On that thought, I was nervous as to whether I was going to be faced with a similar dilemma.

Shortly after getting let go, September rolled around. As it so happens my brother was headed off to university down on the west coast. When he told me the news, I was excited for him. He had been talking about taking mechanical engineering for some time and God knows he finished high school that past June with flying colors. He could take anything he wanted to. Despite my excitement though, it was tough to see him go.

All the memories that we shared and the bond that we had created over the past few years had become solid. Our adventures at 1814 were life changing and I had difficulty coming to terms with the fact that our hang outs would be much less frequent than they ever had before. I tried my best to hide my true feelings towards my brother leaving but I knew I couldn't disguise them forever.

Eric and Lisa had changed their living situation several times while I was at 1814. For almost two years, Eric had been living with Mark, which I thought was great. Mark had been like a father to me for years and to this day I still look up to him in that regard. I was glad he was able to devote his time into being that same figure for my brother.

As a result of Eric living with Mark, I got see Mark often and we'd all get together and debate politics and life and ever so often, play some Texas Hold 'Em poker. I also saw Brian from time to time, which was always an interesting experience. We were both adults now and had put our old conflicts and differences far behind us. Although we never considered each other as good friends at that point, we could still get together, have a good time and joke about the old days.

When it came time for him to head down to the coast, Mark suggested I take his car and drive Eric down to see him off. I was glad to be able to have this opportunity to drive down and spend some time with my brother. I wasn't sure when I was going to see him next so I made the most of it.

The drive down was good and the weather was great so I had no complaints there. Eric and I talked about anything and everything. While I was enjoying this experience with my brother, I couldn't help thinking that I was driving him out here to say goodbye. I tried my best to shrug the thought away, at least for now. I couldn't let anything get in the way of me making the most of our time together. When we got into the city, we crashed for the night at a friend's place and the following morning headed off to the campus where Eric would be living.

I helped him get his stuff up to his dorm and after a couple hours of moving and getting acquainted with the campus (or at least where the map was), it came time for us to say goodbye.

Eric had never really been an emotional guy, or at least presented himself like that. Me on the other hand, I am big wussy when it came to things like this. I knew it wouldn't happen if I didn't do it so I went up to my little brother, gave him a hug and said "Love yah bro." He nodded like he understood and that was good enough for me. With that, I got in the car and waved goodbye as Eric walked back into his dorm and I began the four hour drive back home. The moment I left the campus, I began to weep.

For over an hour I cried. I had so many questions and concerns. Was I a good enough big brother? Was I a good role model? What did Eric really think of me? I loved the guy to death and he was leaving off to university before me. Did this make me a failure? Would he be alright out here in this big city by himself? I knew this was a turning point for him and me. I had little left to teach Eric. Before I knew it, he'd be teaching me.

The weeks that followed after returning home were spent in contemplation. After watching Eric go off to university I wondered what I was doing with my life. I was no longer depressed in the way I once was and every day I was starting to feel better. I knew I wasn't going to find my identity in booze or pot so I put those aside, although I did indulge from time to time.

In many ways my brother heading off to university was a bucket of cold water on the face. I woke up and realized I wasn't doing anything with my life and I had no reasons why I shouldn't be out there living my dreams.

While I continued to struggle with these thoughts it had been nearly a month now since I was unemployed. Knowing I wasn't going to get very far without a job and risked losing this newfound yet reacquainted desire to make something of myself, I desperately threw resumes at every business and person I could think of. Still, the last day of the month rolled around and I had no leads. I was about to storm out of the house and kick inanimate objects lying around outside in sheer frustration and stress, when the phone rang.

I had completely forgotten that I had dropped off a resume at another liquor store on the other side of town, just shortly after getting fired. I was hired over the phone and so on the last possible day I could spare to remain unemployed, I was able to secure a job. Working at a liquor store again wasn't exactly thrilling but knowing the current job market, beggars can't be choosers.

It was strange working at this place. The whole time I was there I felt like I was supposed to be doing something else. I had never felt so empty before and even though I was working a steady job, I still felt unproductive in some way. I was seeking something, I was seeking a face.

Since all my own endeavors had failed too many times to recall, I was at a point where I had given up on my own ability to make things happen. In this state of total defeat I concluded that trying to make life work out for you on your own is quite difficult. It was within this realization that I decided to give everything I had to God.

Giving everything to God was a popular sermon I had heard all too many times growing up. I always thought that if I gave my life and everything I had to God, He'd make me go to Africa and preach to everyone there or something. I was afraid He'd make me do something I didn't want to do and so I never truly gave my life over to Him. Being at the point I was at now however, made it seem like giving my life completely to God would be lifting an immense burden off my shoulders. And so I did. I really did and it felt unbelievable. Then before I knew it, my life started to change yet again.

While working at this new liquor store, every smoke break I'd go outside and pray. I'd tell God that I've always wanted to write a book about my life, about 1814, about everything. I told Him it would take me a million years if I worked at this liquor store to ever finish it. So I asked for time. Time to think, time to write, and time to reflect. So everyday for a month and a half I prayed for time and thanked God that I could trust in Him to lead my life in a good direction.

Sure enough as I was sitting at home on one of my days off, I got a phone call from my boss. Apparently I was being fired for being unreliable, although I'm not sure what exactly it was that I did that made me seem that way. Regardless, I was now unemployed once again.

Realizing that I had an abundance of time on my hands, I wondered if this was the time I had asked for to write my book. I now had time, but only enough money to survive for a month and a half before I'd be broke. Doing my best to have faith, I continued to pray.

I became interested in going back to school. The only downside was that school started in a month and half, which just so happened to be exactly how much money I had left to live on, and the acceptance process seemed like it might take longer than that. Regardless, I continued to trust in God and felt at peace.

For the next month and a bit I wrote a piece of this book every day and made arrangements to try and get into school. Unbelievably enough, I got into school for Culinary Arts and now here we are, approaching the last few pages of this story. It blows my mind.

This last chapter is called "Crossroads" because it's where I feel like I am in life right now. I continue to weigh out the balance of thoughts that revolve around everything from my dad's death to high school to my adventures at 1814. I constantly strive to make sense of things but I have feeling I may never find some of the answers that I am seeking.

I still currently live with Amanda and Ken in our tiny apartment. Although I feel that yet again, the winds of change will blow and we may all take a new direction in life, I enjoy the time I continue to spend here with my friends.

Ryan and Matt still come by often and we all hang out, although lately our hangouts seem to be getting much more mellow and infrequent than they ever have been.

Bret is out working in another city but says he might move back to go to school in a few months. I look forward to seeing him when he returns.

Jack and Leah moved out of 1814 shortly after we did. Although I never thought it could happen, they broke up and went their separate ways. I wish I could say that I still see them often, but because they're both in different cities, I think having them as part of my experience at 1814 is where my relationship with them began and ends, although I know we'll always be friends.

Brian got married this past summer as well as Aaron from the band. It was
crazy to see these kids I grew up with getting hitched but I suppose that's all part of growing up. They're both doing well and I occasionally hang out with Aaron. Unfortunately though, I never see Brian these days.

Jake ended up going through a rough patch in his life similar to my own. It ended up taking a huge toll on him and the lives of those close to him but luckily enough, he is managing to break through his chains and find freedom once again.

Mike finally broke up with Kristy for good and has been in a solid relationship for just over two years now. I'm glad he's found something worthwhile although it sucks because I hardly ever see the guy. I think about him often. I remember him telling me about "The Times" for the first time as I sat there in awe, listening to all the crazy adventures him and James had undergone.

Now here I sit, at the age Mike was when he first told me of "The Times" and I wonder if I will tell someone younger than me about my crazy adventures at 1814, about my "Times." In many ways I feel like Mike must have felt back then. When I asked him how he could just leave "The Times" like that and didn't understand how or why, well, I feel like I'm finally able to see his perspective.

I cannot forget the chance that Edward gave me to start my business. He saved my life. Although I can't right now, I've sworn to repay him one day what is owed, apologize for the mistakes I made, and thank him for what he did for me. I know that was a once in a lifetime chance and before the end, I will have proven to him that I was man enough to take control of my life and he will get his investment returned, with interest in one way or another.

Writing this book has been one of the craziest things I've ever done. I've wanted to tell my story for a long time but was never really in a good enough place to dedicate myself to completing it. It was perhaps the work of one of my favorite authors, Donald Miller that really encouraged me to write all this down. Don's book entitled "Blue Like Jazz" was probably the first piece of literature I've ever read that was written to sound more like somebody relating their thoughts and feelings to you, than some traditional, structured form of non-fiction. It seemed like Don was just talking to me, sharing stories about his life. Sharing his thoughts, feelings, ideas, conclusions, realizations, and revelations. I thought that if Donald Miller could write a New York Times Bestseller and it was simply a collection of the things that made him . . . well him, then I wondered if I could do the same.

I wrote this book to tell a story yes, but I also wrote it to try and understand why everything happened the way it did. I wrote it to try and make some sense of my life. The writing has brought me several answers (although a million more questions remain). I figured if I could relive my life through the words I'd type on my computer, then maybe I'd be able to pick up something I missed the first time around.

Probably my biggest question is where did my depression go? After everything it put me through, I can't just accept that it up and left. Although I enjoy the way I feel these days and have no desire to ever be depressed again, I just feel like I can't move on with life until I find my answer. Yet at the same time, I feel like I can't find my answer until I move on. Ironic isn't it?

A lot of healing is taking place in my life these days. It's a miracle but my mom has been in recovery for about nine months now and for the first time in five long years it seems that she is finally herself again and has beaten this addiction that gripped her for so long. I had lost hope, but it goes to show that nothing is impossible with God and I thank Him every day that I get to talk to my mother.

In talking with my mom lately, connecting, and rebuilding our relationship, she said that it was one conversation in particular that I had with her just before the end of 1814 that changed her life.

It was late August and 1814 was separating in less than two weeks. Downtown was the hot spot for drug addicts and since that's where I lived, I'd always see plenty of them around. Every once in awhile, I'd find my mom in the parks or on the streets. Because no one ever knew where she was, she was often difficult to track down. Despite this I wanted to find my mom because I had something to say that I felt she needed to hear. I walked out my front door and headed to the center of downtown. I didn't know how I was going to find her so I prayed that God would somehow bring us together that day. Miraculously enough, He did. I spotted my mom sitting in the park with some people, a crack pipe in her hand. I walked over to the group of people and got her attention. When she saw me she gave me a hug but was of course noticeably ashamed to be seen like this. I asked her if she wanted to go for a walk and she agreed. So we headed over to a quiet spot on the beach not to far away.

Reaching into my backpack I pulled out two beers and asked if she wanted one. She took it from my hand and so we sat there, probably looking quite dysfunctional, as I told her what was on my mind. I told her I was moving out of 1814 back in with the Williams, so I couldn't just roam downtown looking for her anymore. My mom always said it was her guilt and shame for the pain she caused my siblings and I that made her continue to use. Since that was the biggest reason, I had to take it away from her. Looking her in the eye I told her that no one cares anymore. I told her it had been five years and Eric, Lisa, and I had all moved on with life. I told her she was living in her head thinking that we were upset all the time over what she had done. Sure we still thought about it from time to time but it had been five years and everybody had put the past behind them except for her.

I watched as my mom processed that information. It seemed like she understood. We continued to chat for a little while longer and I tried my best to encourage her before we went our separate ways.

No one heard from my mom after that day for nearly eight months and then one day I got a call from her. She was staying in the hospital. Apparently she had a serious infection in her spine. So serious in fact that the doctor's said that if she had been on the streets for just two more days, she would've died. The fact that my mom was that close to bringing my worst fears to life was unbearable.

It's nothing short of a miracle that my mom is here with me today. She's been in recovery for nearly nine months, making this the longest she's been drug free in the past six years. It's tough for her in many ways but she is learning to come to terms with reality, accept change, and move on with life. I speak to her on the phone almost every day and visit her in person whenever I can.

My brother is doing well and I know that he will go on to do great things in this life. I cherish the memories I have with him and look forward to the new ones that await.

My sister has been with the same foster family for almost two years now and is being officially adopted by them. Although this was difficult for me to hear and come to terms with, she finally found a place where she feels at home, and I am happy for her.

I got into school and am looking forward to see where life will take me next. I no longer fear the ever changing state of this world and instead, have set my eyes on the future.

It's been just over a month since I quit smoking and I am relieved to have finally kicked this habit that I had clung to for so long. It's crazy to think that one miserable day would have led to five years of smoking!

Alcohol is something I rarely indulge in. It's lost its flare and its ability to satisfy my problems (not that it ever did). I still smoke pot from time to time but it's likely that past time will fade as well. I suppose I just can't party like I used too.

So much of the time I still find myself reminiscing about 1814. I'm always trying to develop a possibility of going back there and somehow recreating what I once had. As it stands, I'd give anything to buy that house. Then I'd call up everyone and tell them to come down for a knock-your-socks-off party. The idea seems so perfect and poetic in my head. It would be such a glorious reunion, I think I'd cry.

But then I think about reality and how much has changed and it smashes that whole idea it to bits. We've all changed, and when I think about it, I can't party like I did before. When I do have the odd night of drinking, I'm out of commission the next day. I can't really even smoke weed anymore because I just get so tired afterwards. Not even that but I don't even enjoy myself anymore. I know if I drink and smoke dope often enough, I'll probably start smoking cigarettes again and I certainly don't want that. The thought is tragic to me that I can't really party anymore but it's true. 1814 was in many ways a party house so if I were to go back there and not party, well then what the hell kind of house would it be? Most of my friends are in the same boat; they are married, engaged, traveling the world, or in college or university. They don't party anymore either.

I sometimes just wish I could go back to the first day I moved into 1814, only this time I wouldn't be such a depressed bum. If only.

This book could turn into the size of an encyclopedia if I wasn't careful. There's a million and one people and events that were never mentioned that played a vital role in my story. Many characters seemed to be here one moment and then gone the next, never to be heard from again.

The truth is there's a lot more things I could've put in here or elaborated on, but I feel like if I did, I'd never finish this story because I still have so much to say. But hey, that leaves room for another book doesn't it?

For the first time in my life I feel alive. It is a feeling unlike any other. In all honesty, I was dead for the longest time, just a zombie like creature moving about the earth, with an appetite for booze instead of brains. I've only survived until now, never really living my life, just dragging my body through every messy predicament I had undergone.

When I think back on my life hard, especially on the difficult times I faced in high school and at 1814, it is honestly a miracle I'm alive today. To be suicidal or to be in a state where cutting your wrist is bliss, is something that one can only understand if one has been there, living in such a terrible moment.

My whole life I never understood what possessed people to commit such things but after learning first hand and gaining that comprehension of why people do these things, I feel much more educated. Now I can tell if someone is troubled a mile away. I always see my own reflection when I look at their face. "That was once me!" I want to tell them. "I got out of it, so that means you can to!" When they ask me how though, I won't have an answer for them . . . because I don't even know how I got out of my own mess.

I often wonder if it was God. Perhaps there was a psychological reason behind it. Maybe the healing that time provides was what cured me. Things grew so far in the past, that they had lost their intensity to me. Whatever the reason is, I managed to pull through. How I did, I don't know but one day, I will find the answer.

My advice to anyone undergoing a serious depression like mine is to try and change your surroundings as they have a vast impact on how you feel. If you're feeling trapped you need to tell someone, anyone because if you don't, you'll forget that you have that ability. Time I believe is the one thing that will heal or decay anything, depending on your perspective. You could call it healing, as time had become the scab which covered the wound which was my depression. Or you could call if the decay of time, as over time all things decay, good and bad.

Depression is a very real and frightening condition that few people can truly understand. I hope that this book, that my story, will help anyone who is in a similar predicament. I was at a point where life was not worth living and somehow, now it is. Although it seemed like God wasn't there with me in my darkest times, I know for a fact He was. He really is the only light in such darkness. Regardless of your beliefs, I know that if you reach out to Him, your hand will not come back empty.

And so it ends. As one chapter of life concludes another begins. I'm only twenty two right now but I feel more like forty two in regards to what I've been through. The optimism I thought had left me has returned and my perspective remains positive. My broken family is being repaired. My depression has faded and my desire for substances is all but gone. I have come to find some peace with change, the one thing I loathed for so long. Instead of living in the past, desiring to go back to the way things once were, I live in the present and look forward to the future and all of the good things that await in life. 1814 changed my life. I could never forget the good times I had there with my friends who really were in a sense, my family and more often than not, I long to be back in my living room, hanging out with all my friends just talking about life.

Since I finally feel alive, I figure I should get out there and live my life to the fullest.

And I think I'm finally starting to find a face.

1814 Abbott Street

About the Author

Brandon Krogel is an emerging author and musician. He lives in Kelowna, British Columbia, Canada with two roommates, where he continues to write and perform.

For more information about Brandon Krogel and his work, please visit
www.brandonkrogel.com.

Breinigsville, PA USA
13 December 2010
251225BV00005B/1/P

9 781450 251846